"I know you're risking your life for us."

"I would risk everything for you." His head lowered and his mouth hovered near hers until she let her arms slide around his waist.

"Is there anything you can't take care of?" she asked in what she meant to be a teasing voice. But it came out shaky.

"Nothing," he growled in her ear. "You tempt me. Right now, all I want is to take care of you."

Tracy wanted that, too, her fuzzy mind realized. She wanted to forget about everything and drink him in. He was winning her over, her weak knees said. He was everything Scott hadn't been, or so he was proving himself to be. Did he really want to stay by her side this way forever?

"Tracy," Matt whispered huskily. "I care about you. And Jennifer. I'm not doing this for Scott anymore."

"Then who are you doing it for?"

"For me. For us..."

His To Protect
Patricia Werner

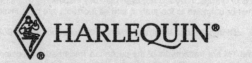

HARLEQUIN®

TORONTO • NEW YORK • LONDON
AMSTERDAM • PARIS • SYDNEY • HAMBURG
STOCKHOLM • ATHENS • TOKYO • MILAN • MADRID
PRAGUE • WARSAW • BUDAPEST • AUCKLAND

Acknowledgments

Many thanks to Jessica Wulf for her insider's knowledge of banking
institutions. Thanks also to Sergeant Mark Olin of the Denver Police
Department for answering questions about police procedure; to
Elizabeth Hill for her information about Washington Park; to Alice Kober
for advice about children with asthma. And, of course, many thanks to my
literary agent, Alice Orr, for her incisive knowledge of the business, and
to my editor, Angela Catalano, for making the experience pleasant.

The initials SWAT stand for Special Weapons and Tactics.

ISBN 0-373-22526-1

HIS TO PROTECT

ABOUT THE AUTHOR

Patricia Werner is the author of twenty-three Medieval, Western historical romance, Gothic and contemporary romantic suspense novels, as well as numerous articles. This is her third Intrigue title. She and her husband reside in Colorado, where they enjoy hiking and attending llama festivals.

Patricia received the 1998 Rocky Mountain Fiction Writers Writer of the Year Award.

Books by Pat Werner

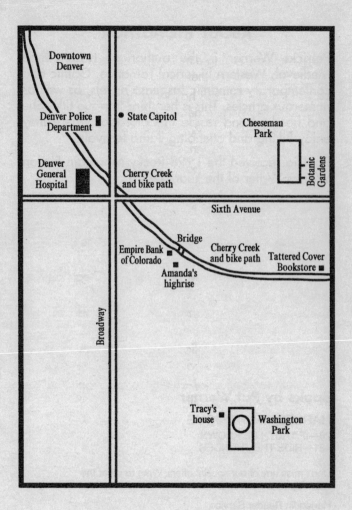

CAST OF CHARACTERS

Tracy Meyer — A single mom who's sworn never to get involved with another cop.

Matt Forrest — The cop holds a grudge against whoever killed his partner.

Jennifer Meyer — Tracy's seven-year-old stepdaughter and an innocent pawn.

Amanda Fielding — A bank president who throws obstacles in Tracy's way.

Carrie Lamb — Jennifer's tutor and a bank employee with a secret past.

Roland Baker — SWAT team sniper. Patient, steady and dangerous.

Rene Baker — She believes in letting her heart be her guide.

Andrew Leigh — He wants to take his granddaughter away from Tracy.

Brad McAllister — A police captain who doesn't like his jurisdiction messed with.

Commander John Udal — He knows that only the most stable officers qualify for SWAT.

Prologue

Tracy Meyer hated appearing nervous and defensive. She tried to keep her hands in her lap instead of twisting the long strands of her curling auburn hair. But the July 1, nine-o'clock meeting in the Empire Bank of Colorado's small basement conference room was nerve-racking. Her survival and that of her stepdaughter, Jennifer, depended on it.

She couldn't understand how blond, immaculate bank president Amanda Fielding could be the mother of a nine-month-old infant and yet be so unfeeling. Tracy had just made a plea to access Jennifer's trust fund, a fund set up as a result of donations following the death of Jennifer's father—and her husband—a year ago. Scott Meyer had been a cop killed in the line of duty, and as such, the trust fund had received considerable contributions from the Denver Police League and concerned citizens who'd read about his little girl's loss in the newspaper. The bad news was that with Scott's death, the family health insurance had lapsed, and Tracy had made expensive insurance payments so at least part of Jennifer's asthma treatments would be covered.

But now Tracy's palms were sweaty with desperation. Her high-stress job as a production manager at a small publishing company had gone by the boards. It just wasn't manageable as a single parent. With Jennifer out of school so much and needing special attention because of her asthma, Tracy stayed home. But the money had run out. There was nowhere else to turn. Thus, this morning's meeting.

Beside her, Jennifer's tutor, Carrie Lamb, sat stone-faced. Her short, wispy black hair had a trendy cut, but her trim, athletic body looked stiff under her houndstooth jacket. Tracy knew Carrie was fond of Jennifer, but perhaps as a teller at the bank, she was afraid to offend her boss. The authoritarian Amanda Fielding had an intimidating bearing, to say the least.

To back up her arguments about her ability as guardian to access the trust funds, Tracy opened the safe-deposit box that lay between them on the laminated wood table. She lifted out the heavy stainless-steel revolver that had been returned to her after Scott's death, and placed it on the table so she could get to the papers underneath it.

"My God, Tracy," said Amanda. "Why do you have a gun?"

"It was Scott's service revolver."

"Not loaded, is it?"

Tracy widened her brown eyes and looked up at the haughty bank president. "I don't know. I hate guns. I wouldn't even know how to check."

Carrie reached for the revolver and with quick movements, opened the cylinder. She removed five bullets and dropped them into the box.

"It was loaded, but not anymore," said Carrie with a shrug.

Tracy stared. Where had she learned to do that?

She retrieved the trust-fund documents from the box and scooted them toward Amanda. "Here."

Amanda barely glanced at them. "I have copies. I know what they say. Legally, you have every right to access the trust. However, as overseer of the trust fund, I advise against it. This money is for Jennifer's college education, possibly for special schooling now. You shouldn't use it for living expenses."

Tracy felt her stomach tighten. "Can't you understand? Jennifer and I don't have any *money*."

It was a horrible feeling. She still had the house, but she had to make the mortgage payments. She couldn't work full-time because Jennifer needed her at home after school. She had to watch like a hawk for all the early-warning signs of an asthma episode. Her fists clenched and her heart beat in quick, shallow thumps as the conversation broke down into an argument about the suit for custody Jennifer's maternal grandfather, Andrew Leigh, was initiating. His daughter, Jennifer's own mother, had died a year prior to Tracy and Scott's marriage.

"I understand your situation," Amanda continued. "But you need to think of how it will look to a judge if you start using the funds now. Jennifer's grandfather will use it as ammunition in court, saying you're irresponsible."

"But Andrew Leigh hardly knows Jennifer," Tracy said with vehemence. "During the four years I've taken care of her, he's only seen her six times."

"Surely he doesn't have a chance of winning custody," said Carrie, coming to her defense at last. "Does he?"

Amanda didn't try to sugarcoat her answer. "I'm afraid so. He's a blood relative and can afford the best attorneys."

Tracy felt herself on the verge of tears of frustration. Amanda didn't understand a thing. She felt a surge of resentment for Amanda's good-paying job and healthy child. It wasn't the same at all.

Something clunked against the door, interrupting Tracy's thoughts.

Amanda frowned at the interruption. "We're busy in here," she called out.

Then a man dressed in black and wearing a ski mask broke into the room. He pointed a semiautomatic rifle which was slung from a shoulder strap.

"Let's go. Now!" the man ordered.

Tracy's heart stopped beating. "What's happening?"

"Bank robbery," said Amanda, paling.

The man grabbed Amanda's arm. "You the lady bank president with the combination to the vault?"

Amanda winced in pain, but nodded.

Tracy saw Carrie's hand dart for the revolver on the table. But the ski-masked man forced her hand down.

"Don't," he told her.

He picked up the gun and slipped it into his belt. Then to all of them, he barked, "Move it! All of you!" He waved the weapon at them.

Tracy's instinct was to shrink under the table, away from the gun, but she felt Carrie grip her arm to steady her. The man was shoving Amanda through the door and waving the gun at Carrie and Tracy.

Carrie spoke evenly into Tracy's ear. "Do what he says."

Numb with fright, Tracy followed Amanda up the stairs. Belatedly, she realized the safe-deposit box had been left open, the contents scattered on the table. She heard Carrie speaking to the masked man, but she was too terrified to understand what they were talking about.

Upstairs, Tracy gasped when she saw two more masked men waving guns over the customers and employees lying facedown on the marble floor. One of the robbers was big, with the look of more brawn than brain. The other one was lankier, but with a dull, stoned look in the eyes behind the ski mask. Her fears turned to dread when she saw the security guard also lying on the floor, bleeding from the head.

"Oh, my God," Tracy whispered. *Was he dead?*

The robber pushed the three women toward the vault, then Tracy heard Amanda speaking about the key. Blood pulsed in her ears as she tried to think. Tried to summon her courage. She turned to see Amanda's white but determined face. There was still a sense of unreality about the scene, and she leaned against the teller counter, grasping its edge for support.

One of the robbers started to kick a woman on the floor who was curled into a ball, but Amanda intervened. Then Carrie bent down to the woman, retrieved a key and stood up again. Gunfire burst from the two other robbers' weapons, and Tracy crouched, covering her ears. She glanced desperately toward Carrie and Amanda to see if they'd been hit, but they were standing together near the first robber.

The biggest of the three robbers barked, "Quit playing games. Open the goddamned vault. Now!"

She watched Carrie and Amanda move to unlock the vault. The tall robber stepped inside, pulling a dolly after him. Compassion flowed from Tracy toward the terrified woman curled up on the floor. She started to kneel to comfort her, but the big thug who'd tried to kick the woman shoved the barrel of his automatic weapon in her face.

"Back off."

Tracy glared at him. "I'm not armed. I just want to help her."

"I said back off," the mean thug threatened again.

Tracy took a step backward until she pressed up against the teller counter once more. She didn't want to die.

Then Carrie and Amanda were herded beside her again. The three of them huddled together while the two thugs kept watch outside the vault. Tracy could hear the third robber working inside, stacking money on the dolly. On the floor, some of the bank customers and staff whimpered and cried. Let him take the money and get out of here. These people needed help.

Over the thug's shoulder, she saw out the big windows facing the parking lot that police cars were pulling up outside. Thank God. She swallowed, but tried not to react. The second robber saw them, too.

"Hey," he yelled toward the vault. "We got company."

Then one of the men on the floor moved, pulled out a gun and fired. Tracy gripped Amanda's waist and recoiled. One of the masked robbers screamed and let loose a barrage of fire as Tracy pulled Amanda down under the teller counter to get out of the way. She breathed in the hot smell of gunfire and heard screaming.

She looked across the marble floor toward the gray-haired man who'd fired his gun. He was lying still and bleeding. Oh, God! Let this end! She and Amanda and Carrie clung together tightly, whispering to each other.

Then Carrie said in a firmer tone, "We're going to get out of here."

The robber from the vault was outside now, arguing with the one who'd been shot. The one giving orders prevailed and the wounded robber eased down to the floor. But he waved his gun and shouted, "All of you, shut up!"

The customers and employees continued to whimper, some in pain, some frightened for their lives. The first robber was talking on a cell phone. Negotiating?

The red-and-blue lights flashed from the police cars in the parking lot outside. The sight of police nearby ought to reassure her, but instead an unwanted image formed behind her closed eyelids. Another bank robbery a year ago. Another police attempt to intervene. A dispatcher call. Scott unable to raise backup because the rest of the SWAT team was busy elsewhere. Her husband had died that day because of it. She felt queasiness and a dull stab of pain remembering it.

She opened her eyes. The robber on the phone said something about hostages and an ambulance. She started to shake again. With the robbers in control, more people could get hurt.

Then the robber with the phone started barking orders.

"You two," he said to three male hostages in business suits. "Carry this injured man outside and put him on the grass. Move slowly and don't try anything else. Understand me?"

The three businessmen got to their feet and started to move the wounded man. Someone else helped the bleeding security guard to his feet, draped the guard's arm around his shoulders and walked him toward the front door.

"They're going to let us go," Tracy whispered hopefully.

"Maybe," said Carrie. There was a hard edge to her voice. "Stay on your guard. Do as they say."

The first robber continued to organize the retreat of the remaining hostages. But as Tracy, Amanda and Carrie started to inch toward the door, he swung around.

"Not you three. We need hostages."

"Not them," Amanda said, stepping forward. "I'm responsible here."

The big, gorilla-like thug said, "Sorry, honey. You're not enough."

Amanda turned to confront him. Though she only came to about his shoulder, she spoke defiantly. "Let the others go. I insist."

The big thug muttered something else.

Amanda stuck her chin forward. "Do you know who I am?"

"Yeah," he sneered. "You're a hostage."

"You have to let these other women go."

"Don't push me, or you'll be a dead hostage."

She turned to Tracy. Embracing her, she whispered, "Tracy, I'm sorry."

"It's okay."

Amanda turned to confront the robber again. "I insist—"

The big man made his move, swinging the butt of his rifle toward her temple. Tracy choked off a scream and tried to grab Amanda as she sank to the floor.

Chapter One

The Denver Police SWAT team site commander went over the blueprints of the bank with the rest of the team as they rode in the unmarked van to the call-out. Matthew Forrest listened to the commander's remarks pointing out the layout of the bank that was in the control of the robbers. At the same time, he rechecked the ammo in the 20-round extended magazine for his 9 mm automatic pistol. While the use of deadly force would be the last, desperate choice of the SWAT team commander, the team was trained within an inch of their lives for high-risk assaults and had to be prepared.

There was something eerie about this bank-robbery call-out. Fortunately, the squad had been downtown today, and so only minutes had elapsed before they had all piled into the van equipped with communications equipment, weapons and heavy-duty tools they might need. But a year ago, this very team had been busy serving a high-risk warrant in a high-crime neighborhood when the call-out had come for help at the Crestmoor State Bank. Matt's buddy, Scott Meyer, had been in the neighborhood and was the first to respond to the patrol officer's call. But without the rest of the SWAT team, he had been shot with a .38-caliber bullet in the head and died instantly. The robbers got away.

Now the adrenaline flowed, sharpening all Matt's senses. He was never so alert as just before a call-out, when he knew that split-second timing could mean life or death.

"We don't know how many perpetrators are in there," said Commander John Udal, a fortyish man with sharp, decisive features. Matt trusted him implicitly. With his twenty years of experience and even-handed leadership, the whole team had come to trust and admire him. Commander Udal didn't give orders unless they were well thought out.

Udal continued the briefing as the van rolled along the street. "No time to rehearse the assault. Patrol cars are already covering the inner perimeter. Captain McAllister jumped the gun. He's already talking to the perp who seems to be in charge in there."

Udal frowned at Juergen Biggs, the SWAT team's negotiator. "If he hadn't blown it, we might have had a chance of persuading the perpetrators to release their hostages and come on out."

"How many hostages?" asked Matt.

"Three women. And there's already been gunfire. We don't know if any of the hostages have been hurt."

Matt stuffed his gun back into the holster strapped to his right thigh and placed extra ammo in a pocket of his load-bearing vest. His energy level and heightened perceptions went into overdrive. He'd been chosen for this prestigious but demanding job because he had the skills and agility. If a little anger surfaced when he knew he was about to face criminals, so be it. Anger that lawbreakers endangered the lives of innocent bystanders kept his attitude balanced toward the use of deadly force when it was necessary.

"Forrest," said Commander Udal. "You and Hobbs

will be the first entry team if the hostages haven't been released by the time we get there.''

"Yes, sir," replied Matt. He and Hobbs leaned over the blueprints and followed the commander's finger tracings as he deployed the rest of the team.

"Seeing as how we don't know the positions of the perpetrators and the hostages," said Udal, "stun grenades will be in order."

Matt nodded. Stun grenades, or "flash-bangs," as they called them, were less-lethal distractions used to create noise and smoke to allow the entry team to get inside and make a rescue before the perpetrators could fire at them. There was still some risk that the grenades, loaded with flash powder and low explosive, could injure. But it was a calculated risk. The grenades would daze and disorient the perpetrators, giving the entry team the precious seconds they would need.

"We're going in this side door, then," said Matt.

"Right. McAllister has them busy enough at the front door." Commander Udal looked at Roland Baker, the team's sniper. Roland, a tall, quiet man with an angular jaw and calm blue eyes, was Matt's trusted friend.

"There won't be time to set you up for observation. We'll try to get you to the roof of the bank before we go in so you can cover in case of a getaway attempt. But I won't give the order to fire if any innocent bystanders are in the way."

Roland nodded. The sniper had to be the most stable of the entire team. He never fired without the green light from the commander.

They felt the van round a corner and quietly pull up at a curb behind a small, two-story bank that overlooked a busy street this side of Cherry Creek. So far, they were still incognito, but not for long. This side of Speer Boulevard, the quiet old neighborhood with brick 1920s bungalows and a couple of modern high-rises a block or so away, buzzed with curious onlookers.

Matt groaned, ran a hand through his sandy blond hair and shook his head. "Why can't people stay indoors when there's a threat?"

"Don't know," answered Hobbs. "Maybe they want to catch a flying bullet. Never made any sense to me."

Commander Udal ordered some of the rest of the team to clear the area around the bank, getting the bystanders out of the way before they made their entry. Out of the corner of his eye, Matt saw a *Channel 7 News* truck arrive. Another headache. Though the Denver Police Department had a pretty good relationship with the press, it was still tough to make sure they didn't broadcast the SWAT team's deployment, providing a picture of their efforts to any perpetrators who might be watching a television inside.

Matt had to hold his irritation for the press in check. Instead, he concentrated on his job as they received last-minute orders from Commander Udal and checked the earpieces attached to portable radios in the pouches of their vests, through which they would keep the commander updated as to what they found inside.

Matt and the rest of the team sprang stealthily into action. The back doors of the van swung open, and the first man leaped out and sprinted across the street. He swung a grappling hook attached to a knotted nylon rope upward to catch securely on the roof. Scarcely had it caught when the lightest man on the team pulled himself upward, hand over hand, using his feet on the brick wall for added leverage. As soon as he was on top, he made sure the line was secure and Roland, the sniper, followed.

Matt and Hobbs hightailed it across the street, crouching against the brick wall on either side of the door. Every

nerve came alive in Matt's body in the heat of the excitement. In the split second following the flash-bang, the
perps inside would be ordered to drop their weapons and
put their hands up. Should they fail to do so, and Matt had
to shoot, the lives of whoever was inside would depend
on the accuracy of his aim. Every fiber of his nervous
system was charged, and his mind was keenly prepared to
take in the scene instantly and respond. At least Brad Mc-
Allister and his flashing red-and-blue lights ought to be
keeping the perps distracted for a moment longer while the
rest of the SWAT team was deployed.

The grenade thrower was ready to slide in the side door
ahead of them, toss the grenade and dive. He took his
position and nodded to Matt, who spoke into the radio to
their commander.

"Entry team ready, sir," he said. Then he tucked the
radio back into its pouch. Hobbs gave him a quick nod
from the other side of the door from where he would play
his part in their well-choreographed entry.

"On my signal," said Udal into his ear.

THE ROBBERS ARGUED as Tracy and Carrie tried to help
Amanda. She looked deathly pale, her mouth slack, her
eyelids drooping. Tracy felt for her pulse. It was weak,
and her skin was clammy. She moved around to cradle
Amanda's head in her lap. The robber with the phone
paced back toward them. Tracy saw him look at Carrie,
who pleaded to him, "She's badly hurt. She needs a doctor."

The robber crouched down beside them to remove his
mask and talk to Carrie while Tracy gently tried to feel
Amanda's head to see how serious the blow had been. The
head wound was bleeding, and there could be internal in-

juries. It scared her, but at the same time she used all the first-aid training she knew to try to be effective.

She was dimly aware of the dark-haired robber talking. Then he moved away and talked on the phone some more. Without his mask, Tracy could see that he wore his hair pulled back in a ponytail.

"He's got to get her out of here," Tracy said. "Amanda needs a doctor. She's going into shock."

Amanda's lips moved as if she were trying to speak. Her eyebrows drew down, then she groaned and her eyelids fluttered open. Her pupils were dilated.

"What should we do?" Carried asked.

"Keep her flat," said Tracy. "Since it's a head injury, we shouldn't try to raise her feet."

"There must be something else," said Carrie.

"We need to keep her warm. She needs to conserve her body heat. And loosen her clothing. It will help her circulation."

Carrie peeled off her own jacket and tucked the material over Amanda's upper torso. Tracy looked around for something to put under Amanda, as well. Carrie rose to her feet.

"Dallas." Tracy heard Carrie call one of the robbers by his name. "We need you."

Tracy drew in a sharp breath as the injured robber on the floor aimed his weapon at Carrie. "Sit down and shut up," he said firmly.

The robber called Dallas strode across the floor toward Carrie, as if they knew each other. "What is it?"

The two of them exchanged a few words about Amanda needing to be covered for warmth, then he took off his black windbreaker and hunkered down to place the jacket over Amanda. Tracy instinctively recoiled. He withdrew his hand and gave the windbreaker to Carrie instead.

"It should only be a few more minutes," he told them.

What was going on here? How was Carrie able to carry on with this stranger as if they knew each other?

Carrie spread the windbreaker around Amanda as the robber walked away, again talking into the phone.

"Do you think he's right?" Tracy asked. "Will we be out of here soon?"

"I hope so." Carrie seemed to concentrate on Amanda. "How do you know all this first-aid stuff?"

Tracy shrugged off-handedly. "When you have a sick kid, it only makes sense to know as many emergency techniques as possible. I took some classes."

Tracy suspected that Carrie was trying to keep her mind off the danger, but she wasn't fooled. She changed the subject. "I have a favor to ask."

"Sure."

Tracy hesitated before asking such a big favor, but they were in a tight spot. If she were going to speak, it had to be now.

She drew a big breath. "You and Jennifer have gotten really close."

Carrie gave a desperate smile. "She's a good kid. Smart, too."

Tracy reached out and squeezed Carrie's arm. "Carrie, if I don't get out of here alive, I want you to take care of Jennifer. Don't let her go to her grandfather."

"Stop thinking like that," said Carrie. She squeezed Tracy's hand and glanced toward the center of the room, as if keeping an eye on what was happening with the robbers. "You'll get out of here alive. We all will."

"But if I don't..." She forced Carrie's attention back to her and looked intently into the other woman's gray eyes. "I want Jennifer to be raised with love, and I know you love her. Please promise me you'll take care of her."

She saw the hesitation flicker in Carrie's eyes, but she continued her plea desperately, "Please, Carrie. You know Jennifer's grandfather wasn't close to Scott, for reasons I don't quite understand, and I don't want her poisoned against her father. He was a good man. I'm afraid her grandfather will poison her against me, too."

Carrie gave her a doubtful look. "Jennifer's smarter than that."

Amanda stirred, and Tracy returned her attention to the injured bank president. Beside her, she heard Carrie murmur, "I can't promise anything."

Amanda was trying to speak. Tracy leaned her head closer, her long, curling auburn hair falling forward as she strained to listen.

"What did you say?" asked Tracy.

"I'll look after…Jennifer." Amanda drew a ragged breath. "I won't let her forget…you love her."

Tears sprang to Tracy's eyes, and she glanced at Carrie, whose own eyes were glistening. She didn't want to believe that any of them was going to die. But in that moment, the three women's hearts reached out to touch each other in a way that was deeply moving.

Then the moment was lost as the robber with the dark brown ponytail made a dive toward them from the far end of the teller counter.

"Get down!" he ordered. "Cover your heads."

His body shielded them, and Tracy ducked. A deafening explosion rocked the room, followed by the sound of shattered and tinkling glass. The other two robbers returned a barrage of fire, and terror flooded Tracy as she crouched beside Amanda, clutching the injured woman on the floor.

The first robber had thrown himself across Carrie, but now sprang up and scooped Amanda into his arms. Out of the corner of her eye, Tracy saw Carrie relieve the robber of the gun he'd taken from the conference room downstairs. Her gun, Scott's weapon, the one that had been in her own safe-deposit box.

"Open the front door," the robber ordered Carrie.

Carrie got up and opened the door facing Speer Boulevard, the street that bordered Cherry Creek. She heard Carrie calling out, "Don't shoot. We're hostages. Don't shoot."

Behind her, from the far side of the bank lobby, Tracy heard a voice shout, "Drop your weapons."

She turned, recognizing that voice. But smoke from the explosion stung her eyes and she rubbed them, unable to see.

Shots exploded. Tracy ducked, feeling blindly along the teller counter in the direction of sunlight coming from the front door.

The robber carried Amanda out and Tracy followed, numb and blinded by the hot July sunlight. The robber placed Amanda on the grass. In the sun, Tracy could see the ugly wound on her temple even more clearly and started toward her.

In the corners of her vision, she saw more black-jumpsuited, armed men she recognized as being from the Denver SWAT team. Everything erupted into confusion. She thought she heard someone call out to her, "I'm sorry."

Then she saw the robber twist Carrie's arm around her back, forcing her to drop the unloaded gun to the grass. Carrie winced but didn't struggle as he grasped her around the waist and held a gun to her temple. Tracy gasped and half rose to her feet, her adrenaline pumping hard.

"She's dead if anyone makes a move," the robber shouted.

From within the bank, more gunfire erupted and Tracy

crouched toward Amanda again, more to have someone to hold on to than to be able to help her. The fight wasn't over, and they were in the open now. She glanced around for cover, but there was nothing. Even the bushes were a good five yards away.

Carrie was being dragged away by the robber, who was calling out that he would shoot her if anyone came any closer. The SWAT team would only shoot as a last resort, but she cringed at the danger. A stray bullet could be deadly. Another heavily armed SWAT team cop kicked open the front door and entered the bank.

The robber dragging Carrie got her to a black motorcycle and pushed her onto the back as he climbed onto the front. Tracy's heart beat even harder. A familiar figure came out of the bank and crouched two car lengths away. Tracy's pulse raced with new hope and fear. She knew she'd heard him inside. He must have gone out again when he saw the robber taking a hostage with him.

If anyone could save Carrie, it was Matt Forrest, who was in peak physical condition and highly trained. His sandy blond hair and tanned face contrasted with the sturdy black jumpsuit and vest. His tight, muscular physique was poised, ready to spring. Automatically, she glanced behind him to see who was covering his approach.

But the motorcycle roared to life before Matt could reach them. She caught a glimpse of Carrie's white face just before they screeched away. Tracy's heart crashed into her ribs as some of the police fired at the getaway vehicle.

"They'll hit Carrie," she cried out, wondering who was stupid enough to fire at an open motorcycle with a hostage on it. The life of a hostage was supposed to be the first priority in any situation.

Then she was aware of the acrid smell of smoke and blood as the sound of gunfire stopped. In another moment, the doors to the bank opened and four black-clad SWAT team officers led out the other two robbers, disarmed and handcuffed and looking sullen. Then the medics carried in a stretcher, presumably for the injured security guard.

She felt dizzy as someone nearby said, "It's over."

Matt got up from his crouched position near the cars and stared straight at Tracy. The black utility trousers were stuffed into heavy laced boots. He wasted no time in striding across the grass toward her, fastening the safety catch and shoving his pistol back into its holster as he moved. In that moment, the past flooded back full force to hit her. She felt frozen in time, one irrational thought running rampant through her mind.

She would never be out of danger.

IN HIS EARPIECE, Matt heard his commander inform them that the building had been cleared and two of the perps had been apprehended. Patrol cars had roared off after the escaped robber and the hostage. Paramedics were working on the wounded. Matt crossed the grass to where Tracy Meyer knelt beside one of the victims.

Still keyed up from the precision assault, Matt felt his throat tighten. The blood still pulsed in his ears. No one had told him Tracy Meyer was inside the bank. He stopped a small distance from where the medics were transferring the woman on the grass onto a stretcher from the ambulance. Tracy only backed off from the patient when the medics took over. Then she stood slowly and raised her wide-eyed gaze to meet his. She looked so vulnerable in the bright sunlight, he felt a wave of emotion engulf him. He wanted to reach over and tuck her into his arms to comfort her. But he also saw the iron will flash from the depths of those dark brown eyes and knew of the inner strength she'd had to rely on this past year.

"Tracy," he said hoarsely. "Are you all right?"

She seemed to waver in the aftereffects, and then he moved over to her, steadying her with his hands on her chilled arms. The color was returning to her face, and he felt her sway in his grasp. She nodded her head, the thick auburn hair tangled around her face. A hand went to her face and then down again as she looked deep into his eyes again. He knew what she was thinking.

He felt the old simmering anger as he saw the moisture at the corners of her eyes. She was thinking about Scott, shot dead a year ago. Damn! Why did this have to happen to her? To reopen the old wound.

She shook her head as if to herself. "I'm all right. I was worried about…" She looked vaguely in the direction of the ambulance that had taken the woman away.

"Would you like to go with her to the hospital?" he asked.

"No, I don't know." She looked up again, a confused expression on her face. "We're not…it's not that we're close. But she said something…in there, that I…" She paused to draw a deep breath, her hand on her diaphragm. "I think I should sit down."

"Over here."

With his professional eye still on the rest of the proceedings, he led Tracy to the concrete edge of a low retaining wall on the property next to the bank. The police information officer was giving an interview to the press on the outer perimeter. The ambulances had pulled away with the wounded, and the patrol cars with the prisoners had driven off. Bystanders still stood around talking about what had happened. He pulled out his radio to talk to his partner.

"Hobbs," he spoke into the radio. "Matt. I'm with a witness. Everything okay?"

"We're clear," came the answer into his earpiece. "You need some time?"

"Right."

"Commander says we'll be here for a few. Udal's mad. Whoever fired at that getaway vehicle, it wasn't one of us."

"Didn't think so. They have the ID on the girl yet?"

"Yeah, bank employee."

"I'm here if you need me," said Matt, and signed off.

"I can tell you who she is," murmured Tracy.

Matt sat down on the concrete wall beside her and unconsciously reached over to give her hand a squeeze. She returned the light pressure, and he felt the bond between them. A bond built of mutual sympathy and loss. It was as much a shield as a bond.

It was hard to face Tracy again. Hard because he still felt somehow at fault that Scott had gotten killed last year at a call-out where Matt and the rest of the squad should have been. It had left a bitter taste in his mouth and a gulf in his life. It was hell losing a team member who'd been a close friend, as well, and it was even harder confronting his widow.

"Who is she?"

He heard the hardness in his voice as he tried to keep the conversation in the present. Now wasn't the time to fight the demons of the past.

"Carrie Lamb. She's Jennifer's tutor. You met her at Scott's funeral."

"Sorry. I didn't recognize her."

"That's okay."

He saw her lips start to tremble and he had to force his hand to stay down and not reach up to smooth the tangled hair on the back of her shoulders. The dark blue cloth of her short, belted dress contrasted with the deep red of her hair, and he was conscious of confused emotions inside of him. Never good at sorting out his feelings in the first place, he felt the situation getting more awkward by the moment.

"Tell me what happened," he said as smoothly as he could. She would be asked to give a statement later. In fact, he felt a twinge of conscience that he didn't have her talking to the investigators now. They'd want a description of the robber that had gotten away and anything she'd heard him say.

Tracy placed both hands on the ledge beside her and held herself up stiffly. "We were having a meeting," she explained. "It was about Jennifer's trust fund."

Matt frowned. "I see."

"I…" she glanced at him quickly, and he saw the doubt in her eyes, as if she didn't want to tell him.

He spoke softly. "You know I just want to help." It wasn't his place to pry into her private life.

Tracy struggled with her words. "I wanted to access some of the money in the trust fund. For Jennifer. She's being treated for her asthma. I'm using some alternative therapies that even her doctors agree are helping. But the insurance…" She broke off and turned her head away. "Sorry. I sound like I'm complaining. None of this is your problem."

Matt frowned. "You mean you were discussing the money when the robbery happened?"

She gave a slow nod. "I had Scott's revolver out on the table. It had been in my safe-deposit box. Anyway, the robber took it upstairs. I guess it's out there on the grass somewhere. I saw Carrie grab it when we went outside. But the robber made her drop it."

"Scott's revolver?"

She nodded. "The one they returned to me after the funeral."

She squeezed her eyes shut, and he didn't press her further. Loud voices were drifting their way from the perimeter around the bank where officers were taking statements. He heard Commander Udal raising his voice with someone. Matt tried to keep his attention focused on Tracy a moment longer.

"Are you up to giving a statement now?"

She nodded and stood up. In spite of her ramrod spine and the way she squared her shoulders when she stood up, he could still see the anguish in her brown eyes. Her cheeks looked hollow, and there were faint worry lines across her forehead where there shouldn't have been. Damn! The situation was getting to him. He had to see her alone and find out what was really going on with Jennifer and her. He knew about the trust fund and had been glad when the Denver Police League had come up with a flood of donations. He had thought that would see her through. But there must be some hang-up that he hadn't foreseen.

Placing a hand gently on her back, he guided her toward the scene and into the midst of an argument. Captain Brad McAllister was near the front door, legs spread, hands on hips, glaring at SWAT team Commander Udal.

"You've done your job, Udal. This is my turf now. If you don't mind, I have a crime scene to secure."

"You can secure it all you like," replied the tall, normally unruffled Udal. "I just want to know why you took it upon yourself to negotiate with perpetrators and then open fire when a hostage's life was in danger."

"If you don't like what I did, why don't you take it to the division commander? I didn't see your squad preventing that suspect from escaping for all your fancy training."

Udal's jaw clenched, but Matt could see that his commander knew this argument would get them nowhere. "We'll get out of your way, then."

McAllister looked over Udal's shoulder and seemed to just now recognize Tracy. His belligerent expression changed to one of compassion and sympathy a bit too smoothly for Matt's taste. The large, square-built captain came forward.

"Mrs. Meyer. I'm so sorry to involve you in this. Would you like to sit down?"

"Thank you, I've been sitting. I can give you a statement if you wish."

Matt admired the way she stood up to him, as if she didn't care for McAllister's solicitousness very much, either.

"The sergeant will take your statement, then, when you're ready."

Matt saw her give a little frown, but let her go. He knew McAllister wouldn't want him nosing around any further, especially since there seemed to be a turf war going on.

But there was something funny here. The revolver Tracy mentioned clearly hadn't been Scott Meyer's gun at all. While it was true that the officers in the Denver Police Department purchased their own weapons, and any weapon of Scott's would be part of his personal effects, SWAT team members used automatic pistols for the extra rounds they needed. Not revolvers.

He crossed the grass to where he remembered the robber taking his hostage with him. The crime-scene investigators had marked off a perimeter, and the photographer was snapping pictures. Matt didn't see any gun. Maybe it had already been confiscated as evidence.

But if it wasn't Scott's gun, whose was it?

Chapter Two

By the time she finished giving her statement to the sergeant, Tracy just wanted to go home. She had to take Jennifer for her chiropractic visit today. She ground her teeth, swallowing the resentment she couldn't help feeling at having to do all this alone. Much of the time, she just told herself to put one foot in front of the other. Nobody ever said being a single parent was easy, but sometimes the problems she'd had to deal with since Scott's death were too much. She used to talk to Carrie about it sometimes. But now Carrie was God knew where.

"We'll have your statement typed up," the sergeant said. "Then you'll need to come downtown to sign it. I'm sorry, Mrs. Meyer."

"It's all right."

The young sergeant had the sorrowful look she'd seen in so many eyes since Scott had been killed. She winced inwardly. Didn't they understand? It wasn't sympathy she wanted anymore. Gradually, during the past year, grief over her loss had been supplanted by the struggle of daily living. She couldn't afford to dwell in the past, with only memories of Scott to sustain her.

She forced her expression into one of acknowledgment and turned to go. Up ahead she saw Matt tossing his vest and equipment into the back of the van. She tried not to look at him. Something inside her felt glad he'd been there today, but she didn't dare talk to him. Feelings were still too raw between them.

Scott had been his partner and friend. It was hard for Tracy to come to grips with the fact that the living, breathing man she'd been married to had departed his capable, virile body. She knew Matt had trouble dealing with it, too. It felt almost like cheating that she and Matt were still on earth, while the man they had both cared about had gone on to the next life.

But she felt cheated, too. She bit back a new source of bitterness and helplessness as she walked to her car. Her financial dilemma hadn't been settled and wouldn't be with Amanda in the hospital. Tracy shook her head, inserted the key into the red Mazda Protégé and unlocked it.

"Tracy." Her heart bolted into her throat.

Matt crossed the street to the shade, stopped a foot away from her and glanced back at the SWAT team van. "I just didn't want you to leave without seeing if you were okay."

"Thanks. I guess I'm done here." Even she could tell her voice had a resentful quality to it. "Sorry, I don't mean to sound..."

"Tracy." His voice was mellow, full of compassion and a strength that warmed her. "You don't have to punish yourself. You've just been through a trauma. Are you sure you won't go to the hospital to let the doctors check you out?"

"I don't have time," she said firmly.

"Okay, sorry. It's just that I'm worried about you." His tanned face frowned in concern.

"I know, I know. And I'm sorry, Matt. I guess I'm a little on edge." She drew a deep breath and sighed.

Matt still hovered near her, and she was aware of the

awkward sensation of comfort his presence offered. He was several inches taller than her, but he wasn't a hulk. His keen physical condition was a job requirement. And his face was handsome without being glamorous. His manners had always been pleasing. Now they had taken on a quality of what, extra concern? She saw the same anguish reflected in his hazel eyes that she knew he must read in hers.

Being with Matt reminded her of good times long ago. But it also reminded her of the terrible hours after the shooting. Identifying Scott's body in the morgue, answering questions. As she stood there staring into Matt's handsome face, it jolted her that she still blamed the SWAT team for her husband's death. She knew Matt felt that guilt, too, had tried to express it in a hundred ways.

"Matt," she said, turning to him and lowering her head a little so she didn't have to look up into his eyes. "You don't have to feel responsible for me. I can take care of myself."

She lifted her head, summoning her resilience. "What happened here today just…happened." She frowned. "But I am worried about Carrie. Will you let me know what you learn about her?"

He nodded solemnly. "I will." His brow creased in frustration. "I don't understand what happened here. The patrol cars gave chase, but that bastard got away with your friend. Don't worry. They can't get far. We have the ID on the motorcycle, and an all-points bulletin went out immediately. We'll find her."

Tracy closed her eyes and leaned against her car. "If anything happens to her…"

"Don't think that," Matt said, his jaw stiffening. "We'll find her."

Tracy opened her eyes, her heart doing a figure eight in

her chest. "Okay. I believe you." She turned to open the door. "I have to go."

Matt placed his hand on the door, still looking at her. "Listen, I'd like to come around later to check on you."

He glanced away again, as if he, too, felt a little awkward. "We really haven't had a chance to talk."

She swallowed. Hadn't she just been thinking she needed to talk about her situation with someone? If only he wouldn't think she was trying to take advantage of him.

"All right. You can come. Jennifer would like that."

At the mention of Scott's daughter, Matt's eyes filled with a hopeful look, and his attractive lips smiled in that boyish way she'd forgotten until now. She suddenly realized with a twist in her heart, how long it had been since she'd seen that smile.

"I could fix something to eat if you want to come around when you get off." She arched one of her dark eyebrows in a query. "If you get off."

"Yeah, no problem. I can make it. And maybe by then I'll be able to tell you what's happened to your friend."

"Good."

She knew the rules. SWAT team members did regular shifts, but there was no guaranteeing when they'd be called out for an emergency. Long hours and the pay wasn't any greater than regular police work. Why did they do it? she wondered for the thousandth time in her life.

He waited while she got into the car and pulled away. She drove slowly along the narrow residential blocks in the old neighborhood, where tall oaks and elms leaned toward the street. If Matt was coming for supper, she'd better think about what to fix. There would just be time to shop for groceries before she needed to pick up Jennifer.

AN HOUR LATER, Tracy pulled up next to the curb at the Washington Park Elementary School, where summer day camp was in progress. The sound of children's voices filled the air as clusters of brightly clad kids romped on the fenced-in playground. Tracy searched for Jennifer among the exuberant children flying from swings to jungle gym to sandpit. She prayed it had been a good day for her stepdaughter.

Then she spotted Jennifer with her day-camp counselor, coming out the front door, and went to meet them. She smiled and waved, relieved to see Jennifer's round face with color in her cheeks. Her long blond braids had loosened, and wisps of hair floated around her face in the light breeze. Her gray eyes gleamed with mischief, and she didn't look out of breath at all. A good day.

Tracy ruffled Jennifer's hair, knowing Jennifer would be embarrassed by the hug Tracy longed to give her. In her own emotionally distraught state, she longed to kneel and grasp the little girl in her arms, holding on to her for loving warmth and to reassure herself that at least they had love. Instead, she let Jennifer slip her hand into her own and smiled at Jennifer's counselor, Malla Luethe.

"Jennifer made a beautiful plaster-of-paris horse in craft session today," said Malla, a young woman with light brown hair twisted into a long French braid.

"You did?" asked Tracy. "Let me see it."

Jennifer held out a white horse that did look rather realistic. "I have to leave him here so I can paint him tomorrow."

Tracy took the figure. "Why, that's wonderful, Jennifer. Did you give him a name yet?"

Jennifer frowned thoughtfully, taking the figure back and turning it over in her hands. "No, not yet. I haven't decided if he's a girl or a boy."

The three of them laughed, and Tracy felt a twinge in

her heart. How desperately she wanted such normal exchanges to be the very stuff of which her life was made. If only she could find a way.

Malla held out her hands for the unnamed, dubiously gendered horse. "I'll take it back inside and put it on the shelf for you, Jennifer. He or she will be waiting for you tomorrow."

Jennifer surrendered the horse and then tightly clutched Tracy's hand as they walked to the car. Tracy pressed her lips together, hoping Jennifer wouldn't ask about Carrie today. The little girl had undergone so much tragedy at such an early age that Tracy didn't dare introduce another loss into her fragile existence. It had taken a lot to hold Jennifer's world together after her father had been killed. After a year, Tracy knew Jennifer must still feel the loss, but life was beginning to have some good days. Except that they still lived on the edge, never knowing when the next asthma attack would come.

As she waited for Jennifer to get into the front seat and strap herself in, Tracy fought the feeling of imminent disaster. Closing the door carefully, she braced herself momentarily on the top of the car. The very environment seemed full of threats after this morning. On such a beautiful summer day, in such a pleasant neighborhood, it shouldn't seem that way. She calmed her own labored breathing in an effort to keep going and to preserve the mask of normalcy for Jennifer's sake.

"So, how was your day?" Tracy asked as she climbed into the driver's side.

"We had a history project today. It was about the Colorado gold rush. Mrs. Luethe told us about the gold discovered in Cherry Creek. We're going to have a field trip where one of the first homesteads was."

"That's nice, Poops. Maybe I can go, too, as an extra helper."

"Would you?"

"Sure. Just tell me when."

Out of the corner of her eye, she could see Jennifer looking pleased. She was playing with her braids, which were certain to be a complete mess by the time they got home from the chiropractic clinic.

They negotiated the traffic on Colorado Boulevard and pulled into the parking lot of a tall office complex. Tracy kept up a stream of conversation, trying to keep Jennifer's mind off her health problems. In the waiting room at the chiropractor's office, they looked at picture books together until the assistant came for them. Tracy sat in on the examination so she would know exactly what the chiropractor was doing. She also felt it reassured Jennifer to have her in the treatment room.

Dr. Hanson was a pleasant, attractive woman approaching fifty, with gray touching her curly brown hair. She had a broad background in health-care-related fields, in addition to more hours of training than most medical doctors.

"That's my girl," said Dr. Hanson as she tested Jennifer's muscles for strength. "Jennifer is looking very well today," she told Tracy. "She has more strength in her diaphragm. That's going to help her breathing efforts."

She had Jennifer lie down on the treatment table so she could adjust her.

"Keep up that healthy diet," said Dr. Hanson. "The stronger her immune system, the more likely she may be able to grow out of this."

"Yes, of course," replied Tracy.

It cost more to shop for the healthiest foods, and it took extra time to prepare them, but Tracy was committed to the healthy life-style if it gave Jennifer more of a chance.

She still had the inhalers for use in an emergency and for when she had trouble breathing at night. But with ample research documenting the relationship between the spinal column, the nervous system and the respiratory system, Tracy had asked Jennifer's primary-care physician to refer her to a chiropractor for treatments. The natural treatments relieved the nerve interference that caused the bronchial tubes to contract and reduced the risk of side effects from drugs.

Jennifer's gray eyes gleamed as she grinned at Dr. Hanson, who patted the girl's shoulder. "Now, you do what Tracy says and eat a big, healthy dinner tonight, all right?"

Jennifer nodded enthusiastically and rubbed her tummy. "We're having turkey burgers on buns and a salad. We're having company."

"Oh? That's nice," said the doctor.

"Lieutenant Matt Forrest," said Jennifer proudly.

"A lieutenant? Well, that is something special." Dr. Hanson smiled as she reached for Jennifer's chart to make notations.

"He was a friend of Scott's," Tracy said, feeling an unreasonable need to explain.

Dr. Hanson mouthed an "Oh."

Tracy got up. "Thank you, Doctor."

She realized her step was lighter as they left the chiropractor's office. Maybe, just maybe, as long as she kept Jennifer living a healthy life-style and stayed on top of the early-warning signs of an asthma attack, maybe Jennifer would be able to live a completely normal life someday.

"Ouch, you're squeezing my hand too hard."

"Sorry." Tracy loosened her grip, then let go altogether as they reached the car.

With the doctor's appointment over, Tracy found herself thinking about the evening. Matt's visit caused her mixed feelings indeed. She was conscious of the awkwardness between them. She'd been almost rude to him in the months following Scott's death. Maybe he understood that in her grief, she needed to blame somebody for Scott's getting killed. Then she had become even more ill-tempered because of her desperate financial straits and her worry over taking care of Jennifer alone.

All the SWAT team cops were just like Scott, dedicated to the job and motivated by a sense of honor and duty about protecting the public. But men like that had a hard time seeing that their families needed them first. She had cried and cried over Scott's death, realizing they had missed their chance to be a real family. His long hours had kept him away from home so much. She had begun to feel abandoned even before he'd been killed. But then his death was the final blow.

Maybe their relationship hadn't been the very best it could have been. But after he'd died, she was so acutely aware of having no one there at all to talk to. There had been times when she'd felt so low, she hadn't known how she would keep going. But she had. For Jennifer. And she had learned to get through each day. Learned to combat the loneliness. Slowly, she'd climbed out of her depression and decided she had to keep going. That she would learn to be a single parent.

Tracy's home was located a few blocks from Washington Park in an old residential neighborhood in central Denver. Dormered brick bungalows sat on small lawns with no driveways. Tall, mature oaks and elms provided shade.

The cool interior of the small brick house greeted them as Tracy carried the groceries through the house to the old linoleum-floored kitchen. Jennifer dashed down the hall to her room at the back of the house, while Tracy checked the answering machine on the small white kitchen table. No messages. No news about Carrie, then.

She bit her lip, fighting back worry. She just couldn't take it if something awful had happened to her. She tried to think of whom to call. It made her realize, suddenly, how little she knew about Carrie Lamb. She'd never mentioned any family and didn't seem to have anyone in Denver. Whom would the authorities have called about this predicament?

She also wondered about Amanda Fielding. Only this morning, she'd considered the bank president an adversary. Now she was surprised and confused about Amanda's offer to take care of Jennifer if anything happened to Tracy. She shook her head. Strange things happened sometimes in a crisis. She hardly knew Amanda and, of course, the woman had been wounded when she'd made the offer. Still, it gave her a curiously empathetic feeling toward the woman. She might be clinging to life by a thread right now. Surely Tracy ought to call the hospital.

She was relieved to learn that Amanda was conscious. The doctors had found no serious internal injuries. Tracy asked the nurse at the desk to relay the message that she had called to ask about her.

That taken care of, Tracy flew around the house picking up the clutter and then organizing in the kitchen. The house was already spotless because of her rigorous cleaning to reduce dust and molds, which could trigger Jennifer's asthma. Now she took extra care cutting up the fresh vegetables for the salad and mixing up the ground turkey with egg and onion for burgers. She molded each patty carefully, thinking about how she wanted them to cook evenly.

Matt was just a friend, she reminded herself. If she was excited about having him over, it was because of this morning's scare. And she knew she was just clutching at straws in her loneliness for adult companionship.

She and Matt had shared a loss. And emotions could make you do funny things.

"Not with Matt," she said out loud as she slid the burgers into the oven to await broiling.

He was a cop, even if a compassionate one. But she shouldn't let Matt get the wrong impression. Those strong shoulders and his concern today had done something to her insides, met a need she'd suppressed for a long time. A woman liked to be looked after in that kind, caring way. God, she'd been bearing the burden alone for too long. She obviously needed a shoulder to lean on.

She gave a little laugh of derision at herself for where her thoughts were going. SWAT team officers were not the sort to rely on for punctuality. She couldn't even be sure he'd show up on her doorstep at seven o'clock for dinner. He might be on a call-out. A SWAT team cop's life wasn't his own.

She ran a bath in the claw-footed bathtub to freshen up, and afterward she studied her uninspiring wardrobe. This was not a special occasion, she reminded herself. He was just dropping by for dinner. Because it was so warm, she chose a light pink, lace-trimmed tank top and crisp white, loose-cut shorts with cuffs. She looked casual but clean. They would eat on the deck built onto the screened-in back porch. Just before seven, she called Jennifer to help set the round redwood table.

When the doorbell rang at straight-up seven, she and Jennifer exchanged looks across the table. Jennifer had laid the blue quilted place mats in three places and set out the silverware. Tracy read the expectant look in her stepdaughter's round gray eyes.

"Okay, Jenn, you can answer the door."

The girl sped across the redwood deck, banged the screen door to the enclosed porch and raced through the house. One knee on the redwood bench, Tracy appraised the table. Perhaps she'd been working Jennifer too hard. Worried that she had fallen behind when she'd been sick so often during the school year, Tracy was desperately trying to get Jennifer up to speed by September. Of course she used to have Carrie to help tutor. Her heart clenched at the thought. She hoped Carrie was okay.

Thinking of Carrie made something niggle at the back of her mind, but there was no time to think of it, for jubilant voices were coming through the house. She waited as Jennifer's excited giggles preceded the two of them, and then Matt followed her out and stood on the deck.

For a moment, Tracy caught her breath. It was a blissful summer evening, the kind that lasted a long time in Colorado. The sun was still high over the mountains to the west, but this side of the house was in shade. Matt looked devastatingly handsome standing there in an olive short-sleeved, collared shirt and belted fatigue-green shorts that covered his thighs. On his feet were dark brown leather loafers. His hair still gleamed with the dampness that must have come from a shower. He smiled hesitantly from beside the steps to the porch. Jennifer skipped across, waving an armful of roses.

"Hi," she greeted him, then took the flowers from Jennifer.

"Look, look," squealed Jennifer. "Roses. They're for us both," she said importantly.

"Well, of course. Jenn, go find us a big vase under the sink. I think these flowers deserve special treatment."

She breathed deeply, inhaling their delicate scent. "Mmm, they're beautiful."

How had he remembered that roses were not likely to

trigger an asthma attack in Jennifer? She was sensitive to some wildflowers and some pollens, but not to the mild scent of roses.

When he moved across the deck, the breeze caught his hair and lifted it slightly as his gaze roamed the backyard and her small herb garden. She was aware of his masculinity in a startling way. Then he brought his eyes back to her face.

"The place looks nice."

"Thanks."

She felt self-conscious and glanced awkwardly around. It was pleasant just to stand there and enjoy the end of the day while Jennifer rummaged for a vase. But she guessed what Matt was probably thinking. That she was doing all right with the house in spite of having to do it alone. She turned and headed for the door. "I haven't used the grill since..."

Her gaze met his and she shrugged. "Anyway, I'm just broiling the burgers inside. It'll only take a second."

"Can I help?"

"I'll hand you things to bring out."

Between Jennifer's bubbly excitement and his easy way of making himself at home in the kitchen, Tracy began to relax. They sat down and stuffed themselves on the burgers and salad. After the meal, Matt and Jennifer tossed a Frisbee. When Tracy thought Jennifer had roughhoused enough, she called out to them.

"Jenn, it's time to get ready for bed."

She loved seeing her stepdaughter have a chance to play with a grown-up, but she couldn't let her overdo it. If she got herself too out of breath, it might bring on an attack.

Matt brought her up to the porch and promised he'd come in later to say good-night before he left.

"All right," Jennifer finally said, letting go of his hand. "I guess I'll let you have grown-up talk now."

"Thank you," said Tracy, smiling. "You go clean up and get into your pajamas. I'll be in to tuck you in."

"Sure." She looked up at both of them hopefully. "Will you read me a story, both of you?"

Tracy and Matt glanced at each other, and she felt her cheeks flush. He gave her an amused smile, and she answered his grin. "Well, sure, if Matt's still here by then," she said.

"I'll be here," he said quietly. "Now do as Tracy says, and we'll read you a story in a little while."

AS MATT WATCHED Jennifer trudge out of the kitchen to the narrow wood-floored hallway that led to her bedroom, he felt a tug at his heart. The evening had been pleasant in a way he'd forgotten. He hated the idea of infringing on that with serious matters; however, he wanted to find out more about this trust-fund problem.

He looked around the kitchen with a critical eye. Guilt stung him as Tracy headed out the screened-in porch to the deck to finish bringing everything in. He had told her to call him if she ever needed any help with anything, but she never had. Perhaps he should have come over to check on things more often. If she was trying to access the trust fund, that meant she was having financial problems and it made his heart ache. Well, it was time he found out what he could do to help.

Not that it would be an unpleasant task. Maybe he'd kept his distance for another reason this past year. He'd realized when he saw her this morning how beautiful she looked in that short cotton navy dress, belted at the waist. It emphasized the curve of her hips. And the color of the dress and her luxuriant hair brought out the vitality in her face. A face he found he wanted to touch. There'd been an instant connection between them, but one he couldn't afford to acknowledge.

He stuck his head out the door to see if she needed any more help. "Anything else?"

She shook that mane of dark red hair and gave him a relaxed smile. "That's everything."

He held the door for her and smelled her fresh, clean scent as she passed in front of him to the sink.

"Give me those dishes," he said. "I'm an expert in washing up. Bachelor, you know."

"Just scrape and rinse and we'll throw them in the dishwasher. Coffee?"

"You bet." He was glad they'd have some time to talk alone while Jennifer was in her room.

The aromatic coffee brewed and gurgled, and then they took their cups into the living room. The furniture was old, but it had a homey feel. Framed old photos filled the far wall above the small dining table, and a large pastel watercolor hung above the overstuffed burgundy sofa. Tracy pulled the chain under an antique lamp shade to cast a soft glow about the room, and they sat on the cushy sofa facing the brick fireplace.

Tracy sat sideways, her attractive legs pressed back against the sofa. She sipped her coffee before setting it on the natural-wood coffee table.

"Any news about Carrie?"

He shook his head and set his cup down, as well. "None yet. They lost them. On that motorcycle, the robber outfoxed the patrol cars. Doubled back on some alleys. In that dense neighborhood, there wasn't room to maneuver fast enough to keep up with them without endangering pedestrians and hitting the cars parked on both sides of the streets."

Tracy's face seemed to lose color, and her brown eyes widened. "You mean she's still a hostage?"

He pulled his mouth sideways and flicked his gaze away from hers for an instant. From the deep frown formed by her brows and the examining look she gave him, he knew he wouldn't be able to hide his other doubts from her.

"Afraid so."

He paused for a minute. It tortured him to add any more worries to what Tracy already had to deal with. He stretched his arm across the back of the sofa in an unconscious gesture of protection, even though he wasn't touching her.

"Tracy, how much do you know about Carrie Lamb?"

The question seemed to startle her. "Why? What do you mean?"

When she leaned closer, he was distracted by the shadow visible behind the lace of her scoop-necked tank top. He looked away, then picked up his coffee cup to give him time to gather his thoughts. After a swallow, he faced her again.

"They tried to do a background check on her and got nowhere."

He heard her soft intake of breath. "Why, what do you want to know?"

"I don't want to frighten you, Tracy. But the investigators are already considering that the attempted robbery might have been an inside job."

He waited for that to sink in and saw the reaction on her face before he continued. He leaned forward again, holding the coffee cup in both hands.

"I've seen a lot of hostage situations," he said, shaking his head. "There was something about the way she went with him that made me wonder." He looked Tracy directly in the eye.

"She didn't even try to get off that motorcycle once he had her on it."

Tracy sat bolt upright and immediately came to her friend's defense. "Well, he would have shot her."

"How? Once he was on the cycle with her behind, he couldn't aim for her while he was making the getaway. She could have jumped off, even if she'd sustained a minor injury. She didn't."

The shock registered on Tracy's face. "No," she said, exhaling a sudden breath. "You must be mistaken. She would never have gone with a thief willingly."

"I hope not. And I hope she's safe. But the fact that they haven't even located the bike yet makes me worry. This guy was slick, not your common bank robber."

"But you have two other perpetrators in custody. Haven't you made a deal with them yet?" He could hear the irritation rising in her voice.

"One of them is in the hospital, heavily sedated for his injuries. The other one might talk. That's all the feds on the case will tell us, but they're still working on it."

Tracy sat dumbfounded, and he could see the wheels turning in her head. Damn! He hated doing this to her, but he had to find out if she knew anything that could help. And she needed to know where things stood for her own safety, as well. A bad feeling in his gut told him they weren't through with all of this. And he still hadn't told her about the gun.

Even more disconcerting were the feelings that were smoldering inside him. In spite of the danger this morning and his anger at the patrol officers who'd showed up at the scene and made a mess of it before the SWAT team could get there, Matt was conscious of the warmth of Tracy's home. It made him not want to leave. He'd feasted his eyes on her all evening, and he honestly took pleasure in little Jennifer's company.

Now he found himself wanting to lean closer to Tracy, to pull her into the curve of his arm. She was incredibly sexy in the loose-fitting shorts and pink tank top. He had to make an effort not to stare at the curve of her calves against the sofa. And he had to force his hand to stay away from the springy softness of her hair. He wanted to scoop her up in his arms and tell her things would be all right. Instead, he met her worried gaze with his own.

He hated interrogating her about her friend, but something wasn't right there. And where he had a personal interest, he wasn't about to leave it to the official investigation. He was quite aware that he had done that once before and regretted it.

Tracy's lips tightened. She grasped the arm of the sofa with her right hand and held her body rigid. "I can't believe Carrie would do anything wrong."

"I hope you're right."

She drained her cup of coffee and got up to get a refill. "More?" she asked him.

"Sure." He handed her his cup.

After she turned away, he shook his head, still bothered by the way she was arousing him. As she walked back to the kitchen, he tried to shift his attention to the fireplace. She was an attractive woman, and he cared what happened to her. But she'd been his best friend's wife. Surely she would be offended if he offered any advances. And what would be the motive behind those advances anyway? They hadn't seen each other in several months. Wasn't this just the hunger of two lonely people caught up in the aftermath of a crisis?

Or maybe she wanted his reassuring touch as much as he wanted hers....

Chapter Three

Tracy used the time in the kitchen to steady her jangling nerves. She was conscious of an attraction growing inside her caused by Matt's nearness. It shocked her how attractive he had looked to her all evening. In the midst of the growing worry about what had happened this morning, she was aware of tingling sensations that she thought had been dead for the past year. Matt's all too male presence in the house fanned a slow-burning ember deep within her that she hadn't looked to rekindle any time soon. And she felt a twinge of guilt about finding Scott's partner attractive. It seemed disloyal, somehow.

She paused after pouring her second cup of decaffeinated coffee and fiddled with the cream just to have a few extra seconds to catch her breath. Did he know the way his sandy blond hair fell over his brow made her want to run her fingers through it? Had she been so starved for a man that she was reaching out to her friend like the needy widow she truly was? She had caught Matt gazing at her breasts, though he'd tried to hide it. Okay, so they were human. She had thought she'd dressed conservatively, but maybe she should have worn an ankle-length skirt to cover her legs.

She placed a hand on her midriff and straightened her

back. Then she marched into the living room. But when she sat down again, she pressed herself farther into the corner of the engulfing couch. Matt, too, had moved farther away and was slouched down on the couch, his hands folded across his taut stomach, his legs stretched forward under the coffee table.

When she set the coffee cups down, he scooted himself back up so he could turn his head toward her again. "Now, tell me about this trust-fund problem. I'd just like to know if there's anything I can do to help."

She lifted her chin. Though she didn't like to sound pitiful, at least talking about money would help distract her from the feelings that were starting to be too evident between them.

She drew a breath. "As you know, I've had to take Jennifer to a lot of doctors. I wanted second opinions, so I consulted a nutritionist and a chiropractor for allergy testing. Fortunately, her medical doctor agrees that the results are positive." She shook her head regretfully. "But the insurance only covers about half of it."

He frowned. "I take it you bought new insurance after...."

She nodded. "With Scott's death, I had to shop around for another plan. It's not cheap."

His brow furrowed. "I hear you. Go on."

She lifted her shoulders and let them drop in a shrug. "There just wasn't a question of going back to work. Jennifer needs me to manage her condition. Not that I don't want to work. I loved working. But I have to find something I can do that has flexible hours."

She hesitated to go into the litany of details about washing Jennifer's pillows once a week, keeping the house dust free, shopping for healthy food.

She just said, "I've had to take her to the doctors so

often, and if she has an episode at school or day camp, I have to bring her home.''

He started to reach a hand toward her shoulder and then seemed to think better of it and swung it to the back of the couch instead. ''So things have been even rougher than I'd thought,'' he said pensively.

'''Fraid so,'' she admitted. ''That's what we were arguing about this morning. I thought if I could access some of the donations that had gone into the trust fund for Jennifer, it would help. Amanda said no.''

''Why not?''

''Because it would weaken my position against Andrew Leigh, Jennifer's maternal grandfather. He wants custody.'' She felt the anger and desperation creeping into her voice and caught the emotion reflected in Matt's eyes.

''You didn't tell me he was suing for custody.''

''I only recently found out.''

Matt let a long sigh escape, and they sat in silence for a moment. She leaned sideways against the sofa back, feeling low. Her irrational urges aside, she was thankful at that moment that Matt was here. Just to have someone who cared about her dilemma was a help. Except for doctors and teachers, Tracy realized how much she'd cut herself off from adult company. Especially male adult company.

Was that why gazing at Matt's long, tightly packed physique stretched out on the other end of the sofa gave her such a warm feeling? His muscled thighs rippled where they peeked out from under the green fatigue shorts. And her heart pattered when she let her gaze drift to his strong shoulders.

Stop it! she told herself. Just because she hadn't been with a man for so long, it wouldn't be right to throw herself at her late husband's partner. He would realize anyway that she was in a desperate situation. These were not his problems, and probably the last thing he wanted was a woman clinging to him in her time of need.

Then he turned his hazel eyes on her, and she caught her breath. His worried look burned with something else. She saw the muscles in his cheek tense as his eyes swept her hair and face, darting to her neckline and then to the coffee table. The heat between them simmered again, and she felt a sharp jolt of desire.

Matt seemed to be forcing his gaze to the coffee table, but she noticed how his left hand clenched the padded arm of the sofa. He frowned and lifted his head.

"There's something else, Tracy. I know you well enough to be certain you'd rather I be honest with you."

Apprehension darted through her. "About what?"

"I want to know about that gun the police confiscated today."

She blinked. The gun was definitely not something she'd expected to be discussing. "The gun?"

He nodded slowly. "Yes, you said it had been in your safe-deposit box."

Confused thoughts tumbled through her mind, and she tried to focus on this new topic. Tried to ignore the sexy look of his firm, sensual mouth and jaw and concentrate on the subject at hand.

Drawing a breath, she said, "The gun was returned to me after Scott's funeral, along with his other belongings. Since all the officers purchase their own guns, I guess they thought I might like to keep it." She frowned, remembering. "It was a .38 Smith and Wesson."

The crease between his brows deepened. "I knew Scott's weapons. That wasn't Scott's gun."

"What?"

He leaned closer, as if trying to convey the significance of what he was saying.

"SWAT teams don't use revolvers. There aren't enough rounds of ammunition. Six shots isn't enough if we get into a tight spot. There isn't time to reload."

She swallowed, trying to relieve the dryness in her throat. "Go on."

She could tell he didn't like bringing this up. But from the urgency in his voice, she believed he wouldn't if he didn't have to. He must be vitally concerned about something related to the gun.

"Scott carried a SIG-Sauer P-226 automatic pistol with an extended magazine of twenty rounds. All of us on the team had them."

She nodded, beginning to grasp the significance of what he was saying. "Then you're wondering if that gun ever really belonged to Scott."

"That's right."

His gaze wandered over his shoulder toward the door to the hallway that led to Jennifer's bedroom. The way he glanced that way told Tracy that whatever he had to say, he didn't want Jennifer to hear.

"Maybe I should go read Jennifer that story now," he suggested with a lift of one eyebrow.

"All right, she'd like that. You can read to her while I take care of these cups."

"Good idea. Then after we've tucked her in, how 'bout you and I sit out on the deck for a while?"

She nodded at the suggestion. "Sounds good to me."

Best invitation I've had in a long time, she couldn't help but think. He was in no hurry to leave. But he seemed to have something more to tell her that might be important. Why would the department give her a gun that wasn't Scott's? The thought made her uneasy, and she hoped Matt could shed some light on it.

She could hear his good-humored baritone voice joking

with Jennifer as they selected the story. She finished with the dishes and turned on the dishwasher, its hum covering up the giggles coming from the back room. When she walked in to join them, Jennifer was under the covers and Matt was in the rocking chair beside the bed. He was acting out the part of a dragon in one of Jennifer's favorite tales.

Tracy's heart turned over to see them together, and she pressed her lips together in a moment of wistfulness. She knew Jennifer missed her father but, stoically, rarely referred to it.

After Tracy got Jennifer settled, Matt followed her out onto the deck. It was getting dark, but the sky would retain its light cast for another hour. The backyard was shadowy, and a pleasant breeze tickled her skin as she and Matt unfolded aluminum chairs and placed them side by side on the other side of the deck, away from Jennifer's open window.

"Now, what did you want to tell me?" she asked.

Matt struggled with what he wanted to say to Tracy. It was made all the harder because of the mixed signals he was getting from her. He had come here out of a sense of duty and concern. But he had to wonder now if there was something else going on. Something neither of them would readily admit aloud.

He hadn't yet gotten over his frustration that she'd been in danger this morning. And he knew the police would lean on her further, since she had been a hostage and a witness.

Damn, he was getting in too deep. A SWAT team member was supposed to be emotionally stable and able to control himself in the aftermath of situations. But sitting here with Tracy reminded him of the festering dissatisfaction he'd felt ever since Scott had been killed in the line of duty.

He shifted in his aluminum chair so he could face her in the fading light. He could still see the glimmer in her warm brown eyes, and the softness about her mouth. He frowned, concentrating harder on what he had to say. They kept their voices low, so Jennifer wouldn't be disturbed.

"Tracy, you know I'd never say anything to hurt or worry you, if I could help it."

A little crease of worry marred her brow. "I know, Matt. But tell me what's bothering you. It'll be better to get it out in the open."

"Since the revolver that was in your safe-deposit box wasn't Scott's service revolver, I just want to make sure it wasn't a gun he might have bought for practice shooting when off duty."

Her narrow shoulders lifted and released in a shrug. "Not that I know of. I don't like guns, so I didn't pay any attention. But he wasn't a collector, if that's what you mean."

He noticed she tilted her chin as she moved her face away an inch.

"Scott did keep up with his training, pushed himself pretty hard. Sometimes I wondered if...well...if he enjoyed work more than family." She stopped for a moment, pressed her lips together, and then plunged on. "Maybe it was because Jennifer couldn't do the things with him he wanted to do if she'd been a boy. I don't know."

She was treading on territory he thought she might not want to speak of. And when he saw her lip tremble, he had the urge to comfort her. Instead, he squeezed the aluminum arms of the folding chair.

"Go on."

She shrugged her shoulders. "I just didn't think anything of it when that gun was returned to me. I didn't want to keep it at the house. Too dangerous with a child. So I just put it in the box at the bank.''

She turned to stare straight into his eyes. ''Why is it so important?''

''It might not be. It's just that that gun is the same caliber and make that killed Scott.''

An icy chill swept down Tracy's back. She knew where he was headed. The weapon that had killed Scott had never been found. Everyone assumed the criminals had gotten away with it. But this coincidence was just a little eerie.

The apprehension she'd tried to push down ever since leaving the bank this morning returned to engulf her. Her mouth felt dry again, but she moistened her lips as she formed the words she knew she had to say.

''That gun wasn't fired this morning,'' she told him. ''It was empty.''

The aluminum chair creaked as he leaned forward. ''How do you know?''

She repeated the scene as it had occurred in the basement conference room near the safe-deposit vault. Even in the near darkness, she could see the grim lines that etched deeper into his face.

''Then the bullets are still at the bank?''

''I suppose so,'' she answered. ''They wouldn't let me back in after they took my statement. I was angry that I couldn't get back to my valuables, but that sergeant guaranteed nothing would be disturbed. I'm supposed to go back in the morning to check the contents and sign a form confirming that everything else is as it was when I left the safe-deposit box open during the robbery. Then I can lock it back up again.''

He nodded thoughtfully, but didn't speak for a minute.

He was obviously thinking seriously about what she'd said.

"Tracy, I think I should go back to the bank now. It might be important."

Small hairs pricked at the back of her neck and along her shoulders. "Why?"

"If someone seized that gun, there might be a reason."

"But it was evidence. They thought it had been fired. Maybe they wanted to check it for fingerprints."

He leaned back again. "Maybe. You said Carrie and the robber handled it?"

"Yes, and I guess I did, too, when I lifted it out."

"If they can get Carrie's prints off it, that might be useful, but it's doubtful they'll be able to get anything clear enough. And you told me the robber had gloves on."

"I think so. He might have taken them off later."

He stood up. "I want to see the ballistics on that gun for myself. And I want to see if the investigators took the bullets in for evidence, as well."

She also stood up and moved closer to him, scrutinizing his intensity. Her pulse pounded with the urgency of the situation as Matt had painted it. His seriousness was frightening her, but she didn't want him to leave her alone yet to contemplate what he was saying.

"Are you going to the bank, then?" she asked softly.

He nodded almost imperceptibly. "There will still be a patrol on guard there, but I have rank. With luck, I'll be able to get in and look for myself."

She straightened her spine. "Then I'm going with you. You'll need me to show you where the safe-deposit box was left on the table."

"But you can't leave Jennifer."

She hesitated. "My next-door neighbor is an older woman and a close friend. She sometimes doesn't mind coming over and sitting up when I have an emergency errand to run. She knows what to do if Jennifer has a bad asthma attack. I can see if she's home.''

Matt ran a hand through his thick hair. ''All right. If you're sure. I don't like dragging you into this, Tracy. Your place is at home.''

''I'm already in it, aren't I, Matt?'' She heard the sardonic edge to her voice, but she didn't stop to apologize.

She hurried into her bedroom and picked up the phone there, dialing the familiar number. Mrs. McCaffrey was home and said she didn't mind at all. In a few moments, Tracy let her neighbor in and introduced her to Matt. As they shook hands, the woman beamed at his good looks.

''Yes, I remember seeing you here before.''

She sent Tracy an approving glance that made her blush.

''We won't be too long.''

''Take your time, dear. I've brought some gardening magazines I haven't had a chance to go through yet. Don't worry about a thing.''

After a few last-minute instructions about where to find the inhalers if she should need them, Tracy led Matt out the front door. He opened the door to his Chevy Blazer, and she slid in. The car smelled masculine and leathery, but clean—just like Matt. A clamor in the back of her mind wouldn't be ignored. They were just friends, weren't they? So why this attention to Matt's strong, male desirability?

She chalked it up to her year of loneliness and her traumatic day. Who wouldn't want to lean on a strong, capable friend? But she forced herself to remember just where all his capability came from. He was a cop, well trained and able to take care of business, to be sure. But SWAT team cops didn't have time for personal lives. As soon as they cleared up Matt's questions about the gun, he would be back to business as usual.

In a few minutes, they were driving slowly along Pearl Street, approaching the bank. Tracy glanced out her open window at the well-lit high-rise that towered on the corner of Second and Pearl. She thought Carrie had mentioned that Amanda Fielding lived there in a luxury condo. It made her shiver again, wondering if the bank president were going to be all right.

Matt swung into the bank parking lot and turned off the engine. The small, two-story building was still encircled with yellow police tape reading Police Line, Do Not Cross, and the shattered windows were boarded and sealed with plastic. The patrolman watching the premises came over to Matt, who got out of the car and showed his police ID.

"Lieutenant Matt Forrest," he said. "I was on the assault team this morning."

"Yes, sir, Lieutenant. What can I do for you?"

"This is Mrs. Meyer. She was a hostage during the crisis."

The young sergeant's smooth face turned to acknowledge her. His dark hair was clipped above his ears. "I see. Is there something you need here?"

Matt turned on a charming smile. "Actually, yes. Mrs. Meyer debriefed her experience to me. We need to go down to the safe-deposit room where her things were tossed aside when the gunman entered the room. She said something in her statement that she's not sure of now. Seeing the scene of the incident may jar her memory."

"Uh, well, I wasn't supposed to let anyone in tonight."

Matt frowned as if he were a busy man, and this minor barrier disrupted his important schedule. "Surely they've finished lifting prints and taking photographs."

"Well, yes, sir. I believe so. My only orders are to protect the place."

Matt smiled again. "And you're doing a fine job of that. I'll be sure your commander knows of your cooperation."

Matt was already walking and had grasped Tracy's elbow to escort her in. The sergeant acquiesced to Matt's seniority and bravado. He lifted a heavy key ring and unlocked the double lock to the front doors.

"Thank you, Sergeant. We won't be very long down there. You can lock the door up again, and I'll tap on the glass when we want out."

"Very well, sir."

The electricity was out, but a milky glow from all-night security lights gave the place an eerie feel. Matt turned on his flashlight. They crossed the marble floor to the stairs leading to the safe-deposit-vault area below, and Tracy could see that the scene was still a mess. Obviously the bank would be closed for business.

Office equipment still lay on the floor, and papers were scattered. Someone must have put the money away, for the timed vault appeared to be locked up tight. But the acrid, smoky smell still hadn't left the place.

Just being here again caused a tremor to race through her. She saw again in her mind's eye the people lying on the floor, fearing for their lives. The man who'd been shot and taken out bleeding. She hadn't even thought to inquire whether he still lived. Matt seemed to sense her discomfort and tightened his hold on her arm in a reassuring way.

"Don't trip," he said. "Hold on to the railing while I go first."

She waited until light from his flashlight made a pool in the darkness. Then she went down. "We were in here," she said, pointing the way.

"Stay there," said Matt. He used his foot to push the door open.

Her heart missed a beat when she looked into the room.

The table had been cleared. Then she saw her safe-deposit box at the side. She opened it quickly to see if the papers were all inside. When everything appeared to be in order, she breathed easier.

"Everything seems to be here. They must have been planning to have me check it and put it away tomorrow morning."

"What about the bullets?"

She shook her head. "Not here. They must've taken them."

"That's strange. Why would the investigating team come all the way down here and pick up bullets from a gun that obviously hadn't even been fired?"

She knew enough about police work to know that didn't make sense. "You're right. Whoever took them might have recognized them as matching the revolver that was on the grass."

She couldn't see Matt's face in the dark, but she could imagine that his brows were arched high in speculative query.

"They might have at that."

When he flicked the flashlight around the rest of the room, the shadows made her jump.

"I'm going to check with ballistics myself to see what happened to that gun," he said.

"Because it's the same type of gun that killed Scott?"

He paused for a heartbeat, and she trembled.

"I hope there's no connection. But I want to rule out that possibility. If it is the gun that killed Scott, we have a big problem."

She gave a shiver in the darkness. If it had been the gun that killed Scott, then someone may have known that— may have purposely given it to her in lieu of his real weapon, thinking, perhaps, that she would keep it out of sight. No one would think to search the widow's own house for the weapon that had killed him.

They returned upstairs, their shoes crunching on broken glass on the marble floor. Matt tapped on the door, and the sergeant came to let them out. The fresh summer air and the light breeze never felt so good. She stayed close to Matt as they crossed the parking lot to his car. Then they drove through the old residential neighborhood in strained silence.

Tracy wanted to tell herself that his fears were unfounded. For a year since Scott had died, she had struggled to give Jennifer as normal a life as possible. True, the financial strain was eating away at her, but she just didn't need the evil specter of Scott's death coming back to haunt them now.

They passed the busy intersection at Downing and Alameda and soon were cruising beside Washington Park. The park was dark now, its broad expanse of grass leading to a lake around which runners jogged during the day. Fragrances from the formal gardens softened the night air.

A sigh escaped Tracy's lips. What she wanted more than anything in the world was a quiet life with Jennifer. The doctors were giving her hope that with the proper nutrition and care, Jennifer might grow out of her asthma. If only they could hang on. They had lost Scott. Nothing would bring him back. She half decided to tell Matt he was chasing a phantom and to leave the past alone. She didn't want to look back anymore.

She had almost decided to unload her sentiments once they were inside the house, but Mrs. McCaffrey got up with a worried look on her face when they entered the living room. Tracy's heart immediately leaped to her throat.

"What is it?" she asked urgently, thinking something had happened to Jennifer.

"Jennifer's fine, my dear. But you had a phone call."

"From whom?"

"It was rather hurried. The caller didn't seem to have much time."

"Who was it?"

"I'm sorry, she didn't leave a number. She said she'd call back when she had a chance. She said to tell you she was all right."

Tracy froze, waiting for Mrs. McCaffrey to finish.

"I wrote her name down before I'd forget. She even spelled it for me."

The neighbor handed Tracy a small piece of paper. On it was scrawled the name *Carrie Lamb*.

Chapter Four

"What else did she say?" Tracy asked. "Where is she?"

"I'm sorry." Mrs. McCaffrey looked apologetically first at Tracy and then at Matt. "The call was very hurried. I'm not sure I caught everything. She was speaking so softly. She just said to tell you she was all right and that she was sorry."

Tracy felt her veins turn to lead, but she tried not to show her agitation in front of her neighbor. "That's all right, Mrs. McCaffrey. I'm sure she'll call back. I hope we weren't gone too long."

"Not at all, dear. And Jennifer didn't even wake up."

Matt offered to see Mrs. McCaffrey to her house. When he came back in, he had his cell phone with him. His cheeks were tense, his hazel eyes serious.

"I'll arrange for a wiretap. She might call again."

Tracy nodded woodenly. "Do what you have to."

She sank down onto the sofa while Matt made the call. He paced away from her so she didn't have to listen to the details.

Carrie had said she was sorry. Sorry for what? If she could call here, she could call the police to come help her if she were in trouble.

Matt made a second call. When he hung up, his look in

the dim light cast from her living-room lamp told her it wasn't good news.

"The motorcycle they got away on was apparently stolen. The owner lost it over six months ago. They haven't found them yet."

Tracy swallowed a lump in her throat. "Then she's still with that bank robber. What does he want?"

Matt shook his head, his golden eyes flickering with knowledge she had the feeling he hesitated to impart.

"There have been no demands. If he abducted her to use as a hostage, he would have reached the police by now and made a deal."

She could tell from the look on his features that he was trying to communicate what she didn't want to hear.

"Maybe she just can't get away from him," she suggested. "He might have locked her up in a motel room somewhere and she had a chance for a quick phone call," she said.

"Then why didn't she call the police?"

Her heart dropped to her feet, and they stared at each other for a moment. She read the suspicion written all over his face. He continued his patient reasoning.

"When Amanda Fielding's doctor allows her to be questioned, the FBI agents will have some hard questions for her. Carrie Lamb's background seems to stop with her arrival in Denver. If Amanda Fielding hired her, she must know some things about her we don't." One eyebrow arched in grim cynicism.

Tracy's lips parted in shock. "What about her fingerprints? Aren't all bank employees fingerprinted?"

"They're checking on that now."

Tracy slumped against the sofa. "She never talked much about her past. But I assumed it was because she had things in her life she didn't want to remember. She let it slip out that she'd been married once, but she hadn't wanted to talk about it. I could understand that.''

Matt put his phone down and lowered himself into the easy chair next to the fireplace. He leaned forward, his elbows on his knees.

"I'm sorry your friend is mixed up in this."

She caught a glimpse of his eyes flicking in the direction of the hallway and Jennifer's bedroom. She shivered, knowing what Matt was thinking. But at the same time, she just couldn't believe his suspicions.

"You're worried that Jennifer was being tutored by a criminal."

"I didn't say that, Tracy. But it does look like Carrie has something to hide."

"Well, whatever it is, I can assure you that since I've known Carrie Lamb, her behavior has been exemplary. She truly likes children and is a good tutor. It was as if Carrie missed her old profession and was grateful for the opportunity to be able to teach someone."

Matt gave her a penetrating stare. "Then why wasn't she a teacher here in Denver? There are job openings all the time, at least at the substitute level. If she liked to teach so much, why was she working as a bank teller?"

"I...I don't know." Tracy's mind raced for an explanation. She'd never even considered the reasons before. "She did know Amanda prior to getting the job here. Maybe Amanda arranged the job before Carrie moved to Denver so she'd have employment right away. I don't know."

Matt's voice softened. "I don't mean to be giving you the third degree. It's just that I know these are questions the FBI is going to research. They'll probably want to talk to you, as well."

"I know."

They let the heavy silence hover over them for a moment. Tracy felt a series of overwhelming sensations—regret, worry, a growing dependence on Matt that scared her.

"Are you sure you'll be all right? I can arrange for some extra protection for you."

Tracy hugged herself. She'd never liked living in the house alone with Jennifer after Scott had died. And now that real trouble was afoot, she ought to take Matt up on his offer. But there wasn't a real need for him to stay here. A bank had been robbed. There was no reason trouble should follow her home. If Carrie called again, she would try to keep her on the line long enough for the call to be traced. There was nothing else to be done.

"No, thank you, Matt. We'll be all right. If Carrie calls again…"

Matt nodded. "Keep her on the line. The sooner this is resolved, the better. Until then, you'd better get some rest. I'll go."

His eyes blazed across the room at her, and it made her heart skitter. The words to ask him to stay were on the tip of her tongue. But that wasn't fair. He was working overtime just by involving himself in something that should have ended for him when the crisis was over this morning. And he would have his regular shift tomorrow, as well.

She got up. "Thank you," she said in a husky voice. "You've done more than your share already."

"Anytime."

She could hear the emotion in his voice. The old bond between them was still there. As if he owed her something because he hadn't been there the day Scott had been killed. She saw the pain in his eyes every time he was reminded of it. She wanted to wrap her arms around him and lay her head against his shoulder, to tell him to stop thinking about his friend's death, that it hadn't been his fault.

But she didn't say anything except good-night. Their eyes locked for a moment, and then he turned to go. She shut the door after him and locked it.

After Matt left, Tracy peeked into Jennifer's room. The soft night-light in the outlet by the door cast dim outlines of the furniture in the room. A sliver of moonlight slipped between the curtains and splayed across Jennifer's face. She lay sleeping and breathing fairly normally. Tracy felt a clutch of tenderness as she tiptoed to the bed and pulled the covers straighter, making sure Jennifer had plenty of room to breathe if she turned over.

It made Tracy think again about Andrew Leigh, Jennifer's grandfather. Surely if she talked to the man, she could persuade him that she could take care of Jennifer. She would get to see her grandfather anytime he wanted. But Tracy just couldn't let this little girl be torn from her. A sob clutched her heart.

Was she being selfish? Did she really want what was best for Jennifer? Tracy swallowed hard as she left the bedroom and quietly made her way down the narrow hallway, past the bathroom to her own bedroom at the front of the house. Jennifer's grandfather had money. He would find the best and most expensive doctors, and could send her to special private schools. A niggling self-doubt pried itself into her desperate determination. She loved Jennifer, but maybe love wasn't enough.

She took off her clothes and tossed them into her laundry basket, donning a cotton knit sleep T-shirt that came to her knees. The ringing phone made her practically jump out of her skin.

Before she snatched it up, she hesitated. It might be Carrie, and she tried to control her thumping heart enough to remember what to do: keep her on the line, try to find out where she was. Her overwhelming concern was for Carrie's safety.

"Hello?"

The hiss of breath that came over the line wasn't Carrie's voice. When the voice came, it was low and tense. And the threatening edge to the words sent a shiver of dread coursing through her veins.

"Where's your friend Carrie?" asked a raspy but distorted voice.

"What?" She heard what he'd said, but she was so startled, she gasped.

"She called you, Mrs. Meyer. Just tell me what she said."

"Who is this?" Her heartbeat rose and hammered even louder. But she kept her voice low to avoid waking Jennifer.

"A friend of Carrie's," he said. "I'm going to help her."

Tracy tried to think. If the police had activated the wiretap, they were picking this up. They could find out where the caller was phoning from. She had to play along.

"What makes you think she needs help?" she asked in what she hoped was a seminormal voice.

"Don't play games, Mrs. Meyer. Your little girl's tutor is in a tight spot. I can fix it for her."

Hearing the caller mention Jennifer made Tracy break out in perspiration. Her chill of dread turned to terror. Where was this caller? And who was he? Still, she tried to think logically, say the right things to find out what she needed to know.

"Listen, mister," she said with a sexy swagger she didn't feel. "I might be willing to tell you what she said if you tell me a little more about who you are. What's Carrie to you?''

Now the voice became impatient and irritated. ''I told you, a friend. If you want to keep safe, you'll cooperate with me. I have a very long reach. Very long indeed.''

Now anger began to accompany her fear. ''How dare you threaten me,'' she said, allowing her voice to get louder than she intended. She glanced toward the hallway but didn't perceive any stirrings from Jennifer's room. ''It so happens that I don't know where Carrie is,'' she said, hoping to be able to bargain. ''I might be able to help you if she calls again, but only if you'll help me.''

She waited, listening to the wheezing breath coming from what sounded like very far away.

''Well?'' he finally asked. ''What do you want me to do for you?''

''I want you to tell me where you think Carrie might have gone. If she's not with that bank robber, why has she disappeared? What reason would she have to hide?''

She thought she heard the voice chuckle, but it was muffled and sarcastic. The sound was not reassuring.

''You ask a lot of questions, Mrs. Meyer. That cop friend of yours putting ideas into your head?''

She squeezed the phone with one hand, her other hand curling up into a ball. She glanced toward the windows, wondering if the caller were watching her now. Icy fear gripped her, but she tried to keep that from seeping into the sound of her voice.

''Maybe my friends have a long reach themselves, Mr. Whoever You Are. Can I give a message to Carrie if she calls again?'' She prayed the call was being traced.

''Tell her I'm waiting for her with open arms.''

''Who? Who is waiting for her?''

The line clicked off. For several seconds, Tracy just sat

on the edge of her bed staring at the phone in her hand. She was petrified. Who was the mysterious caller, and how did he know Carrie had called here? She pressed her lips between her teeth and gnawed on her lower lip. Then she started to shake. In a delayed reaction to the threats and danger, she perceived the fact that the caller knew an awful lot about her personal life. She shivered and shook so hard, she could barely get the receiver back into its cradle.

Then she sat upright, hugging herself, trying to decide what to do. She'd refused Matt's offer of putting someone outside to watch her house. Now she didn't feel so brave.

She forced her fingers to stop shaking long enough to dial Matt's cell phone. He answered on the second ring.

"Matt." She didn't even have to identify herself. Her desperation was communicated through that one word.

"What's wrong?"

"I had a phone call."

She suddenly realized that the mysterious caller may have already tapped into her phone line. How else would he have known that Carrie had called? She didn't want to say too much.

"I'm reconsidering your earlier offer," she said, hoping Matt would know what she was talking about.

It only took him a breath. "I'm coming back," he told her. "An officer is patrolling your street now. I'll have him sit outside and wait until I get through traffic. Don't worry, Tracy. Nothing is going to happen to you or Jennifer."

She allowed herself to breathe. In spite of her refusing the offer of protective surveillance, he must have told someone to drive by and keep an eye out anyway. Silently, she thanked him.

"I'll be waiting," she whispered.

MATT REACTED TO THE SOUND of Tracy's voice and swung the car around instantly, adrenaline pulsing. Carrie must have called back. Picking up the microphone, he contacted the dispatcher and made sure that patrol car was covering Tracy's house. Then, because police bands were so commonly monitored by felons, he used his cell phone to contact communications control. The officer monitoring the phone line was a fellow he knew and trusted, Leo Tully.

"We'd barely got patched in," Leo told him. "We taped the caller, but lost him before we nailed his location."

"Damn! I take it the feds are running this one."

"You got it. Rules are we turn over everything we uncover to the special agent who's been designated task-force leader. They're supposed to cooperate with us on the assault charges. The male gunshot victim they pulled out of there was in surgery all afternoon. The wounded suspect is still in the hospital with a blood-clot complication. But the other one is thinking about talking."

"Keep me posted."

Fifteen minutes later, Matt pulled up in front of Tracy's house. When she opened the door, he could see the terror in her eyes. She pushed the door shut after he entered the room, then she turned around, her fists curled up in balls against her sides as if to keep herself from shaking.

He pulled her against him silently, letting his body protect and comfort her immediate fears. He wanted to hold her close all night, but an inner instinct told him she wanted to be strong. He knew she'd decided long ago that she had to learn to take care of herself and Jennifer. So he stepped away, making sure she was steady.

"Tell me about it."

She motioned him inside and drew a deep breath. "I'll go close Jennifer's door," she said.

He looked around, noticing the bright lights everywhere, something a woman alone would do if she was worried about an intruder.

"It was horrible," she said when she returned. He could hear the shudder in her voice, and her brown eyes were round with fright. "A man called. He had a weird voice. He asked where Carrie was. He knew she'd called. What's worse, he knew all about us."

Matt tilted his head in a query as she went on.

"He said if I wanted to keep Jennifer safe, I'd better cooperate. He knew about you. I tried to keep him on the phone." She looked up at his eyes. "Did they find him?"

He hated having to tell her the truth. "They recorded the call, but they couldn't track it fast enough. You did fine, Tracy, just fine. Don't worry."

She seemed to sway then, as if at the end of her strength. She came into his arms again, and he could almost feel the relief in her body that someone was there to support her. He gently slid his arm around her back and tucked her into his shoulder. His chin rested beside her head, and he had to struggle not to dip his mouth toward her ear.

He was even more attracted to her than he had thought. Her soft breasts brushed up against him, and he worried suddenly that his arousal would make itself felt against her naked thighs. He shifted her, guessing that in her vulnerable state, she probably wouldn't take kindly to male aggression.

He clasped her hand and pulled her down on the sofa. Sitting down, he could hide his evident arousal more easily. Besides, satisfying himself sexually would serve little purpose. His ache for Tracy demanded more. He suddenly knew that he needed to make her trust him. But more than that, he realized he needed to do some hard thinking about why it was that he was getting so involved with her right now. Feelings for a beautiful friend were one thing, but the complications of a relationship with a child involved were quite something else.

He kept hold of her hand and frowned in concentration. "I don't like this," he murmured. "Whoever this person is, he knows too much. But we'll get him. I promise you that."

She bit her lip as if doubting the truth of that. He squeezed her hand. "I'll stay here tonight and sleep on the sofa. The patrol car is outside. You won't be in any danger."

She sighed. "I'm grateful for that. But what about tomorrow? We can't live in fear that we're being watched all the time. I don't want Jennifer to know there's any threat."

He nodded. Then an idea surfaced and he grinned. "I've got the perfect solution. Tomorrow is the Denver Police Department's annual picnic at Elitch's. They had it on Thursday because the park will be less crowded. The picnic goes from about three o'clock until the park closes. I'll take you and Jennifer with me. Where could you be safer than at the police family picnic?"

He waited while she considered this. Thoughts fluttered across her face, and he could imagine what she was thinking. It would be a strong reminder that she was a department cop's widow. She might feel awkward seeing Scott's old acquaintances, but he knew he was right about taking her with him.

"It's been a year, Tracy," he said softly. "There are people who will want to see you and Jennifer, make sure you're doing all right."

She ground her teeth and then said grimly, "We aren't doing all right. Not right now. They don't know that the money they so generously donated is locked up in a bank and can't help Jennifer now. And that someone out there is threatening us.''

''No, they don't know all that,'' he said steadily. ''But we're going to take care of it.''

''How?''

''I'm committed to helping you sort out things with Jennifer's grandfather and with the bank. I won't see you struggle, Tracy.'' Then, self-conscious at this declaration, he covered his bravado by adding, ''I owe it to Scott.''

Her beautiful brows wrinkled as she thought it all over. My God, did she know how pretty she was with that thick hair, and those soulful, sexy eyes? He cleared his throat, trying to keep his thoughts away from lust. He also loosened her hand, realizing he was crushing it.

Gradually, she seemed to relax. ''All right. We'll go.''

She glanced away, as if not wanting to look at him. For a moment, hope surged that she was feeling the same desire he was. But then he cooled those flames. They were in danger and needed to remain alert. It just wasn't the right time.

''Good girl. I'll just get some things from the car.''

She left him to go find some extra bedding. He went outside, more to let the breezy night air cool him off than to rummage in the back of his car. But he brought in the cell phone and a small kit he kept in the car for emergencies when he'd been on an all-night stakeout and couldn't get home to freshen up. He also had to bring in his SWAT equipment for security.

He noticed when he returned to the living room how Tracy avoided direct eye contact. She had made up a bed for him on the couch and piled thick towels and washcloths on top of a pillow.

''I hope you'll be comfortable,'' she said.

''I'll be fine. Beats sitting up all night in the back room

of a mom-and-pop store waiting for suspects to hold up the place.''

She pulled a corner of her mouth to the side at his joke. Then he wished he hadn't said it. Everything that reminded her of SWAT team work must turn her off. He didn't say any more. Finally, she faced him.

''You can use the bathroom first,'' she said. ''I'm too wired to sleep yet.''

''Make yourself some hot milk.''

Her mouth softened, but he didn't trust himself to gaze at her for too long. He strode on through to shower. He paused at the hallway with his hand on the doorjamb. Tracy paused, too, just before stepping through the opening from the dining area to the still brightly lit kitchen. They held each other's eyes for a moment, but he couldn't read her thoughts.

TRACY SIPPED THE HOT MILK, knowing it wasn't the warm liquid alone that steadied her. She was moved by Matt's friendship and knew the only reason she'd be able to sleep at all was that he was in the house.

She checked on Jennifer again to make sure she hadn't cooled off too much. Then she tiptoed down the wood-floored hallway, pausing beside the bathroom. The sound of the shower and of Matt moving around inside caused a warm, prickly feeling. She could picture his strong, well-formed, thoroughly fit physique pushing the shower curtain back and stepping into the hot water.

She hurried on to her bedroom, where a small table lamp cast its glow on the one object in the room that frightened her. She felt tempted to disconnect the phone so she wouldn't have to deal with any more calls tonight. She clenched her jaw as her bare feet came in contact with a chenille throw rug.

But the fatigue was overwhelming as she lowered herself into the bed and tucked feet beneath a sheet. It would be too warm to use the blanket. She turned the light out, then lay awake listening to the shower, straining to hear any changes in Jennifer's breathing. Gradually, she became attuned to the night outside her open window. But it was a night full of danger. Her heart rate kept up its patter as she lay in the darkness.

Not being able to do anything further right now about her worsening dilemmas, she simply listened to the sounds around her. She heard the water stop, heard Matt moving about in the bathroom. She felt a quiver at the thought that she might catch a glimpse of him padding across the hall in nothing but a towel.

She turned on her side and decided not to nurse that sensual thought. She must resist the temptations presented by his being here. They might do things they'd later have to disentangle themselves from. The last thing he probably wanted was to get saddled with a woman and child. He simply would not want that weight dragging at him.

As a bachelor, he could devote himself to his demanding job and be a hero. She'd heard very little about the women he'd dated in the past. She thought she remembered Scott saying that one woman Matt had been fairly serious about had thrown him over for someone else. Maybe he'd been burned.

And she wouldn't go to bed with him for a one-night stand, no matter how much that thought tempted her hormones. To be able to drink in his strength, to be caressed and able to forget about life just for a single night…the thoughts still tugged at her, and the flame of need throbbed within her.

No, she instructed her unruly mind. Passion in the night would only lead to the ugly light of day filled with all its problems. Sex would solve nothing and only make them both feel guilty and awkward afterward.

She tossed to her other side and forced herself to think about the soft breeze outside. *Think positive thoughts.* Tomorrow they would find Carrie. Tomorrow a miracle would occur. Andrew Leigh would call and tell her he was dropping his suit for custody. Matt would take them to the picnic. Jennifer would be able to manage some of the rides without any problems.

She had to make tomorrow a good day.

Chapter Five

Matt was up and out of the house before anyone stirred. He always got to work early, but more than that, he felt it would be easier not to see Tracy in the morning. He'd awakened cramped and aware immediately of the temptation of a comfortable bed with a soft, warm, desirable woman in it just on the other side of the wall. When he made his way to the bathroom to shave, he resisted the temptation to peer into her open doorway and try to catch a glimpse of her lovely form sleeping.

Even so, he felt the tug of hormones and shut the bathroom door firmly. Matt hadn't intentionally been celibate these past months, but he'd dated few women who could understand his schedule or his dedication to his job. Or maybe he hadn't met anyone he cared about seeing more than a few times. No one with whom he'd care to communicate deeply.

He stared at his unshaved chin and rumpled hair in the mirror. The word *bond* just hadn't applied to other relationships he'd had in the past.

But he and Tracy had a bond. He could feel it even when they weren't speaking. His diaphragm tightened as he pictured her standing in the opening to the kitchen when their eyes had locked last night. She needed him; he could almost feel it.

He rubbed his scalp and frowned. He was letting his imagination run away with him. She was pretty and sexy, and she had a great kid. Maybe he was just getting pulled into their desperate situation. He needed to be careful not to mistake Tracy's need for a friend with anything else. Hormones didn't think, and he had to think this morning. About a lot of things.

A half hour later, he left the house, softly closing the door behind him. He'd left a note saying he would call before he picked them up for the picnic today. On his way down the steps to where he'd left his car on the street, he let his sharp gaze sweep the neighborhood. He spotted the unmarked police car with its occupant reading the paper. It was best to have the surveillance team keep a low profile until they found out who the mysterious caller was and where Carrie Lamb had disappeared to.

This morning the SWAT team had a classroom training session downtown. Part of the session would be a review of what happened yesterday morning to make sure the team had acted in the most efficient way possible. Since a hostage had been abducted, that wasn't likely, unless the commander decided that negligence on someone else's part had allowed that to happen.

Matt was glad this was a classroom session. He didn't want to take the time necessary to drive all the way out to their tactical range where they practiced regularly. After the class, he should have some time to find out what was going on in ballistics. He'd have to be clever, though, as official channels didn't allow him access to what he wanted to know.

Matt drove the Blazer into the underground lot where police personnel parked beneath the six-story, fortresslike police-administration building at Thirteenth and Bannock. It was still an hour before the SWAT team would assemble, so instead of taking the elevator to the classrooms, he entered the building and went to the basement-level property-management bureau. He was relieved to find Shelly Dunning holding down the reception desk. The ebony-complected woman was an old friend and might help him. At least she wouldn't snitch on him.

"Hi there, Shelly, how ya doing?" he said with his most charming smile as he let the door shut behind him. "In early today?"

She lifted a plucked eyebrow and flexed long red fingernails in his direction. "I'm always here at seven, Matthew. But I haven't seen you prowling this corridor before breakfast. What's on your mind?"

He put on an official tone, though he doubted it would fool the very efficient Shelly. "Wanted to take a look at some of the evidence from yesterday's assault at the Empire Bank of Colorado. Commander's critiquing the team this morning."

Shelly tilted her head to the left. "Room 2. Just sign the sheet on the clipboard."

"Thanks. Won't be a minute."

He didn't want to sign the sheet. He didn't want anyone else to know he was looking at the evidence yet.

He pushed open the door to the small conference room where the confiscated evidence was stored in individual plastic bags with white tags identifying them. Minute particles were stored in plastic containers with sealed lids. Everything was still laid out on one table. It only took him two minutes to ascertain that what he was looking for wasn't here. He referred to the printed list of items and felt a sudden heat of suspicion.

Next, he consulted the list of signatures of officers and

lab technicians who had signed articles out. The FBI had a special agent assigned as task-force leader. But catching the bank robber who'd gotten away yesterday wasn't his concern. He smelled another rat, much closer, and that was his concern.

Shelly saw his frown when he emerged from the room. "Something wrong, Lieutenant?"

He shrugged. "Don't know. Someone picked up a .38 from the scene. Don't see it in there. Ballistics or the lab check it out?"

"No way."

"You're sure?" he queried.

"No .38 on that list. I typed it up myself." She leveled her dark-eyed gaze at him. "It matter?"

He leaned over and rested his hands on her desk, speaking confidentially. "What matters is that no one knows I'm asking. Can I count on that?"

She considered him a minute. Shelly wasn't about to get herself in trouble. But she ought to know Matt well enough to understand that if he had a reason to ask her for a favor, it was a good one. He watched the considerations flicker across her smooth complexion.

Then she nodded and went back to the papers on her desk. "Long as no one else saw you in here, I surely didn't."

"Thanks. I owe you." He glided out and took the stairs two at a time.

Upstairs he hailed his buddy, Roland Baker. The tall, steady sniper was as cool as they came. A dead shot at a hundred yards, he had the self-confidence and patience to get a target in range and keep it there without getting trigger-happy. Matt trusted him with his life.

They had also shared thoughts about circumstances surrounding Scott Meyer's death a year ago. Neither man was satisfied that it couldn't have been prevented. But the official investigation into the matter had found no one at fault.

As the rest of the team drifted into the classroom to slouch down in their seats, some of them sipping from plastic coffee containers, Matt cornered Roland by the water cooler. He lowered his voice.

"You know that missing murder weapon that killed our buddy Meyer last year?"

Roland turned his silent attention to Matt. He gave a slight nod.

"I have a funny feeling it turned up on the grass at the assault yesterday and was confiscated."

Matt saw the muscles in Roland's jaw work. "And?"

Matt glanced over his shoulder, then leaned closer. "It belonged to Tracy Meyer, which was why it was at the bank in her safe-deposit box. Problem is, it's not in the evidence room now."

"Ballistics checking it out?" asked Roland. His sharp eyes scanned the hallway to make sure no one was listening to them.

"Nope. Shelly says it never came in as evidence."

Roland's sharp blue eyes studied his friend. "What're you going to do about it?"

"I'm not sure. There were some bullets in Tracy Meyer's safe-deposit box. They've disappeared, too, just like that." Matt snapped his fingers for emphasis.

When Roland did speak a whole sentence, it came out as a growl, the creases in his weathered face deepening. "It's not our territory. You're not going to get any cooperation."

"I know that," Matt grumbled. "I believe what Tracy told me. She has a right to know what happened to that gun."

Roland gave him an understanding smile. "Lines are drawn in this agency, my friend. You're supposed to know your role and not try to do anybody else's job."

Matt knew that Roland was only giving him a friendly reminder. In an agency as large as this one, it usually didn't pay to buck the system. But his mouth formed a grim line.

"Sorry, I can't let it go," he muttered. "That gun might have killed Meyer."

Roland refilled his paper cup from the water cooler. "You want someone to pay."

Matt nodded slowly, the old anger like lead in his belly. "I don't want the guilty party to get away with it."

"You still think one of our own did it and not the suspects on the run." Roland spoke to Matt but scanned the hallway for listeners.

"You saw the diagrams of the angles of the shots and read the testimony of the witnesses. From where Meyer was deployed, it would have been impossible for those suspects to have shot him in the back."

"The conclusion was that an inside accomplice got away," said Roland blandly.

"Likely story. No accomplice was ever identified."

"Yeah, well, I wish you luck if you're going to try to get the case reopened."

Matt put a noncommittal expression on his face, but his friend read his thoughts correctly. He was going to do this his way.

"Watch your back," warned Roland.

Matt lifted an eyebrow in reply.

TRACY FLIPPED THE PAGES of the morning paper, reading headlines as she sipped her coffee. After Matt had left, she'd gotten herself and Jennifer ready and taken Jennifer to day camp. Then she'd gone to the bank to sign the release form so they could lock her safe-deposit box back up. The police had her statement typed up, and she met them there to sign it, as well.

Back home now, she had time to do some thinking before making the phone call she knew she needed to make. She wanted to talk to Andrew Leigh personally. Try to make him understand why it would be better for Jennifer to remain here.

But before she confronted that task, she fixed herself a bracing cup of coffee and scanned the newspaper. Pictures from the bank robbery were all over pages one and four. She made a sour face looking at them. She didn't even want to read the text; she didn't need to be reminded of what had happened.

Other news also caught her eye. On the page opposite was an item about another incident that had occurred yesterday. Federal felon Jax Schaffer had escaped from the police van that was transporting him from the holding facility to the federal courthouse. The officers guarding him were slain and the prisoner freed. The escape vehicle was eventually found abandoned along Coal Mine Road. Schaffer's mug shot was pictured.

Tracy shook her head at the incident. She didn't like to think that she and Jennifer lived in an area with so much crime. It reminded her again of Carrie, and she glanced over at the phone.

What was wrong with the police that they couldn't find her? That motorcycle couldn't have gone that far. In spite of herself, suspicion niggled at the back of her mind. Like Schaffer, who no doubt had his escape planned with changes of cars and hideouts, Carrie's abductor must have had places he knew he could go to ground. But Carrie was pretty smart. It seemed that she could have left clues along the way if she'd wanted to.

Only then, sitting alone in her kitchen and having the time to ponder what had happened, did Tracy truly wonder if Carrie Lamb was running from something. But the more she tried to figure it out, the less it made any sense.

She got up to refill her coffee cup, then sat down and pushed the newspaper aside, concentrating on what she was going to say to Andrew Leigh. Fifteen minutes later, she had him on the phone.

A grumpy, hurried voice said, "This is Andrew Leigh."

"Tracy Meyer," she said into the phone.

A slight pause. "Mrs. Meyer. I assume your lawyer has received papers from my lawyer."

"I don't have a lawyer yet, Mr. Leigh. It seems to me that if you and I could talk about this sensibly, we might reach an understanding." Tracy squeezed her cold coffee cup. "I'm willing to try."

"I think I understand things clearly, Mrs. Meyer. You're hard up for cash and Jennifer needs care. I wouldn't be in my right mind if I left her there without any blood relatives to make sure she's being taken care of."

Tracy gripped the phone with both hands, speaking into the mouthpiece intently. "I do care for her, Mr. Leigh, to the best of my ability. She needs some stability right now, and a move would be upsetting to her. This is her home."

"I understand your feelings, but I can't agree. My information says she's in a public school, probably not one trained to deal with asthmatics. You can't afford to continue her care without financial aid. You need to go to work, Mrs. Meyer, and that will leave Jennifer without anyone at home."

"I won't do that to Jennifer." Tracy heard her voice rising. "I quit work so I could take care of her."

"I am her grandfather," interrupted the gruff voice. "You can't keep her away from me."

"Blood relations aren't everything, Mr. Leigh. Surely there is a way we can work things out so we both see Jennifer."

"She is blood family, and I want her here in Chicago where I can see her. She's all I've got left. I won't change my mind."

"She is family to me...." Tracy had to stifle a rising sob of frustration. "Surely—"

"You're wasting your time, Mrs. Meyer. Have your attorney call mine."

"I said I didn't have an—" But he hung up.

She stared at the phone, her heart cracking. She couldn't believe it. He had hung up. Exhaling, she replaced the phone in its cradle and sat down at the kitchen table before her wobbly legs gave way. Then she placed her elbows on the table and braced her head in her hands. She would have to get a lawyer. And she couldn't afford one good enough to fight the powerful Andrew Leigh. She might as well hand Jennifer over right now. There was just no winning against him.

After five minutes of rubbing her eyes and slumping over the table, she got up to pour a fresh cup of coffee. She couldn't give up. She just couldn't. But where to turn? Amanda Fielding had not only refused to help with the trust fund, but the poor woman was now also suffering from a blow to the head.

Tracy's hand reached for the phone to call Denver General to find out about Amanda's condition again. She knew it was selfish. She would hardly spare more than an appropriate sympathetic thought for the sophisticated bank president were it not for the fact that she was intricately involved in Jennifer's trust fund.

A quick phone call informed her that Amanda Fielding had gone home and would be resting there. Tracy sighed. Hardly the time to call and badger her. No, she'd have to think of something else.

For the time being, she needed to drag herself around the house and take care of the endless cleaning. It was the day for the bathroom to be scrubbed to guard against mold spores forming that could trigger Jennifer's asthma episodes.

After changing into grubby work clothes and getting out the cleaning supplies, she threw herself into the hard physical work. It was the only thing she could do that would keep her from going crazy.

TRACY WAS READY when Matt rang the doorbell at four o'clock. She had managed to dress, pick up Jennifer and return home in time to splash water on her face before he got here. Vanity prevented her from letting Matt see her looking as hot and frazzled as she felt.

Just before she reached to open the door, a twinge of guilt assailed her. It was almost as if Scott were watching them, and she tried to deal with her reasons for looking forward to seeing Matt so much.

Scott is dead, she reminded herself. *I'm not cheating on him. Matt and I never so much as looked at each other while Scott was alive. He was just another cop on the team, albeit a good-looking one.*

But then she opened the door and stared at Matt's strong, sexy presence standing in the shade on her porch, and her hormones raged. His tight black T-shirt outlined bulging muscles and left his tanned, powerful arms bare from the biceps down. And his tight-fitting jeans outlined trim hips and thighs that bulged against the denim.

It stung her to realize the force of her attraction to him.

She'd never thought of him this way when she'd known him as her husband's friend. But now with Scott gone, she and Matt looked into each other's eyes and heat sprang between them. Her breath became quicker, and she flushed in embarrassment, hoping he would think it was just the sun.

His eyes registered pleasure at her appearance, and she wiped her hands down the sides of her sturdy white cotton shorts. They were cut modestly, with deep pockets and cuffs across her tanned thighs. But she saw his gaze glance across the curve of her breasts, firmly supported in an athletic bra beneath the lime-green T-shirt.

"Come in," she finally said.

His handsome lips lifted in a sensuous smile, and she imagined that if it hadn't been for Jennifer getting ready in her room, she and Matt might have made themselves comfortable on the couch and spent the rest of the afternoon indulging in what single, consenting adults did when aroused to the frenzy she was beginning to feel hovering beneath their social veneers.

He stepped into the living room and shut the door, but she was still aware of the heat of his gaze on her back as she moved into the room.

"All ready?" he asked.

"Yes. Jennifer should be ready in just a minute. Would you like anything to drink before we go?"

"I'm fine."

Dear Lord, I'm not, she thought, feeling wobbly and still not recovered from the anxieties of the night and morning.

She led Matt into the kitchen, giving Jennifer a few more minutes. She purposely didn't hover when Jennifer was changing clothes. It was important that a child with a disease such as she had be as self-reliant as possible. So

Tracy let her make her own decision about what to wear to the picnic.

Matt also seemed to turn his thoughts to the serious matters before them. By the time they'd reached the kitchen, his face had lost its look of anticipation and was replaced by grim concern.

"Did you have any more phone calls?" he asked.

"No. What's happening downtown?"

"Nothing new." He looked down as if thinking about whether he should continue. Tracy sensed he was withholding something.

"What is it?" she asked quickly.

He pulled his lips sideways before he spoke, but then looked into her eyes. "I paid a visit to the evidence room this morning to check on your gun."

"And?"

"It wasn't there." His tone rang with irony. "My friend Shelly, who typed up the list, assured me it hadn't been turned in as evidence."

Tracy frowned. "Why not?"

"You tell me."

It wasn't accusatory. He was just conveying the fact that it made no sense.

He continued. "Why would someone on the scene confiscate a weapon and ammunition and not turn it in?"

"Did you ask?"

Matt gave her a mocking look. "This isn't exactly my territory. The FBI has a task-force leader on the case, and they're rather territorial about their turf. If I'm going to play by the rules, I don't get to ask."

Tracy felt a low thrum of warning. "Then you're not going to play by the rules."

He just lifted his chin stubbornly, but didn't answer.

She shook her head. "But why would anyone take the gun?"

Matt's face seemed to darken slightly, and the creases in his cheeks and forehead revealed themselves a little more sternly. "Someone would take it only if he had something to hide."

Tracy gave a shiver. "And what would that be?" She was afraid she knew the answer. "You think that gun killed Scott."

He nodded. "And whoever took it knew that."

Tracy closed her eyes. Feelings that she thought she'd dealt with and buried rose up to cause a nasty tightening in her throat. She spoke with her eyes still closed. "What good is it? We can't prove anything."

She opened her eyes when she felt his hand on her arm. The heat radiating from his hand communicated a deep intensity that she felt right down to the soles of her feet. She looked up into his eyes.

"You can't let it go, can you?" she asked him.

"Can you?"

She waited a moment before she spoke. "I don't know," she said levelly. "I've let go of Scott. He's gone. My life goes on. I have to survive alone and deal with all these problems."

Her gaze flitted to Jennifer's room, since she didn't want her to overhear. "I feel like I can't take on one more burden."

He loosened his grip, but still rested his hand on her arm.

"I understand. And I want to help you with those problems. But Scott was my partner. I can't let go of something like that. If his death wasn't an accident, I have to find out."

She pulled her arm away slowly. She didn't feel re-sentiment exactly, rather a cynical feeling that contained no sympathy.

"You guys are all alike that way. Obsessed with everything about your jobs."

The intense desire she'd been feeling for Matt cooled a little, and she stepped away. It helped her get some perspective on him to remind herself that he was like Scott in many ways.

Starting to rely on another member of the high-and-mighty SWAT team would be a mistake. Here one minute, gone the next. Work always coming first. That was the part of her marriage she had never worked out. There just wasn't a choice about it.

She tried not to snap at him, but she tossed her head as she spoke. "Do whatever you like. Whoever may have caused Scott's death, inadvertent or not, plunged me into deep financial problems. I suppose I should want to strangle that person."

Matt looked sympathetic. "Don't you miss Scott?"

"Of course." It came out in an angry tone, and she wasn't able to bite back the bitterness. Her chin went up, and she wasn't able to stop the words from pouring out. "But not in the way you think. Not anymore. Half the time, he wasn't here, anyway. Jennifer wouldn't have known she had a father if she didn't know he slept here."

Matt's brows furrowed, but she went on, circling the kitchen as she spoke.

"Our relationship wasn't the greatest. He was out on call so much of the time or away for training. I guess I was asking too much, wanting a normal family life. I wanted to spend Saturdays with Scott and Jennifer, going to the mountains, feeding the geese in the park, working on the house. She is a special child and she needed his attention. I couldn't do it all myself. I still can't."

Grief and frustration began to well up. She had to raise her hands to her face.

"I'm sorry," she croaked, beginning to break under the stress.

Matt was beside her in a heartbeat. She felt his arms slide around her and pull her to his chest. He held her close and just let her lean on him until she got her feelings under control. He didn't say anything, just pressed her head against his shoulder and rested his cheek and jaw against the side of her head.

She felt him communicate his strength to her. He didn't apologize for the life of a cop, something about which she realized she held deep resentment. He just comforted her. And that made her want to cry all the more.

"It's okay," he finally whispered. "Don't worry. It'll be okay."

She sniffled like a baby against the soft cotton of his black T-shirt, but she grasped his firm torso and drank in his warmth and his fresh masculine scent. He dropped comforting kisses on her ear and stroked her back. It wasn't demanding, but it was all the more arousing because of his gentleness. Scott hadn't had this kind of gentleness, she couldn't help but think. And in the next breath, she admonished herself for making the comparison. She shouldn't be getting involved with Scott's partner.

She wasn't planning to get involved with Matt, but she felt their embrace turn into something else. He held her so close that the desire throbbing through his veins began to make itself felt against her. She twisted her head so the skin of her forehead lay against his neck and felt the heat flood through her. Crazily, she felt her hands stroke his back in answer to his own strokes. But with deep breaths, she began to push herself away from him, swallowing deeply. They couldn't let their lust run amok with Jennifer coming out to join them momentarily.

"All right," she said, taking a deep breath. "I understand you want to find out if Scott was murdered. But you have to understand that I have a list of other, equally important priorities."

Her gaze into his golden, burning eyes was pleading. "I need help sorting out the rest of it, as well."

His jaw thrust forward. "I understand, and I'll help."

She felt a wave of relief and thought for a ridiculous moment that they might shake hands on their newfound understanding, but Jennifer walked into the room at that moment.

"I'm ready," she announced in her high-pitched voice. Her large gray eyes rounded as she looked up at Matt. "Will we get to go on the big rides?"

Matt's face blossomed into a grin as he knelt beside her. "We'll go on whatever rides Tracy thinks are okay for you. But I don't know about the roller coaster," he said with a mock-serious look. "I'm scared of heights."

Jennifer squealed out her girlish laughter. "You are not. You're a cop. Cops aren't afraid of anything."

Chapter Six

Elitch Gardens was a premier family theme park located along the South Platt River next to downtown Denver. The park, which had a hundred-year history, was in its third year in the new location. Matt drove Tracy and Jennifer along Speer Boulevard, cutting diagonally across Denver's street grid, following Cherry Creek. They took the rise on the wide bridge over the old rail yards sprawling from Union Station, and turned at the stoplight in the middle of the bridge. The long, curving street led downward to Elitch's main parking lot.

The late-afternoon sun bore down from a bright blue sky in searing intensity. It would be a few hours yet before the sizzling ball of fire sank to the edge of the clearly outlined Rocky Mountains, which stretched across the western horizon. From the vantage point of the park, the vista was an impressive one.

Jennifer squealed with excitement and happily held Matt's hand after he presented their tickets at the ticket kiosk. Inside the covered pavilion that housed souvenir shops, as well as the restored carousel, Matt paused.

"What do you want to do first?" he asked Tracy. "Do you want to say hello to anyone? Or shall we take Jennifer on some rides?"

She felt herself stiffen slightly at the idea of confronting old acquaintances from the force and opted for the rides.

"We're here to do rides," she said, smiling at Jennifer. "So let's do rides."

"Great." Jennifer tugged on Matt's hand and pulled them both through the pavilion.

Beside them, the carousel started to move slowly, the painted and gilded horses beginning their up-and-down motion, pulling hand-carved chariots as the graceful ride turned, accompanied by traditional organ music. Tracy felt a tug of something like nostalgia as the movement and color pulled her into the aura of amusement-park fantasy.

"We'll do that last," announced Jennifer. "I want to go outside now."

Sharing a smile with Matt, Tracy followed along. Emerging onto Main Street, they walked along a short block of quaint Victorian-style shops and eateries and turned into Kiddieland. Ahead, the adult rides were framed against the blue of the mountains. The big Ferris wheel and the Tower of Doom rose mightily. The Mind Eraser was the ten-story, steel, looping roller coaster that plummeted along at over sixty miles per hour. Not for her, Tracy thought as she felt her stomach react to the memory of similar roller-coaster rides from her younger days.

Jennifer stopped beside a children's ride with small cars supported on octopus-like tentacles that lifted and lowered in a circle. "Can I do this one first?"

"Sure," agreed Tracy.

The kiddie rides didn't seem as if they would excite Jennifer too much to trigger her asthma, so Tracy didn't plan to be too restrictive. And Jennifer herself basically had a level head about what she knew she could and could not do.

They watched her gleefully take a seat in one of the cars, then waved as the ride started up.

While Jennifer rode, Matt took his sunglasses out of his shirt pocket and put them on. The dark lenses and frames gave him a secretive look as he studied the main stream of foot traffic. Tracy could almost feel the wheels turning in his head. With Jennifer occupied, the other matters foremost in his mind pushed everything else aside.

"Looking for someone?" Tracy asked. She stood at an angle to him, their shoulders almost touching, so she could wave to Jennifer.

"Maybe."

Her hope that this afternoon could amount to a pleasant outing fled, and she realized that even here amid the excitement of rides, the squeals of passengers and the splashes coming from Shipwreck Falls, she couldn't forget that life wasn't rosy. She felt her shoulders tighten in resentment and tried not to let bitterness mar the day. She had to keep things on an even keel for Jennifer.

As if he sensed some of what she felt, Matt halted his surveillance of passersby and forced his attention back on her. His hand at his side bumped hers, and then both their hands reached for each other's. His fingers curled around hers, and she felt a spark leap up into her heart. Then he switched hands and turned around to watch the ride slow as Jennifer descended.

Tracy felt a sudden flood of embarrassment. What if mutual acquaintances passed by and saw her holding hands with Matt? She still wasn't over the feeling that the Denver police force knew her as Scott's widow. Logically, no one would condemn her for dating after a year. But this wasn't a date. He had brought them here to keep them safe.

Besides, she hadn't exactly relayed to Jennifer any of her confused new feelings about the man beside her. She broke the handhold, knowing she just wasn't ready to confuse Jennifer with any new relationships in their fragile home life right now.

"That was fun," said Jennifer as she got down and skipped toward them. "What's next?"

Her upturned face was so expectant that Tracy relaxed, determined to have fun. It was a holiday weekend. She shouldn't have to worry about money or about sending Jennifer to her grandfather or about what was to be with Matt. Or even the strange calls from Carrie Lamb and her pursuer. It was the weekend of the most American of holidays, and she wanted desperately to enjoy it.

They moved on to the next ride, and Tracy tried to just let life flow past and admire the setting bubbling over with people having fun. Elitch Gardens was famous for its flowers, and the brilliant beds were riotous with purple, yellow and pink pansies. The old park had featured extensive gardens, a dance floor and a theater. The new amusement park was much more in keeping with modern-day theme parks, but as a tribute to the nostalgia that the old Elitch Gardens evoked in Denver residents, small raised beds and tubs of brilliant flowers were everywhere.

Something of a green thumb herself, Tracy decided she'd like to visit the greenhouse to see what varieties might be growing there. Jennifer was begging to ride in the Teacups, something she could do with Matt. They had stopped to look at the guess-your-weight concession.

"Why don't you two do the rest of these rides?" she suggested. "I'd like to wander over to the greenhouse and take a look, if you wouldn't mind. We can meet at that refreshment stand in half an hour."

Matt judged the length of the line to the Big Wheel and gave a nod. "As long as Jennifer doesn't mind. You're sure you want to go alone?" he asked.

She smiled at him. "It's down the walk under the Twister by the fence. I'll be fine."

She gave Jennifer's shoulder a squeeze. "Have fun and don't leave Matt, okay? I don't want you to go anywhere alone in the park. Got that?"

The little girl nodded soberly. Matt took Jennifer's hand with a look that said he understood the importance that a child not be left without an adult in an amusement park or any public place. And she trusted Matt with her stepdaughter. If she would be safe with anyone, she should be safe with a cop. But it was more than that. Matt seemed to handle responsibility well. With an ironic inward smile, she realized that she'd just chalked up another point in his favor. Something she wasn't really trying to do.

She turned from the two of them and made her way through the crowd. She passed the Tower of Doom, the heart-arresting free-fall ride, then circled past more games and a hot-dog stand to the walkway beneath the stomach-churning Twister Two, the famous roller coaster. The long stretch of white latticework frame supported the looping roller coaster. Above her head, the cars thundered in a dip and passengers screamed. Tracy held her ears until the car made the curve to the far side of the ride. There were fewer people on the walk toward the greenhouse, and it was quieter once she got past the end of the roller coaster.

To her right, a high chain-link fence marked the boundary of the park. On the other side of the fence, a solitary cyclist pedaled on the bike path beside the South Platt. The long white building, with a plastic roof to let in the sun, lay just ahead.

Something made her glance back, and when she did, she saw a man break off from the throng coming off the roller coaster. But his movements held none of the excitement of the fun-loving crowd. He followed them toward the exit, but he didn't walk very quickly.

Paranoia made Tracy quicken her steps. She was probably imagining things, but she gave a silent thanks that Jennifer was safe with Matt. The sidewalk leading to the greenhouse was empty, and she wondered for a moment if guests were not allowed inside. She hesitated for a moment, instinct telling her that she ought to retrace her steps now, while she could still see other people on the walkway under the coaster.

Don't be silly, she told herself. It was still daylight. What could possibly happen?

She reached the door to the greenhouse and put her hand on the doorknob. Then she breathed more comfortably when it pushed inward. She was further relieved to see two other people working on the plants some distance along the rows.

The floral scents assailed her, and she breathed in, enjoying the smell. Her herb garden had few flowering plants due to the risk of pollen triggering one of Jennifer's episodes. For that reason, Tracy indulged in breathing in the sweet air and allowing her eyes to drink in the vivid colors.

She walked along the row, reading the stakes peeking out identifying unfamiliar varieties. Her green thumb twitched, and she realized that when and if things ever got resolved in her life, she would like to become more involved in gardening again.

For a few moments, she wallowed in the fantasy. Enough money for Jennifer to attend Ability Plus, the private school of her dreams, where learning was self-paced—time enough for Tracy to volunteer at the botanical gardens. The aesthetic moment carried her all the way down the row of rosebushes and around the end.

When she looked up again, she noticed that the workers

had gone and she was alone. Looking at her watch, she realized she'd been dawdling and had only another ten minutes before she needed to start back to meet Matt and Jennifer.

The sound of a footstep behind her shot a bolt of fear through her heart, and she turned. No one was there. The heat from the intense western sun coming through the plastic roof, along with the humid roomful of plants, suddenly felt cloying. She would feel better in the outside air.

She made a beeline down the row, looking neither right nor left. When she passed a gap in the tables, she thought she saw a shadow of movement, but didn't stop to find out what it was. Tall shrubs blocked her view now, and she felt a sudden urgency to reach the door. For now she had the queer feeling that someone else was watching her. The thought of the unhurried man under the roller coaster made her throat tighten in warning.

She didn't reach the door in time.

He came out of nowhere as she tried to make it past the next gap in the plants. She only saw a blur of movement as he grabbed her from behind, clamping down on her waist and sticking a rag in her mouth when she tried to scream. She twisted and turned and kicked. But the choking rag and the chemical smell of something over her nose cost her her breath.

She screamed in her mind, struggled to get away. Her will fought on even when her limbs weakened and dizziness forced its way into her head.

Her last thought was of rosebushes, Matt and sweet little Jennifer.

SHE WAS FIRST AWARE of the dizziness as she began to wake up. It was hard to tell what position her body was in. Then tight cords restricting her arms and hands made her aware she was tied to something. Was she sitting?

"Where am I?" she mumbled through thick lips.

The terror seized her again when she opened her eyes and everything was still dark. She began to struggle, until hands gripped her shoulder and a nasty, threatening voice ordered her to stay put.

A blinding circle of light flicked on, aimed at her face. She squeezed her eyes shut then, turning her face to the side. Still, the light blinded her, and she could make out nothing.

"Relax, Mrs. Meyer. We just want to talk."

This voice was different—grating, raspy and it came from opposite her. She realized, finally, that one man was standing behind her to try to keep her from tipping the chair over and that the other man held a large flashlight and was talking to her from about ten feet away. They were probably going to hurt her, at the very least, and tears sprang to her eyes.

Panic seized her, and she almost blurted out that Matt and Jennifer would be looking for her. But she bit her lip. If she was late, they would become concerned. But that would be to her advantage—if she were still in the park, that is—because they would come looking for her.

"Who are you?" she asked, squinting and ducking her head against the shining light.

The man behind the flashlight gave a rasp. "No one you need to know. And you're not going to get hurt if you heed my words."

She didn't say anything, just tried to stifle her fear so that she could concentrate. She tried to remember things she'd learned in self-defense class. But there was little she could do with her arms tied to her torso and her feet bound to the legs of a chair.

She tried to sound courageous but cooperative. "You don't need to threaten me. Just tell me what it is you want, and if I know anything useful, I'll tell you."

"That's more like it."

She didn't voice the fact that she would say anything whether she meant it or not just to keep them from doing something awful to her. And she tried not to think about Jennifer. She was with Matt. Then, with a sinking feeling, she realized that her captors must know that. If they'd followed her in here, it must be because they'd seen her leave Matt and Jennifer in the main part of the park a little while ago.

She kept her eyes downward and tried to see what was on the floor and to the sides in the pool of light. She gradually became aware of a damp, earthy smell.

In the distance were muffled sounds she could make out, sometimes louder, then fading. She felt a spurt of hope when she recognized the screams from the roller coaster, but they were muffled. So she wasn't far from the park, maybe somewhere still on its grounds.

She must have been out cold, for she didn't remember being carried anywhere. Her wrists hurt from the cords, and she tried to wiggle them into a more comfortable position.

"What do you want with me?" She was still terrified, but she didn't want her captors to know it.

"Just a few questions, that's all."

"Was it necessary to tie me up and put me out? I'm a reasonable human being. Couldn't you have just asked me whatever it is you want to know?"

The raspy voice coughed out a laugh. "We thought some privacy might be more convincing."

"Convincing of what?"

Now the raspy voice took on a harsher tone. "Let's just

say you need to be persuaded not to mess with your late husband's memory.''

''Scott?'' She blinked in surprise. ''What's that got to do with anything?''

''Nothing. That's why you need to tell your boyfriend to mind his own business.''

''I really don't know what you're talking about. And he isn't my boyfriend. He's a friend of the family, that's all.''

''Then if you want him to remain healthy enough to take you and your little stepdaughter out to play, he'd better stick to his job.''

Anger made her sputter out her reply. ''Whatever he is doing, I'm sure he considers it his job.''

''Not everyone would agree with that.''

She clamped her teeth together. There were a lot of things she could say, but she was afraid her temper would make her give things away that she shouldn't. Still, she didn't quite understand why this dramatic, gangsterlike setting was necessary to tell her these things.

After she took a breath, she said, ''I don't want any trouble. Since you know all about our lives, you must know that Jennifer is not well. I have my hands full taking care of her. Scott is dead. Nothing I can do will bring him back. Whatever his death was about, I don't even want to know. All I want is to put the past behind me. The present is much too trying, believe me.''

''Good girl,'' wheezed the man with the flashlight.

She squinted in his direction, trying without avail to see anything, a silhouette, height, a piece of clothing. But he stood in darkness.

''Can I go now?'' asked Tracy.

''Not quite.''

She waited.

''Did your friend Carrie just decide to run away with

that bank robber the day they met? Or was she giving it to him before that?''

Tracy was shocked. "I don't know what you're talking about."

"Come now. You were there. When she slipped her legs around his motorcycle and snuggled up against his back, just how well did she know the rascal?"

Tracy couldn't believe her ears, but she could perceive a tightening in the man's hoarse voice. Jealousy? She tried to think. Whatever was going on here was very bizarre. Did this man know Carrie? Her stomach flip-flopped. Since Carrie's disappearance, she'd realized just how little she'd known her. But the coarse man's accusations really shook her belief that Carrie Lamb was the kind, caring tutor she appeared to be.

"I, um, really don't know. I'd never seen the robber before yesterday."

"That's not what I asked you." The words thundered out angrily. Tracy blinked. The man was clearly obsessed with Carrie, and she was too surprised to be able to understand it.

"How do you know her?" she blurted out. "What is Carrie to you, anyway?

Nobody spoke for a minute, and Tracy looked over her shoulder. Where was the other man who'd gripped her shoulders when she'd struggled? She could still hear him breathing behind her.

Finally, the one with the flashlight answered her. "My interest in Carrie is my business."

"Then why is it that you think I can help you? I don't even know where she is. If the police know, they certainly aren't telling me."

He seemed to be considering her words. "That so?" he

finally said. "But she wants to talk to you. She phoned the night she left with her hero."

"I wouldn't know. I wasn't there when she called. My baby-sitter took the message."

"Well, let's just say that I want to know if you know. If she calls you again, I'll be listening."

The thought made her shiver. "So you've got my phone tapped? Well, so do the police. Why don't you just talk to each other and leave me out of it."

She bit her lower lip. If he hadn't known the police were listening for his phone calls, he did now. Oh, well, she couldn't help it. She was losing her control, and the ropes hurt.

"What are you going to do to me?"

At last, the man behind her spoke. His tone was tough, as if being a gangster were the only calling he was qualified for. "Maybe a few cuts would help, eh, boss?"

"No," said the one with the blinding flashlight. "I think she gets the message. If she knows what's good for her, she'll tell her cop boyfriend to lay off poking around where he isn't wanted. If he keeps his nose clean and minds his own business, he and the lady here can have a nice time with each other."

She cringed at his crudeness, but didn't argue. She just wanted out of here.

Then the thug behind her made a suggestion so revolting that she had to fight a sudden nausea. But raspy voice told him to shut up, there wasn't time. Then, just to make sure she understood, he made one final threat.

"We'll be aware if you try to report this little incident to the police. And they know better than to come after me."

"Who are you?" she said in a low, angry voice.

He just gave a laugh and flicked off the flashlight, leaving them in utter darkness. She felt her bonds loosen, but neither man said a word. She waited for her eyes to become accustomed to the darkness and strained to get free as soon as her captor moved away. Her feet were still tied, and she nearly fell over trying to get up. She sat back down and rubbed her wrists. They'd left her to undo the cords at her ankles, giving them time to get away.

Anger and fear turned into tears, but she tried to keep her fingers from shaking so she could untie the knots. When she finally had them free, she raised her head and put out her hands, having to feel her way to the door, which she'd seen them open and shut.

She had one more moment of panic, fearing they'd locked her in. She held her breath as she felt along the wall to the crack of the door and then down to the cool doorknob. A twist of the knob and she was breathing in moist, earthy air.

She blinked. She was in a small passage that stopped at one end of the greenhouse. To her right, she could see the rows of flowering plants. So they hadn't taken her very far. She glanced back at her small prison and pushed the door open farther, gazing in with a shiver. With light spilling from the main room, she could see stacks of potting soil and coils of hose. They had been in a supply room.

The sting of her wrists and the racing of her heart filled her with terror. She almost couldn't believe they'd simply walked off and left her in one piece. Then she broke out of her numb shock and ran between the rows of plants, her sandals slapping on the concrete floor. She flew through the door and sped down the walkway toward the roller coaster. Her vision blurred with her hair whipping around her face.

She took the twisting path, pushing past people who'd

just gotten off the ride. Finally, she saw Matt and Jennifer pounding down the path toward her.

When they met, she scooped Jennifer up in her arms and clutched her tightly.

"Are you all right?" she breathed into the little girl's hair. Her greatest fear had been that they had somehow gotten Jennifer away from Matt and kidnapped her.

She knew her fear communicated itself with widened eyes as she conveyed her terror to Matt, who wrapped his arms around both of them. His hand slid up to her head and then down her shoulders and back as if making sure she was in one piece. The dark frown on his brow and the tinge of anger on the planes of his face threatened violent repercussions if anyone had harmed her.

"What happened?" he asked. "You were late, and we got concerned."

She felt the firm grip of his hand on her shoulder, while his eyes searched the path behind her.

"Are you all right?" asked Jennifer.

She drew in deep breaths, trying to calm herself. She remembered the doctor's words. Emotions didn't cause asthma, but some strong emotional upsets might trigger an asthma episode. She set Jennifer down and met Matt's eyes over her head. She didn't want to frighten Jennifer. When his eyes swept back to hers, she thought from his tightened expression that he understood her dilemma. Tracy knelt beside Jennifer.

"I'm sorry if you were worried," she said, stroking Jennifer's hair. "Everything's all right now. Some people wanted to talk to me in the greenhouse, and we lost track of the time." She glanced up at Matt, who watched her intently.

She stood up, gripping Jennifer's hand. "Let's go back to the rides now. I'll bet Matt will buy us a soft drink."

Jennifer seemed to relax. "Gosh, we were scared. We thought maybe you were lost."

Tracy squeezed her hand. "I'm not lost now."

She managed a smile in Matt's direction. He seemed to understand the fact that she wasn't going to tell him what had happened until they were out of Jennifer's earshot. As they emerged from the white forest of framing for the roller coaster, he swerved his head, looking around. A booth to their right offered some games.

"Look at that. Would you like to try your luck at winning one of those tigers?" he asked Jennifer.

She beamed. "Do you think I can do it?"

His face warmed into a smile and he tousled her hair. "Sure. Come on."

They approached the concession, and Matt patiently showed Jennifer how to toss balls at two-handled milk cans. Then, while she was engaged in that activity, he stepped back to where Tracy waited. They were far enough away to be able to see Jennifer, but she couldn't hear them.

"What happened?" he said through clenched jaws. He turned his back to the concession so he could watch the path they'd come from.

She tried to keep from shaking as she recounted it swiftly. "Someone grabbed me in the greenhouse. They put me out with chloroform, then they must have dragged me into a supply room at the back. I didn't see anything. The man speaking held a flashlight on me. I could only hear his voice."

"What did it sound like?"

She exhaled a breath and tried to remember every detail while it was fresh in her mind. "It was raspy, grating, an odd-sounding voice."

A muscle in Matt's jaw pulsed, and his arm muscles flexed. "Had you ever heard it before?"

She thought for a moment. When she realized where she'd heard the voice before, a chill of dread flooded her limbs. She grasped her arms to hug herself.

"I think he's the one who called me on the phone last night."

Chapter Seven

Matt's automatic SWAT team reactions were triggered when he'd seen Tracy running for her life away from the greenhouse. Once he'd ascertained she hadn't needed medical attention, it had been all he could do to stand still while she'd reassured the child. But now he itched to go after the culprits. Knowing they'd be long gone, he still wanted to look for any clues. Whoever had done this would pay.

Doubting that the attackers would try anything else, having made their point, he still felt uneasy about leaving her alone. But the longer he waited, the more thoroughly the men would have covered their tracks. He saw his solution when he spied Roland Baker sauntering along with a soft drink in his hand. The tall, self-possessed sniper, dressed in a yellow polo shirt and tan trousers, was exactly what he needed.

"Excuse me a minute," he told Tracy. Then he trotted over to Roland.

"I need a favor," he said to his friend.

Roland eyed him. "Something tells me this isn't about feeding hot dogs to Scott Meyer's daughter."

"Actually, it might be. I need you to stick close to them while I check something out. Some culprits just laid hands on Tracy and passed along a rather nasty threat meant for me."

Roland stopped sucking on his straw and narrowed his eyes. When he spotted Tracy, he nodded. "Tell me what you want."

"I'm going to see if I can find anything. Stay with them and don't let them out of your sight."

"You going to report this?" Roland asked, his eyes sweeping their surroundings for anything suspicious. He tossed his drink in a waste can, his hands flexing.

"That depends."

After Tracy and Roland had greeted each other, Matt slid a hand around Tracy's waist, giving her a reassuring squeeze.

"I'll just be gone a minute. You two keep Jennifer busy while I try to see where those bastards have gone."

He felt Tracy grasp his waist. Her voice was low and intense. "Matt, don't go."

He met her pleading gaze. "Why not? Don't you want to know who assaulted you?"

He saw the battle taking place behind her eyes, and her mouth pressed in a determined line. If he'd thought he would impress her by charging after her pursuers like a white knight, he was mistaken.

"No. They're gone by now. I don't want you walking into danger."

Danger was his business. But he knew that wasn't what she wanted to hear. He laid a hand on her shoulder. "They may have left some clue behind. It could be important. I'll be all right."

Still, her jaw stuck out. "Why don't we just report it to park security? Let them handle it."

Matt's words took on a grim quality. "I'm afraid we're

dealing with something beyond the scope of park security. They would only call in the police. We are the police.''

Not trying to be melodramatic, he needed to follow up on this without wasting any more time. Tracy might not understand now, but she'd be grateful later. He'd just have to gamble on that.

"Take care of her, Roland,'' he said, and dashed off toward the greenhouse.

The door was still open, and he slipped in, alert for trouble. Then he spotted an elderly gentleman in an apron watering the plants. Not wanting to draw attention to what he was doing, Matt adopted a casual demeanor, all the while wary that the criminals might still be in the building.

He whistled absently as he strolled along the rows of plants, his hands in his pockets. "How's it goin'?'' he asked the man with the hose.

"Fine, fine,'' replied the gray-haired gentleman with wire-rimmed spectacles. He didn't look up, but bent closer to examine the leaves.

Matt turned to lean against the table and keep the rest of the room in his sight. "You get many visitors in here? I'm surprised the greenhouse is open to the public.''

The man grunted. "Visitors between noon and three o'clock. Least that's what it's supposed to be.''

"Oh, I didn't know that. My friends said they'd been in here about a half hour ago. You see anyone?''

"Not unless you mean that woman running out of here a while ago.'' He moved along the row and reached into the plants, examining leaves. "Ya'd think the devil was after her the way she tore out. Must've been late somewhere.''

"Yep. She told me about that. Dropped her keys somewhere. Mind if I look around for them?''

The man shrugged. "I didn't see any keys.''

"Thanks."

Matt moved off and looked carefully where he walked. It didn't take long to spot the storeroom, and he pushed the door in slowly, letting in light from the main room. The gardener was too far at the other end of the greenhouse to see him go in.

The chair Tracy said she'd been sitting in must have been pushed to the side of the room, and there weren't any cords in plain view. A tear from a bag of potting soil had allowed some of the dirt to spill out onto the concrete floor, and he thought he saw the outline of a footprint.

He felt along the wall for a light switch, but didn't find one. Then he spied the chain swinging from a bare light bulb in the middle of the room and started to reach for it.

He felt a whoosh of air behind him and turned to defend himself. But the solid object struck him on the side of the head before he could land a punch.

MATT HAD BEEN GONE too long. Roland and Tracy had taken Jennifer on the Rainbow ride, which went up in a half circle and down in a swooping motion. From the top of the ride, they had seen this end of the park, and Matt hadn't reappeared.

Now Jennifer was climbing a rope ladder up Pikes Peak, and Tracy and Roland were watching passersby. But the stony expressions on their faces were a dead giveaway that they weren't having any fun.

"Where is he?" she hissed in frustration.

Roland gave a grunt. He turned as Jennifer squealed and fell off the mountain. "I don't like it. Let's go."

Tracy nodded and reached for Jennifer's hand. "Let's go for a walk," she told Jennifer. "We're going to find Uncle Matt."

She used the name they used to call him when he had

been Scott's partner and had stopped at the house occasionally. Somehow using the familiar appellation drew him in as part of the family.

The hairs on the back of her neck prickled a warning as she accompanied Roland down the walkway to the greenhouse. She fell back slightly as they got closer. She didn't want to put Jennifer in any danger, but she dreaded what might have happened to Matt. She increased her grip on Jennifer's hand, ready to turn and run at the slightest threat.

Roland took up a position with his back to the door frame and pushed the door inward with his foot. She closed her eyes at the action, recognizing the all too familiar moves of the SWAT team. When nothing happened, Roland slipped inside. Tracy stayed on the path, Jennifer close in front of her.

"What's in there?" asked Jennifer. "Why are we staying out here? Is Matt in trouble?"

Tracy sighed. Jennifer was too smart to make it possible to continue to keep things from her. "I hope not," she answered honestly. "Roland's gone to find out."

"Is that the greenhouse where you went?"

"Yes, that's the greenhouse."

"Did something bad happen in there?"

She sighed. Jennifer would know if she were lying. "Something bad happened, and Matt went to check it out."

"Is Roland going to find him?"

"Yes, Roland's going to find him."

"Shouldn't we help?"

Tracy grinned even at the same time as a lead weight seemed to drop in her stomach. Her feeling exactly. Jennifer turned to look up at her with wide gray eyes as if to say *What are we waiting for?*

Her heart turned over at the girl's bravery and readiness to help. But she had to remember who her father was. And perhaps Jennifer had the same streak of daring that Tracy feared would be her undoing.

She suddenly realized as they stood there in the shade of the long building that she was in the middle of something she didn't want to be in. Somehow she'd gotten entangled in danger, and she fought back her fright. Why would this never leave her alone?

"Matt might be hurt," Jennifer's voice rang out as she broke away from Tracy and ran toward the greenhouse door.

"Jennifer, wait!"

But with no time to dwell on whether she liked it or not, she chased after her stepdaughter. "Wait, Jenn. We don't know what's going on in there."

A twinge of resentment assailed her at Jennifer's headlong flight to save Matt. All of them, Scott before he had died, Matt, Roland and even Jennifer, had some kind of valor she didn't possess. Always putting their own skins on the line for the good fight. Was it worth it?

Her heart in her throat, they hurried into the greenhouse. A shiver coursed through her as she paused to look to both sides when they came to the junction of the taller bushes with the tables of smaller plants. She heard voices ahead and quickened her pace.

Immense relief flooded her as they approached the end of the long rows and she saw Matt leaning against the storeroom door frame, rubbing the back of his head. Roland was interrogating him, his mouth turned down in a grim expression.

She stopped just short of reaching him. "What happened?"

He glowered. "Someone slugged me. I must have been out for a while."

"We've got to get you to a doctor," Tracy said in a stern voice. "Where did they hit you?"

He turned and pointed to the bump rising at the base of his skull. Tracy winced, but she continued to insist about a doctor.

"You could have a fracture. You should be X-rayed."

Matt grunted. "I don't have time for paperwork."

Tracy felt her body tense with anger. Seeing that an argument was about to ensue, Roland took Jennifer to look at the roses while Tracy talked to Matt.

"Don't do this," she snapped at him.

"Don't do what?" He rubbed his neck, moving his head around to assess the soreness.

"Don't play hero when you need help."

He tried to grin at her, but she could still see the pain in his eyes. "I have all the help I need right here."

"Don't do that, either."

"What?" His question was even more demanding.

"Don't try to charm me out of this."

She'd had it with cops and robbers and decided they all needed some sanity. No matter what games were being played here with all of their lives, it was time to go through regular channels. She straightened her spine and threw her shoulders back. Then she jerked her head toward the door.

"Come with me now, or I'm going to call park security. Someone can look at you at the first-aid station. You can just say you were mugged by teenagers if you don't want to tell them the truth."

He released a jagged sigh. "It might have been teenagers, for all I know." But he meekly followed her out.

Partway along the rows of plants, with Jennifer and Roland going ahead, Matt stopped and swore. Tracy turned to see him glaring at a table full of geraniums receiving a soft spray from the sprinkling system. A clear plastic tube traveled two feet above the table and emitted the spray.

"I'm an idiot," he said, rubbing his neck and glaring at the water, obviously connected to a timer.

"What is it?"

He gave a long, impatient sigh. "So much for kindly old gardeners."

Then he dropped his arm and moved forward, grabbing her elbow to propel her along. "Let's get out of here."

No one argued with her as they plowed through the crowd to the first-aid station. Matt duly reported that he'd been slugged by some kids, but that they hadn't gotten his wallet. His descriptions were fuzzy, and the head of security who questioned him apologized profusely. Matt assured them he wouldn't hold the park responsible.

The doctor pronounced his contusions minor. There were no fractures, but he told Matt to head home and rest. Instead of going to rest, he took Tracy with him to the family-style pub and ordered two cool, foaming glasses of beer.

Roland elected himself baby-sitter, and since Jennifer was hungry, took her with him to the picnic area where the family-day party was being held. There she could fill herself up on burgers, coleslaw and potato salad.

The tension hadn't left Tracy as she and Matt slid into a high-backed booth in the air-conditioned pub. On the other side of the sash windows next to their booth, tables filled a shady patio. Only halfway satisfied that Matt was really all right, she had to ignore how physically fit he looked in spite of having been out cold less than an hour ago. He had his color back, and his hazel eyes were sharp and penetrating. His muscular arms and chest were only too obvious underneath the black T-shirt. He chugged a drink from the tall glass, and she sipped at hers, feeling wary.

Glancing around to make sure no one was paying attention to them, she leaned forward. "Who do you think hit you?" she asked.

His eyes met hers, and she could see the wheels turning in his head. When he spoke, he kept his voice low. "I don't know. But before I passed out, I saw a familiar shoe print."

She lifted her eyebrows in question and took another sip.

Matt drew his eyebrows down in a frown and glanced at the crowd placing orders at the counter. Then he looked at Tracy, matching the intent look in her dark brown eyes. He didn't like telling her what he was thinking.

He didn't want to tell her how many hours he'd spent investigation Scott's murder last year. The official report read that there had been no wrongdoing on anyone's part. It had been just an unfortunate accident. He didn't want to burden Tracy with how he'd agonized over it.

Scott shouldn't have responded to that call without backup he could trust. The cops who'd rushed to the scene had botched it, and Scott was dead.

He didn't want to tell Tracy how many nights he'd stayed up pacing his living room, rethinking it. And how he'd made diagram after diagram of his own, based on the statements of the witnesses and on the sketches of the bank's layout.

But the way she gazed back at him over the rim of her glass made him desperately want to drown in her eyes. He hadn't realized how isolated he'd been all this time. After his last girlfriend had dropped him for someone else, he'd avoided intimate contact with women. He hadn't considered himself lonely. He'd just considered himself a man involved in his work.

Obsessed with his work, maybe, as a bitter place hardened inside him every time a cop was killed on the job. He wanted a reason why these things happened. Coming from an honorable family, who'd brought him up to do his duty and protect the public, he couldn't stomach random acts of violence. And when it was close to home, someone had to pay.

Tracy let her silky eyelashes droop partway over her eyes as she ran a hand through her tousled hair. It bounced to her shoulders. The long fingers of her other hand curled around the beer glass, drumming against its icy smoothness. Her kissable lips pressed together. Then she sat up straighter, raised her eyelids and bored her gaze into his once again.

"What about the shoe print?"

"I'd recognize that print anywhere," he said in a husky voice that rumbled with anger. "Standard issue, rubber soles with markings worn by Denver's finest."

She blinked and swayed slightly. Her beautiful eyes narrowed. "A street cop?"

He nodded a quarter of an inch, feeling his own gaze narrow. He watched her shiver and wished he had a jacket to offer her in the air-conditioning. He couldn't even reach around and put an arm across her shoulders because the Formica tabletop was between them. For a minute, neither one of them spoke.

Then she asked, "What are you going to do about it?"

"Find out what's going on, that's what."

He saw the sparks in her eyes. "That's exactly what the man in the greenhouse warned us not to do." Her voice shook a little. "He said you should stick to your job." She looked a little embarrassed. "I told him you considered what you're doing to be part of your job."

In spite of the seriousness of the situation, he realized he liked the way she said "us." And his heart turned over at the way she must have stood up for him during her scary interrogation. He responded warmly to the camaraderie he hoped she was offering.

"There are only two reasons people like us receive threats. Either to stop us from doing something they don't want us to do, or because they think we know something they don't want us to know."

She nodded pensively and glanced over her shoulder. "Like that man who wants to know where Carrie Lamb is."

She brought her eyes back to Matt's face, and he read the desperation there. "I don't know her past. But if that man is after her, then I don't blame her for running."

He twitched the side of his mouth, keeping his voice down. "What concerns me more is that he's getting close to you."

Tracy's arms pressed down on the table, the curve of her breasts pushing downward against the soft material of her T-shirt. He tried to ignore the increasing arousal he felt every time he was with her.

Damn it, the situation was getting more dangerous. There was enough to figure out without wanting to abscond with her to some safe haven away from prying eyes, where he could pamper and caress her. Instead, they were caught in a web of evil that was threatening to strangle them. Today's threat had definitely been too close for comfort. It was time to make a plan.

He was considering his next move when the door opened and a group of Denver cops came in. Matt narrowed his eyes as the group moved to the counter and placed their orders. Though they were out of uniform, he recognized most of them, especially the square-built man on the end. His golf shirt and chino trousers did nothing to hide his boisterous, self-absorbed attitude.

"Well, well," Matt murmured to Tracy. "Guess these guys don't like the brand of beer they're serving at the picnic. Lucky for me. I see just the man I need to talk to."

She looked at the group by the bar and frowned. But if she recognized Captain Brad McAllister, she didn't give any indication.

"I should be getting Jennifer," she told him. "Roland might need some help."

"Good idea," replied Matt, taking the last slug from his beer glass. "I'll meet you at the picnic grounds in fifteen minutes. I need a word with our friend, Captain McAllister."

He saw the flash of concern in her eyes. But as they slid out of their booth, he gave her a reassuring squeeze on her shoulder, then he dropped his hand. He didn't know how much of a display of his feelings Tracy would appreciate in front of mutual acquaintances.

"Tracy."

"What?"

"Stay in plain sight."

He gave her a wink as she moved toward the door, and felt the urge to follow her outside. But he stopped himself. Surely she would stick to the well-populated areas this time and go find Roland. He turned and glided over to the counter, sliding in next to McAllister. When he asked for another beer, McAllister hefted his body around to face him.

"Well, Forrest. Enjoying yourself?" inquired the beefy captain.

"I suppose so. You?"

McAllister raised his glass, then slurped up some of the foam from the top. Matt waited, giving himself time to gauge the other man's mood and attitude. Finally, he faced him and leveled his words directly.

"Say, McAllister, what happened to the gun that was confiscated from the grass at the bank yesterday morning? Somehow it didn't get turned in with the rest of the evidence."

He saw the flicker in McAllister's eyes. He had surprised him. But the man kept his cool and returned a cold stare. "It's where it's supposed to be, though I don't see what business it is of yours, Mr. Elite SWAT Officer."

Matt forced a laugh. "Someone doesn't want me asking—I got that message loud and clear. But what I don't understand is why that would be."

McAllister shrugged. "I don't know what you're talking about, Forrest. Seems to me you've had a chip on your shoulder for a while now. You talk to your commander about that? They don't like jumpy guys on SWAT."

Matt took the dig. SWAT team members were selected because they were supposed to be able to keep their cool in hot situations.

"I'm not jumpy when I'm doing my job, McAllister. I just want to know what happened to that gun."

"Now, why would that be? You're not a detective, last I checked."

"Is it your turf you care about, McAllister? Or are you trying to hide something?"

McAllister glared at him. "I don't know what you're talking about."

He started to turn his back, but Matt growled low in his ear. "I'm going through proper channels this time, and if that gun isn't in the evidence room and on the list when I look in there again, I think I'll have a chat with the internal-investigation guys.''

McAllister glowered. ''Like I said, I mind my own business, and I'd suggest you mind yours, Forrest. As to the gun, some red-tape slipup, most likely. Relax. You know how things can fall between the cracks.''

''Is that so? I wonder if your division chief would appreciate your sentiments.''

Matt swallowed another slug of his beer and set the icy glass down with a thud. McAllister was hiding something, he was sure of it. As he moved away, he let his gaze drift over the shoes of the cops picking up drinks at the counter. Sneakers rather than uniform shoes rested on the floor and against the booths. He looked at the faces of the men who hung out with McAllister. Any of them might have held Tracy prisoner and stumbled into the potting soil. But if they had, they'd changed their shoes.

The shade had claimed most of the park, since the boiling sun was now behind the mountains. Beyond the roller coaster, a red sunset streamed across the sky. Matt ignored the revelry in the park and the canned music and hurried his steps to where the smell of a barbecue was overpowering.

When he saw Tracy safely talking to a group of friends, he relaxed. Some of the guys had Jennifer off to the side throwing a Frisbee in the grass. He realized how famished he was and stopped long enough to stack a burger, onions, lettuce and tomato on a thick bun and bite into it. Keeping his eyes peeled warily, he ate.

A couple of rookies wandered in, just off duty and still wearing uniforms. He squinted at their shoes—dusty and scuffed, but not rimmed with potting soil. He couldn't tell for certain, of course, unless he examined their soles. But who would be stupid enough to leave that kind of a trace?

But then the kind of man who would lay hands on an innocent victim had to be stupid to begin with. He finished his hamburger, wiped the catsup off his mouth and stuck a plastic fork in his potato salad. It irked him that Tracy had to be worried. While she talked to some of Scott's old friends, he sat down on one of the picnic tables, his feet on the bench, eyeing the crowd.

Someone here was a dirty cop. Not anyone he knew and trusted. But somebody in the department must be involved in these goings-on. The thought made him sick to his stomach. And he wasn't sure what he could do about it.

He ought to report everything to the internal-investigations squad. Let them handle it. But something made him cautious. Internal investigations had looked into the incident when Scott had been killed and they'd come up with nothing. It would take some powerful evidence to make them reopen the case.

He watched the crowd mill around in front of him. Everyone was having a good time but him.

Roland strolled over, leaned on the table and crossed his long arms. "Heavy thoughts behind those sunglasses," he said.

Matt grunted. "Had a little chat with McAllister just now."

"And?"

Matt shrugged. "He told me to mind my own business."

"Good advice, if you want a career."

Matt glanced at his friend. "But you know I don't let things drop."

"I know."

Matt considered his next move. He had a hunch. Someone didn't want Scott Meyer's death dragged out into the open again. The threats were clear. That meant he had to return to the past, painful as that might be for Tracy, as well.

If Scott had been murdered, and it hadn't been just an accident, then it had been for a reason. He had to find out what that reason was.

Chapter Eight

Tracy warmed to the expressions of concern and the interest Scott's former colleagues took in Jennifer and her. She'd forgotten about the outpouring of sympathy when Scott had gone down in the line of duty. The staunch support and regal display of respect shown at his funeral had moved her then. And the generosity that had flooded in had also touched her.

But all that had been washed away in the following months as it had gotten tougher and tougher to manage as a single parent. And now with Andrew Leigh's custody suit looming, all her focus had been geared to just hanging on. Until today.

Still shaken after their unsettling encounters in the greenhouse, Tracy stood on wobbly legs. But as officers and their wives came around to greet her and ask after Jennifer, she began to thaw amid their expressions of friendship and concern. She was still one of them. Oddly, it was something she hadn't necessarily wanted to be. She was part of this group of peace officers, part of their victories and sorrows, part of the everyday struggle to keep the streets safe.

Everyone had heard about the attempted bank holdup, and the women had wanted to hear her version of the story, shaking their heads at the scary situation. All of them patted or hugged her, said they were glad she was okay.

When Matt strolled into the group, she caught his eye briefly, but didn't hold it. Just knowing he was here made her feel safer again. She hadn't mentioned her abduction to anyone else, but the cops all knew Matt had been mugged. Some of the rookies had gone to help security do what they could.

It was eerie to realize that she and Matt were withholding evidence. She should be in the safest place in Denver right now, with nearly the entire police department enjoying the special day in the park for their families. It was ironic that she couldn't just announce what had really happened.

But as she chatted with other women and asked about their children, she realized the truth of the matter. There was something fishy going on, and Matt wanted to solve it alone. She lost track of the conversation with the group of three other women and had to apologize.

"I'm sorry, I was daydreaming," she said to Rene Baker, the brunette who had just addressed her. "You were saying?"

Rene was Roland's sister and had been watching her brother toss the Frisbee with Jennifer and some other kids until Roland had left the children to go lean against a picnic table with Matt. Now her sharp eyes glanced in the direction Tracy had been staring. When she looked back at Tracy, she lifted a dark eyebrow.

"Hmm. Seen much of Matt Forrest lately?"

Tracy shrugged. If her thoughts were this easy to read, she must be like an open book to Matt and everyone else, for that matter. But why not speak the truth? Rene would hardly begrudge her friendship with Matt.

"He did come over last night. He's fond of Jennifer."

Rene nodded and gazed across the thirty yards that separated them from her brother and Matt. The two men seemed to be in an intense conversation, even though they weren't looking at each other. When Rene looked back at Tracy, the sincerity in the other woman's dark eyes was evident.

"Good man, Matt Forrest. A lot like Scott in some ways." Then she bit her lip and looked apologetic.

"It's all right," said Tracy. "I've been making the comparison myself."

"Ooh, I see. Sounds like you're not too sure whether that's a good thing or a bad thing. Take my advice, Tracy, don't be so hard on yourself. I know it must be rough, taking care of Jennifer alone and all."

"You don't know how rough. Her maternal grandfather wants her."

"Oh, I didn't know that. Where does he live?"

"Chicago."

"Oh, my."

Tracy sighed. "I can't bear the thought of her moving away."

"You're very attached to her, aren't you?"

"Of course. And we grew closer after Scott's passing."

Rene put her hand on Tracy's arm. "Good luck, then."

"Thanks."

"And let me know if there's anything I can do. Though from the looks of it, you might be getting some help from other quarters."

Tracy felt a blush threaten and decided to be frank with her friend.

"Darn it, Rene. Even if I like Matt, which I'm not saying I do, I'd be crazy to get involved in all that again." The wave of her hand indicated the police life they were standing in the midst of. She didn't mind aiming her words directly at Rene. "I've already had the pleasure of being a SWAT team widow. It's the last thing I'd want to do again."

A smile touched Rene's wine-colored lips, but she remained sympathetic. "I know it's rough. But who ever said we live by our heads?"

They both stood there for a minute watching Roland and Matt, until Matt slid off the table and came their way. His eyes locked on Tracy's as if reassuring himself she was still all right. Then he pulled his gaze away to greet Rene.

"You two cooking up trouble?" asked Rene in a low, half-joking voice, including her brother in her comment.

"Why? Did you have something in mind?" Matt replied cheekily, waggling his eyebrows at Rene just as some other people approached to speak to the Bakers. He moved closer to Tracy and murmured in her ear. "If you've had enough, there are some things we need to do. Get Jennifer and meet me by the sidewalk over there in five minutes."

She nodded without looking at him. But she felt her blood respond to his protective nearness. She caught Rene studying her just as she stepped away to call Jennifer from her game. Rene's words sang in her mind, *Who ever said we live by our heads?*

Jennifer's laughter rang out across the soft grass. It was good for her to have fun and run and play. But she shouldn't overexert herself, either. The rides had been exciting, and if she didn't start to wind down now, she might bring an attack upon herself tonight.

"Jennifer," she called, interrupting the Frisbee game. "Sorry, hon, but we need to go now."

"We do?" Jennifer ran over to her, and Tracy saw the grass stains on her shorts. Her braids were a wreck, but it was good that she wore these signs of healthy play.

"Yes. Matt needs to take us home. He has some work to do."

Jennifer's pale skin wrinkled in question. "Work? But it's a holiday weekend."

"Well," Tracy teased her. "The official holiday isn't until Saturday. This is only Thursday."

"Oh."

Tracy held out a hand. "Come on. You've had enough fun for the afternoon. Time for a little bit of rest."

"All right."

It amazed Tracy how obedient the child was. She didn't know anything about how her mother had raised her, and Scott had been around only in the evenings. But neither Scott nor Tracy had wanted to spoil Jennifer, either. She shook her head, thinking about it. Somehow, among all of them, Jennifer had learned some restraint and wisdom.

In the Blazer on the way home, Tracy gnawed on the problems facing her, not the least of which was her growing relationship with the man beside her. She was all too conscious of the body language developing between them. Matt was a gentleman and no doubt restraining himself. And now he was even putting himself on the line for her.

Or was it for her? A man of action, he was clearly used to taking matters into his own hands. They couldn't talk with Jennifer in the car, but she found herself doubting his methods.

With relief, she opened the door and stepped out onto the curb in front of the house. Jennifer took Matt's hand and pulled him along to the porch, where they waited for Tracy to dig out her key. She didn't even have to ask to know that Matt was coming in.

"Go brush out your hair, Jenn," said Tracy. "It's a mess."

Jennifer skipped off to her room, and Tracy went to the

kitchen to check the answering machine. The red light was steady, indicating no calls. She realized what trepidation she felt at the thought of playing back messages. Too many bad things could be on that tape.

"Nobody's called," she said on a breath.

"Oh?"

She went to the sink to wash her hands, as much to give herself a chance to think as because she needed to get rid of the grime from the amusement park.

"Want anything to drink?" she asked Matt.

"No, thanks. I'm okay."

When she turned around, she was conscious of the way he was looking at her. The evening shadows wrapped around them, drawing them together. But he didn't touch her, just looked at her face, as if examining every small detail he saw there. Finally he spoke, tilting his head toward the back stairway that led to the attic room.

"You go up to Scott's den much?"

The house had no basement. But the steep roof allowed a single attic room that had been made into an extra bedroom by the former owners of the house. Scott had adapted it into his den.

She shook her head. "I always told myself I'd make it into a guest room. But every time I went up there to work on things, it made me depressed. I haven't touched his papers, except for what I needed, like insurance."

Matt rubbed his chin, looking upward. "That might be a good thing. Mind if I have a look?"

She straightened her spine. "What are you looking for?"

"Something that will tell me why he got killed."

She shivered. "Matt, why don't we just go to the division chief? We can't fight this thing alone."

He gave her a stony look. "If that's what you really

want me to do, I'll do it. I'm not here to mess with your life. You're already in too much danger.''

She moved closer, lifting her face to meet his gaze. "You don't play by the rules, do you?"

She could see a muscle in his jaw flinch.

"Not if the rules get in the way. I saw a cop's shoe print in that room today. If I report that, there'll be a flap. Chief Bartola won't reopen the investigation into your husband's death without solid evidence. And someone in the department will see that it isn't reopened. Chief'll say I have a chip on my shoulder."

"Well, don't you?" She regretted saying the words as soon as she spoke them.

"You didn't mean that, Tracy."

She half turned away. "Maybe not. I'm sorry. It's just that...I'm so tired." She slumped against the kitchen counter.

Matt came over and massaged her shoulders. "I know you are. And I want to help you."

Fatigue seeped into her every limb. "How can you help me? You're not a lawyer."

"No, I'm just a cop. But I have some powers of observation, and I don't like what's going on."

She turned, placing herself in the circle of his arms. "Then why not report what happened today to the federal investigators looking into the attempted bank robbery? If that raspy-voiced maniac is chasing Carrie Lamb, isn't that connected with her disappearance? And you told me she's now a suspect, as well as a victim. Shouldn't we be telling someone about all of this?"

"I will, I will. Just give me a chance to follow up on this hunch first."

His face was very close. His hand was caressing the back of her head, and he was making her hair dance around his fingers. He rested his forehead on hers for a minute, and she felt her breath grow shallow. Consenting adults. *Who ever said we live by our heads?*

"What do you think you'll find upstairs?" she said breathlessly.

He sobered and pulled away an inch.

"Maybe someone got rid of Scott because he knew something."

He backed away and let his hands slide from her shoulders down her arms. "Did Scott ever imply any suspicions about anyone else on the force?"

She shook her head. "No, not that I remember."

"You're sure."

"I don't know. I think I'm sure. He said nothing to arouse my suspicions." She looked away. "He didn't confide in me about work that much."

"What did he confide in you about?"

She jerked her head back around. "Isn't that getting rather personal?"

His hold on her arms increased slightly. "Aren't we getting personal?"

She heard the huskiness in his voice and felt the swell of desire. Damn him for being so…so…desirable. His masculinity invaded every pore of her body, making her blood sing out for more. Her loneliness cried out to him to hold her, comfort her, make her forget everything. She was losing control, and fast.

"Damn it," she swore as he slid his arms around her back.

"What?"

"This," she whispered as he lowered his mouth to kiss her lips.

She felt her lips respond to his as the kiss deepened. They hadn't turned the light on in the kitchen, and it remained dim and secretive as their bodies began to respond to each other.

He pulled her tighter as if he didn't care anymore if he hid the physical presence of his desire. Her breasts pushed against him, aching with arousal. When one of his hands strayed up to brush across her erect nipple, he stopped to gently pinch it, and a scorching flame ignited deep between her legs. Damn it, she wanted him.

Urgency increased their breathing as they held and caressed each other. Finally, sense penetrated the haze in her mind, and she whispered into his ear, "We can't."

"Why not?" was his answer.

Why not indeed, except that a seven-year-old might walk in on them at any minute. "Jennifer," she managed to croak in his ear.

She heard his tight grunt. Still he kissed her. But she could tell he realized where they were. After one more long moment of clutching each other, he took a deep breath. She tried to steady herself and stepped back when he released her. She couldn't speak for the effect he'd had on her.

She wanted him. And why not? She was a healthy young woman who enjoyed sex when she had a reliable, steady partner. But sex with Scott had never felt like that. And all Matt had done was kiss her!

She tried to still her excited breathing and calm her beating heart. Something told her that she would make love to Matt someday if all their dire complications could be sorted out. And if she did, it would be like nothing she'd ever experienced in her life. Her hand went down hard on the countertop. His searing gaze told her he felt the same way.

But they had to hold back. She wasn't the kind of woman to indulge in sex merely for the physical pleasure.

And she had told herself she didn't want a relationship with a SWAT team cop. She didn't want that all over again.

Matt satisfied himself by bending over and swiping his lips across hers one more time as if he wanted to savor the taste of her mouth. Then he drew in a large breath and looked toward the stairs again.

"I want to go up there."

She swallowed. "I've got to help Jennifer get ready for bed. Go ahead. You know where things are. I never locked his desk. I'll join you after Jennifer's tucked in."

MATT HAD TO USE all his mental powers to cool his desire for Tracy. It was beginning to seem kinky to want to make love to his old buddy's gorgeous widow. Almost as if he needed permission. But the man had been dead for a year. Scott Meyer was gone. Some people said that the spirit was reborn into a new body and started over again. But wherever Scott had gone, even if he were still hovering around the house as a ghost, Matt hoped he understood. It was just him and Tracy now.

"I'm doing this for you, old buddy," he whispered as he pushed open the door to the attic room and walked across to the desk.

Their dire circumstances made him put aside his overwhelming desire for Tracy. His professional instincts told him it would be foolish to immerse himself in a bout of lovemaking that would make them both more vulnerable to the threats that were closing in on them. They weren't secure, and he needed to keep that foremost in his mind.

Already the responsibility of keeping Tracy and Jennifer safe was making him reconsider his plans. They could no longer stay alone. And the sooner he figured out what this was all about, the sooner they could get on with their lives.

Whether those lives had room for him in them, it was too soon to tell. But as he stepped into the room that had been Scott's den and sometime family playroom, he realized in an ironic way how close to this family he already was.

Putting personal thoughts out of his mind, he began to examine Scott's desk. His sharp eyes and trained senses sought anything that might help him.

"Sorry to invade your privacy like this," he whispered to his dead friend. "But I have to find out what you knew."

He poked in the slots where some old letters and papers were folded. He glanced over all of those, but they seemed to offer little.

Opening the drawers below, he saw that Tracy had sorted through things and stacked papers in categories. Car insurance, health insurance, tax returns. He paused over the tax returns. He knew approximately what salary Scott had made, and nothing unusual showed up on his taxable income. No large sums of money, at least none had been declared.

He heard soft footsteps behind him and knew that Tracy had joined him. He felt himself wishing she would come over and lay a hand on his shoulder. He craved her touch. But she simply moved up beside him and hugged herself in that protective gesture he recognized as meaning that she needed to keep herself apart and that she was confronting something unpleasant.

"Any luck?" she asked.

"Not yet." He turned to look up at her. "Did Scott ever come into unusual sums of money?"

She brushed some hair back over her ear and shook her head. "Not that I know of. We lived on both our salaries. I did the budget, so I knew what went into the bank account."

So it wasn't money they were after. Matt felt some measure of relief. He couldn't believe his old partner had been on the take, but he had to make sure. He put away the tax returns and dug elsewhere.

Giving up on the drawer, he returned to the main part of the desk, drumming his fingers slowly on the clean blotter. Then he stopped. Small indentations showed where a pen had pressed down on paper on top of it. He drew his hand away.

"Have you changed the blotter since Scott used this desk?" he asked Tracy.

"No. Like I said, I didn't do any more than I had to up here."

"Good."

He picked up the blotter and held it near the lamplight. "Daylight will work better than this. We might be able to see impressions of what he wrote if he pressed hard."

"What do you think you're going to find?" she asked.

"I'm not sure."

He squinted at the marks there. If he took the blotter to the lab, they could probably do even more with it. But this wasn't an official investigation.

He set the blotter upright beside the desk for a better look tomorrow.

"I'll know it when I find it," he added. His fingers drifted across a zipper-bound, black leather Day-Timer. He pulled it out, saw that it was for the previous year and began to thumb through it. Most of the pages were blank.

"Did Scott write down his appointments or just keep them in his head?" he asked. He never remembered Scott using this book on the job.

She shrugged. "He wasn't very good about writing things down. I bought that for him as a gift." She sighed.

"I'd hoped it would encourage him to plan dates with us. It didn't seem to help much."

Matt frowned at the little book. There were some things noted that he didn't understand. A few phone numbers, some locations, but they didn't reveal a lot. A bowling night was noted, along with the name of a liquor store on that same day. Matt searched his memory. The liquor store might have been one where they'd served a high-risk warrant. He'd have to check that out.

He flipped several weeks ahead. There was the bowling night again, and then again two weeks later. He looked at Tracy. "I didn't know Scott was into bowling."

"He wasn't," said Tracy.

He held her gaze. "Then he was awfully interested in someone who was. Look at these." He showed her the entries, sniffing a trail.

Then he swiveled the chair and gazed vaguely at the bookshelves on the other side of the room and at the closet with its half-open door. "Did internal investigations ever come here after the incident that killed him?"

"No. Commander Udal assured me the incident was being looked into, but it was more along the line of condolences than investigation. I guess he didn't think Scott was murdered."

She grimaced, and he knew it meant that she still wished it weren't so. He couldn't resist reaching out to wrap his hand around hers. "I wish he hadn't been," he said softly.

She lifted her chin as if to acknowledge that they had a job to do, even if she didn't like it. Matt had to make a decision. There wasn't any time to waste, and he couldn't risk exposing Tracy to any more danger.

"I don't want you to stay here," he said. "Can you and Jennifer spend the night at Rene Baker's house?"

If he had to be out chasing clues, then he would have

to rely on some help. Nobody was going to mess with the house where the SWAT team sniper and his sister lived. Not if he had any brains. And Matt thought that whoever was behind all this had some brains.

Tracy tightened her lips, then gave a quick nod. "I'll get Jennifer ready. Do you want me to call Rene?"

"No, I'll call Roland. He'll tell her what we need."

Tracy's eyes dwelled on his for a second, opened wider as if allowing a slight amount of help. That was good, he thought. In her fight for self-reliance, she didn't realize that she was shutting out people who wanted to help. But there wasn't time for the sentiment to be voiced. He touched both her arms and spoke gently.

"Okay. Go pack. And bring along a photo of Scott, if you have one."

IT WAS TIME to tell Jennifer the truth. Tracy dreaded doing that, but she knew she had to. As she walked down the narrow, carpeted stairs and through the kitchen to the hall closet, her stomach clenched tightly. She couldn't allow herself to feel the tremors of fear that drove her thoughts. And the sour resentment that curled in her stomach. Her parents' cautions about marrying a police officer echoed in her mind as she yanked open the door and pushed back coats to reach for the suitcase hidden in the depths.

Was she bent on a course of self-destruction, then? She'd just fanned the flames of intimacy with Matt, and now they were on a wild-goose chase, trying to solve what Matt was certain was a murder.

"The trail is cold," she said to the closet, as if arguing with it over what they were about to do.

She wanted to pack the suitcase and take Jennifer away, all right, far away from everything. Then let Matt charge around on his white horse and take care of whoever was hounding them.

A twinge of guilt assailed her as she threw the suitcase on her bed. If she needed to get Jennifer away from danger, oughtn't she take her to her grandfather, Andrew Leigh? He had the resources to keep her safe. She considered it. She would do anything for Jennifer. Even if she had painted herself into a corner, Jennifer deserved a chance.

She swore under her breath. She tossed her own undergarments and toiletries into the suitcase, putting off going into Jennifer's room. She hated running. But she knew she couldn't sleep another night in her own bed, waiting for a stranger's voice to call on the phone and tell her he was watching. It was better to go.

But if she took Jennifer to Grandfather Leigh, she might never get her back. The thought of surrendering the child made her feel bereft, and she wanted to kick herself for failing to adopt her right after she'd married Scott. What had seemed like respect for Jennifer's memory of her own mother at the time had grown into a bond deeper than either of them could have imagined. Now it was too late. She would adopt Jennifer now, but she had to fight Andrew Leigh first.

She finally walked down the hall to where Jennifer had put on her pajamas and combed out her braids as best she could. She was sitting on her bed playing with her teddy bear. Tracy went in and sat on the bed with them.

"Telling him about your day at the park?" she inquired.

"Yes," said Jennifer. "He liked hearing about the Big Wheel."

Tracy reached for Teddy and squeezed him on the head. "How would you and Teddy like to go spend the night at Rene Baker's house?"

"Hmm. Will you go with us?"

"Yes, I will. Matt will take us over there. I'll help you pack."

"Why are we going?"

She felt her heart turn over. She wanted to protect her little girl, but Jennifer needed to know some of the truth. If worse came to worst and Jennifer were threatened, God forbid, there would be some things she could do for herself. Nonetheless, Tracy chose her words carefully.

"You know that Matt is a police officer, don't you?"

"Yes, like Daddy was."

"Uh-huh. Well, Matt is chasing some bad men. There are some things he has to find out about, and he needs my help."

"He does?"

"Yes."

She swallowed and forced herself to go on. "When your father was killed last year, it was so sudden he didn't have a chance to tell us some things about the bad guys. Matt needs to find out what Scott knew and didn't have time to tell us."

Jennifer's eyes were round, and she listened seriously. But Tracy was relieved to see she wasn't afraid.

"Will Matt catch the bad guys?" asked Jennifer.

He'd better, Tracy thought. *Or we might all get hurt.* She said, "He'll do his best. But until he does, we thought Rene and her brother could take care of you. I'll help Matt find out what he needs to know, then I'll come back to Rene's house and sleep there. Okay?"

"Okay." Jennifer moved off the bed and chose the things she wanted to take with her while Tracy stacked some clothes on her arm.

By the time she had the suitcase zipped up and Jennifer ready in the living room, Matt had finished talking on the phone. She left some lights on to make it look as if they were home and then grabbed the keys off the lamp table.

"Are you going to stay with us at Rene's?" Jennifer asked, looking up at Matt.

He caught Tracy's glance before he smiled at Jennifer and squatted down to talk to her. "I just might do that. Would it be okay with you if I did?"

"Yes. We could have a slumber party."

"Okay, then."

He straightened, tucked the appointment diary they'd found upstairs under one arm, and took Jennifer by the hand. They headed out together, and Matt stood outside the car, scanning the neighborhood, while Tracy fastened Jennifer's seat belt. Then he slid in and started the engine.

They drove in silence down the quiet residential street. Light from the corner streetlamps bathed them as they slowed at the intersections. Then they turned onto the major thoroughfare and headed east.

She saw Matt glance in the rearview mirror after every stoplight, and she turned to look out the back herself. But it didn't seem that they were being followed. Even so, she felt the unwelcome sensations that came with being on the run.

On the run. As if she didn't have enough problems to deal with, now she was caught up in some dangerous web that was life threatening. She didn't know whether she should thank Matt for his protection or be angry with him for wanting to handle it his way.

At least he trusted Roland Baker. She gritted her teeth, remembering what a tight group the SWAT team cops were. No wonder there was territorialism within the police department. The SWAT team guys got the best training. After that, how could they trust anyone else to save their skins but themselves?

Rene and Roland had inherited from their grandparents one of the old farmhouses still left in the eastern suburb of Aurora. Small brick duplexes and frame houses had multiplied as subdivisions ate up the original farmstead. But the two-story white house with fieldstone foundation and chimney sat back on an acre of grass. Behind the house, a barking Doberman pinscher paced the length of a chain-link fence.

Jennifer was half-asleep by the time they got there. Matt picked her up in his arms and carried her from the gravel driveway to the covered porch.

The porch light was on, and movement of the curtain behind the oval glass in the door was followed by Rene's opening the door. She reached for Jennifer and patted her on the back while admiring Teddy.

"I've fixed up the extra bedroom for you and Jennifer," she told Tracy. "You staying here, too?" she asked Matt.

Matt looked at Tracy briefly. "Yes," he answered.

"Fold-out sofa in the study upstairs is fixed up."

She nodded to a set of buttons and a steady red light on a box on the wall next to the door. "Lock the door. Alarms are set."

Matt followed Tracy up to the guest room and waited until she had Jennifer tucked into one of the two chenille-covered twin beds. Then Tracy followed him out into the hall so they could talk. He kept his voice low.

"I'm going to follow up on these leads. Roland will be back soon to take care of anything that might come up."

"Where are you going?"

In answer, he held up the appointment book he'd brought from Scott's desk. "Liquor store, bowling alley."

"Now?"

He jerked his head in a nod. "Now's as good a time as any. I'll need that photo of Scott."

She made her decision. "I'm coming with you."

He seemed to hesitate. "You know I'm not going by the book."

Her voice was tight. "I know. But I can't just lie here and go to sleep."

"Why not?

"I can help you."

He seemed to weigh the possible dangers against having her along. She herself wondered at her impulsive decision to go with him. Jennifer's safety came first. But Jennifer was soundly sleeping in a burglar-alarmed house with a guard dog. And the SWAT team sniper himself was on his way here to sit on the porch with a shotgun across his knees if necessary.

With all that security so she wouldn't have to worry, Tracy realized that she was as curious about what those appointments in the Day-Timer meant as Matt was. She'd never questioned Scott about his work much, realizing now how she hadn't really wanted him to bring it home. But if he'd been involved in something that ultimately had gotten him killed, she felt a sense of duty to help find out what it was, like it or not.

Matt's fierce expression softened, and his eyelids relaxed over his hazel eyes. He didn't even touch her, yet she could feel the warmth emanating from his solid torso and flexed arms.

"I can't guarantee what we might be getting into," he said. "Wouldn't you rather rest?"

Her hand went to his chest of its own volition, though she didn't look up at his face. "I won't rest. Not until I know why we're being hounded."

She felt his breath in her hair. His hand slid up to her waist.

"All right," he murmured. "I'll take you with me. Bring the picture."

Her limbs trembling, she returned to the room and quietly opened the suitcase to pull out the brown envelope in which she had a photograph of Scott.

When the two of them returned downstairs, they saw Roland sprawled on one of the sofas in the living room. Rene sat on the edge of the other sofa across from him, leaning forward, a glass-topped coffee table between them. They rose when Matt and Tracy stopped in the wide-arched entryway. Roland crossed to them and stood, hands on hipbones, as he looked at Matt.

"We're secured here," said Roland in the tone that reminded Tracy of the military-like tactics they were trained in. But Scott had also been one of them, and Scott was dead.

Matt told Rene and Roland where they were going, and then Rene let them out, locking up securely behind them. As they walked to the car, a cool breeze blessed them, and the old maples and giant oaks that had stood here on the original farm rattled their leaves and swayed their branches. It was the kind of summer night lovers basked in...if they weren't being hunted.

Tracy fastened her seat belt and locked her door as they got under way. Matt drove in silence while Tracy flipped slowly through the Day-Timer. A sting of regret washed over her as she noticed that neither her birthday nor Jennifer's was circled. Nothing but a few notations here and there about training days and the unexplained times and places she and Matt were now following up.

Then she turned to the previous July, beginning with the Fourth of July weekend, exactly a year ago today. As she might expect, the Denver Police family day was duly noted. It had been held at the YMCA camp last year. She flipped forward to the next week, the next, and then the next.

She stared at a date that had been circled in green ink. Friday, August 1. The day Scott had been killed. She felt the blood pound in her ears. No one had touched this Day-Timer, which had lain in Scott's desk for the past year. She even recognized the green ink from the green ballpoint pens he used to keep at his desk.

She lifted her head and looked out the window at the lights of Colfax Avenue as they headed downtown. She watched Matt's determined profile while he glanced in his mirrors and at the sides of the streets as they drove.

"It's circled," she said, feeling a chill creep along her spine. "August 1 is circled."

Matt didn't speak for a second. Then he frowned. "The day Scott was killed."

She nodded, not taking her eyes from his shadowed face as he stared out the windshield.

"Why would a man circle the day he was going to die?"

Chapter Nine

Matt didn't answer for a moment as he slowed for a stoplight. Finally, he asked, "Are you sure?"

The date she'd never forget had been heavily circled in green ink. "He knew," she whispered to herself.

Matt reached over to squeeze her hand. It was a comforting gesture. Then he returned his hand to the wheel. "We just need to find out what he knew," he said.

She stared out the window at the closed shops with gates across their windows. Colfax Avenue changed its appearance at night. Only a block away, fine old mansions had been renovated for use as offices and bed-and-breakfast inns. But this close to downtown, a block with chic boutiques and restaurants might be located next to a block where winos congregated on the steps of a church.

They turned down a side street and parked. Matt opened the glove compartment and removed his automatic pistol. He checked the magazine and safety and then strapped on a shoulder holster. To conceal the bulk, he reached into the back seat and retrieved a khaki vest with pockets.

"You sure you don't want to wait in the car?" he asked.

She shook her head. "I'm sure."

Looking around to see whether they'd been followed, he started to open his door. "Stay close to me."

She stepped onto a sidewalk sprinkled with broken glass. It wasn't the kind of neighborhood she would ordinarily visit at night, but for a SWAT team cop it must seem routine. When she caught Matt's face in the light from the streetlamp, she could see the steely glint in his slightly narrowed eyes. His jaw was set and his muscles flexed. Everything about him seemed coiled tightly, as if ready to spring into action.

Even so, the protective grip of his arm around her shoulders was warm and reassuring as they crossed the street to the liquor store.

Inside, several T-shirted clerks stocked shelves and took money. They looked as if they could handle any trouble that came through the door. Matt glanced around briefly and then approached the clerk behind the counter. He opened his wallet to show his badge. The blue-eyed, tattooed clerk in a sleeveless, cutoff T-shirt met his gaze evenly.

"What can I do for you?"

Matt reached for the photo. "If you have a memory for faces, I need to know if you saw this man in here about a year ago. He was a cop."

The clerk shook his head. "I never saw him. Hey, Nico, ever seen this guy? Man says he was a cop."

The dark-complected clerk addressed as Nico came over and took a look. "Who's asking?" He spoke with a Latin accent.

"Another cop," said the first clerk, nodding at Matt.

Matt adopted a relaxed manner. "He wrote down this address in a date book he had. He was here several times about a year ago. Any idea why?"

Nico looked at the picture for a long time. He finally looked up. "Never saw him."

From the way he said it and from his guarded gaze,

Tracy knew he was lying. She looked at Matt and felt certain in her gut that Matt knew it, too.

Matt shook his head. "Too bad."

"Why's that?" asked Nico.

Matt placed both his hands on the counter and leaned forward, forcing Nico and the blue-eyed Romeo to look at him.

"Someone shot him. I think whoever shot him was in here at the same times he was. It'd be helpful if you remembered anything."

He reached for a stubby pencil and wrote something on the back of a flyer advertising the motorcycle shop next door.

"Here's my cell phone number. You call me if you think of anything." He put his hand on Tracy's waist and guided her toward the door.

She was glad to leave the high-crime neighborhood behind as they drove east on Fourteenth Avenue. Matt was thoughtful, and Tracy tried to relax some of her tense muscles.

Twenty minutes later, they pulled into the parking lot at the bowling alley located in southeast Denver. Inside, the lanes were busy, and the familiar sound of heavy balls thumping on the wood lanes and knocking into the pins reverberated every few seconds. A glass partition separated a restaurant from the rest of the bowling alley. Matt steered her inside and they took seats at the counter.

"Decaf coffee, please," said Tracy when a middle-aged waitress with dyed-red hair came to serve them. Matt had the same.

When the woman returned with their cups, Matt showed her the picture. "This man look familiar to you at all? He was in here several times about a year ago."

The waitress took the picture and drew her penciled eyebrows together in concentration. "Good-lookin' face. Yeah, I seen him. Couldn't tell you when. Been a long time. A year, you say?"

Matt leaned his elbows on the counter and nodded toward Tracy. "This is his widow. We're trying to find out who killed him."

The waitress widened her blue eyes into sympathy. "Oh, I'm sorry, honey. That's a shame."

"Thank you," said Tracy.

She left the rest to Matt, who played on the woman's sympathetic feelings. His voice was deeply intent, as if he were taking the waitress into his confidence.

"He left behind some notes that indicate his interest in this location. Anything you can remember might help us. Who he was with, what he did while he was here, whether he came and left alone."

The waitress cocked her head and frowned into the air above their heads as if trying to remember. "I served him coffee a couple of times," she began. "He always sat over there." She indicated a seat at a small table next to the glass partition.

"Alone?"

She shrugged. "Don't remember anybody else with him."

Matt slid off the stool and picked up his coffee cup. "You mind?" He headed for the seat she'd indicated.

Tracy felt a wave of queasiness as they took seats at the little table where Scott had sat. It was a little eerie to be following her deceased husband's trail. Matt broke off from narrowing his gaze through the glass at the bowling alley. He settled a look of concern on her as if to make sure she was doing okay.

"It's all right," she whispered hoarsely. "What do you think he was doing here?"

Matt returned his gaze to the lanes visible through the glass. The sound of toppling bowling pins was muted.

"Watching someone."

She, too, looked at the bowling teams. From here, she could see every lane to the right and left. Then she craned her neck around to see where Matt was looking past her head. Through the glass behind them, on the other side of the main entrance, was the counter where people rented shoes. When she turned back around, she read the look on Matt's face. Seated where Matt was, Scott could watch whoever came in and see where he or she was playing. She swallowed.

"Who do you think he was watching for?"

He brought his steely gaze back to her eyes. "Give me the appointment book."

She reached into her bag and handed Matt the black leather Day-Timer. He flipped to the pages where Scott had marked down the bowling alley. "Tuesday nights," he said. "Whoever he was here to meet or to spy on isn't here now."

"Don't tell me," she responded. "We can't wait around until Tuesday to see what he saw."

"Right you are."

He told the waitress they were ready for their check and handed her an extremely generous tip. "Anything special happen around here on Tuesday nights?" he asked her as she ripped the check from her pad and pocketed the ten.

"Some of the leagues play. Which one you interested in?"

"Police league?" guessed Matt.

She gave a shrug. "Schedule's marked on the wall over there. Harry can show you."

When they finished their coffee, they strolled out toward the rental counter. Matt gave a friendly nod to the man with hairy arms leaning across the counter talking with a crony, but he didn't stop to talk. They found the schedule and lifted the calendar pages. "Police league" was scrawled in heavy black ink on the third Tuesday of every month. A chill raced down Tracy's spine.

"Police again," she whispered under her breath.

"Let's not talk here," he said. "I think we've got what we came for."

Tracy didn't see what he was so certain about, but trusted his judgment. Back in the car, he settled in his seat but didn't start the engine.

"More police," she said with an odd sinking feeling. "What do you think's going on?"

"Ugly picture, isn't it? Police shoe print in the place where you were held. Scott had a definite interest in the police bowling league, but he didn't play. The gun that may have killed him is removed from evidence. And he gets killed on the day the rest of the SWAT team is busy elsewhere."

The full truth stared her in the face. "Police corruption. He really did know something, didn't he? And he was killed because of it." Her voice shook as she said it.

Matt reached over, took her hand and warmed it in his. "I'd better take you back. It's late and you need your sleep."

The compassion in his voice was almost her undoing. He suddenly slid an arm around her shoulders and pulled her closer to him. She felt the heat emanating from his strong body and wanted to curl up against it. Perhaps the danger they both knew they were in made her cling to him all the harder.

The subtle scent of his aftershave mingled with his natural masculine scent and drew her to him. She wanted, needed his protection, even while the other, more logical side of her cautioned her against doing the wrong thing for all of them.

His embrace steadied her and she pulled away, back to her side of the car, so she could fasten her seat belt. She still trembled with the realization that Scott's finding out something someone didn't want him to know had gotten him killed.

She didn't say any more. Finally, they pulled up the Bakers' driveway. The growling Doberman barked his warning, until Matt got out and called the dog by name.

"Quiet, Paolo, we're friends."

The growls muted to a few gruff woofs.

After checking on Jennifer in the other bed, Tracy fell gratefully into her comfortable twin bed. The old-fashioned furnishings inherited from Rene and Roland's grandparents gave the room a cozy feel. The warmth and protection of family surrounded her in a way she'd longed for.

She'd been left alone after Scott's death; her own family had been sympathetic but they couldn't help. Her parents struggled to keep their farm in Nebraska going, and she couldn't saddle them with an asthmatic child. While her family would gladly welcome Jennifer and Tracy home, even their feed store in town couldn't support two extra hungry mouths.

More than that, Tracy couldn't risk taking Jennifer so far away from doctors and treatments right now. Her sister in New York was a free spirit, struggling with running a new business. Not the time to lean on her. No, Tracy had to be self-reliant in this dilemma, counting only on friends to help. Friends like Matt.

In spite of warning herself that she didn't want to be with another cop, she couldn't put aside the sensual heat between them. He knew it and she knew it. Images of him disrobing her and gazing at her body warmed her blood. And thoughts of his well-formed, muscular body without anything on made her insides turn somersaults.

As the mental pictures rolled around in her mind, she surrendered to the emotional and physical exhaustion that claimed her. The night felt safe for the moment. The uncertainty of Matt's forging ahead where he'd been warned off frightened her. If only things were different. But she had to let everything else wait for tomorrow.

TRACY WAS AWARE of strong summer light thrusting around the edges of the old-fashioned window shade and curtains and of a soft knock on her door. She had a momentary panic when she looked over to see Jennifer's bed empty, the covers tossed back.

"What is it?" she cried out in a semihysterical voice.

Rene slipped into the room and closed the door behind her. Seeing Tracy's fright, she put up a hand.

"Relax, Jennifer's downstairs eating a bowl of cereal. But you have a visitor waiting for you."

Tracy sat up and shoved the covers back. "Who?"

Rene paused to let Tracy get herself fully awake before telling her anything more. When Tracy had gotten into her robe and reached for her hairbrush, she added her second question.

"What time is it, anyway?" From the strength of the sun, it had to be late.

"I let you sleep in since you and Matt were out late last night," Rene said. "It's eight o'clock."

Tracy frowned. She was normally up at six-thirty to get herself ready and see that Jennifer was ready for day camp. But today was Friday, and camp was canceled today to celebrate tomorrow's Fourth of July holiday, which fell on Saturday this year.

She rummaged in the suitcase for clothes to put on. "So who's waiting for me downstairs? Is Matt still here?"

"Matt left for work, but he told me not to let you out of my sight without telling him where you're going. And you're not to go anywhere alone."

Rene's evasive answers finally penetrated Tracy's anxious mind, and she paused before stepping out into the hall to use the shared bathroom. She straightened up and looked at Rene, who cocked her head and glanced toward the door.

"Prepare yourself for a shock. Jennifer's grandfather is downstairs. Your next-door neighbor told him you'd left with Matt, so he called all the squad members until he reached us here."

The shock was even more than Tracy had expected. She nearly bolted toward the stairs, still dressed in pajamas and bathrobe, her hair disarranged. But she gripped the doorjamb instead.

"You left him alone with Jennifer?" her voice was a high-pitched screech.

"Calm down, it's all right. Roland is in the kitchen eating breakfast with them. He won't let the old man snatch her out from under you."

"Good God, my worst nightmare." She cast Rene a pleading look. "I have to look decent when I see him. He probably already thinks I'm irresponsible, sleeping in like this."

No matter that she'd been out late the previous night trying to track Jennifer's father's killer. She had to hurry and get down there. Damn! What else could make matters worse?

"Tell him I'll be down as soon as I'm presentable. Tell him Jennifer has no camp today. Oh, damn!"

"Relax," said Rene. "Roland's got him occupied. His shift doesn't start till later. You've got time."

She didn't feel that she had time. As she hurried through her morning preparations, the sinking feeling in her stomach only got worse. By the time she was dressed in crisp white slacks and a royal-blue short-sleeved top, her heart pounded in her chest. She took a deep breath at the top of the stairs and then held on to the railing as she walked down.

Voices coming from the big kitchen at the back of the house told her everyone was congregated there. As her sandals squeaked on the veneer of the wooden hallway, she squinted at the bright light coming in through the large kitchen windows.

A trim, gray-haired gentleman sat hunched over the tiled pine breakfast table, talking to Jennifer, who sat at an angle to him. At the other end of the table, Roland polished off bacon and eggs, while Rene poured coffee. Everyone stopped talking when Tracy walked through the doorway.

"Good morning, Mr. Leigh. This is unexpected."

"Mrs. Meyer."

He got up to greet her, and she had a moment to assess the look in his cunning eyes. They were light green, unlike Jennifer's. As soon as he stood to face Tracy, all her defensiveness and territoriality rushed upon her, along with an adrenaline surge that made her ready to stand her ground.

Andrew Leigh was a healthy-looking sixty-year-old, with short silver hair, a long Roman nose and a square jaw. His tanned face was weathered, but he was the kind of man who seemed used to getting what he wanted. His blue mesh golf shirt, with embroidered monogram on the pocket, under a navy sport jacket with casual tan trousers, somehow did not lessen the urbane look of a man of wealth and power. He seemed oddly incongruous in the homey kitchen, and he did nothing to change that impression.

He shook her hand, but she didn't miss the sharp examination of his eyes. His authoritarian stare sent tremors through her, which she did everything she could not to show.

"Have you had coffee?" she asked to give herself time to get her bearings. Her eyes flew to Jennifer, who was peacefully eating her cereal.

"Yes, thank you. Please sit down," he ordered as if this were his office.

She walked over to the counter and poured herself a cup of coffee, taking her time with the cream. Then she remained standing, leaning against the counter.

"I see Jennifer has been entertaining you."

She tried to say it in a neutral voice. If she and Andrew Leigh were going to have a showdown, she'd be damned if it was going to be in front of Jennifer.

"That she has," responded Andrew. A hint of pleasure lit his otherwise hard facade. "She's been telling me about day camp."

"Oh?"

He looked up at Tracy, clearly resenting the fact that she remained standing. But it was too late for him to make an issue of it.

"I was hoping to spend some time with Jennifer today, if that doesn't interfere with your plans, of course."

She was sure he didn't care whether it interfered or not. He was just negotiating. And he wouldn't reveal his true reason for being here in front of everyone else.

"Jennifer," said Rene from the other side of the kitchen. "Why don't you come help me make the beds upstairs while Tracy and your grandfather visit?"

"All right."

Jennifer slid off her chair and carried her bowl over to the sink, reaching over the edge to place it with the other dirty dishes.

Tracy met Andrew's eyes, feeling proud that Jennifer was behaving like the well-brought-up child she was. Tracy wanted Grandfather Leigh to witness for himself just how well she was raising his granddaughter.

Her heart welled up as she saw Jennifer march out of the room to help Rene with chores, but she wouldn't allow Mr. Leigh to see any sentimentality. He might misinterpret it for weakness. After everyone cleared out of the kitchen, she carried her coffee cup to the table and sat down.

A feeling of dread crept along her spine. What if Jennifer's grandfather were going to simply abduct his granddaughter? Tracy couldn't bear just letting Jennifer be scooped up and taken away like that. She felt her eyes round as she faced the tycoon across the corner of the table. The thought that he would do something underhanded like that seemed monstrous. But with the many reports of kidnapping in the news over the past decade, it was a frightening prospect. Why else would he show up here unannounced?

Instead of revealing her horrors, she faced him in a grim, businesslike manner. "What can I do for you?" she asked.

He took a sip from his coffee mug and leaned back in the oak kitchen chair. His steady gaze was not as mean as she expected, although she sensed an underlying cunning. His tanned features were distinguished, the firm jaw decisive, as if he were not a man to be messed with. His fit body still looked capable of taking action, and she imagined that in younger years he had been quite appealing to women. The hardness engraved in the lines of his face seemed more from fighting for what he wanted than from the wrinkles of age. A formidable opponent. Tracy dug in her heels.

He assessed her. "I came to see my granddaughter. I want to know how she is getting along with her illness."

Tracy jutted her chin forward. "You can see for yourself. I've written to you about the treatments and you have the doctors' reports. Even the medical doctors have to admit that the chiropractic treatments have restored the nerves and that her breathing is better. Her lymphatic drainage seems to be clearing out the bacteria and debris faster now. She's having fewer attacks, so that means her immune system is getting stronger."

For a minute, their eyes locked in challenge. Then Andrew cleared his throat and took another sip of coffee. "I know you insist that she is getting the best treatment here. I also know you cannot expect to support a child now that you've left your employment."

Tracy straightened her spine, seeing red. "I left a very demanding job in a publishing company so that I could take care of Jennifer. She is my greatest and only responsibility."

His coffee mug banged down on the tile in the table surface. "She is my granddaughter and should be my responsibility."

Tracy swallowed, trying to even her temper. "I know how you must feel. And I'm sure Jennifer wants to get to know her grandfather. But if you care about her, you will not uproot her from all that is familiar to her here."

She leaned forward, begging not for herself, but for Jennifer.

"Can't you see? Her father died last year. We're just now establishing a life routine that is healthy for her. She likes her school. The teachers love her, and she has friends there."

She stopped her litany before she brought up her tutor. It would only add fuel to Andrew Leigh's arguments that the caring tutor was herself now missing.

Thoughts of Matt's easy relationship with Jennifer also crossed her mind. She closed her eyes for a moment, allowing the reassuring feeling to wash over her. When Matt had been with them at dinner on their porch the other night, it had been like a dream. She only now realized how much she was beginning to want that dream to come true. She frowned and opened her eyes.

That dream included Jennifer, and she wasn't about to let this man rip her stepdaughter from her home, not if she could help it.

"I certainly would never dream of trying to keep you from seeing her. Scott was perhaps at fault for not making a greater effort to make sure you saw her. I can't answer for that."

A glower darkened Andrew's face. "Scott Meyer was at fault for a great many things."

The anger underlying his words surprised her, and she blinked. For a moment, she could think of nothing to say.

"Well, if your argument is with Scott, it's too late to do anything about it. But please don't equate what he did with what I'm doing."

The shadows slid across Andrew's face as he seemed to weigh her words. She sensed a sharp mind there, a lawyer's mind, but she didn't trust him. Suddenly, Andrew looked away as if dealing with some private battle. He sipped his coffee, thinking. When he brought his gaze back to Tracy, he seemed to have gathered his thoughts.

"I appreciate what you've done for Jennifer. But these are things I should have done for her myself. I have few regrets, Mrs. Meyer, and I'm determined to see that this doesn't become one of them." He lowered his gaze almost with a trace of humility. "I didn't have time for my daughters when they were young. Now it's too late...."

Surprised at this sudden exposure of raw feeling, Tracy was taken aback. They sat quietly for a moment, awkwardly, as the sun bathed them with its light. Andrew Leigh must miss Jennifer's mother very much. Was that why he wanted Jennifer now?

"I'm sorry," she managed to say slowly. "But feeling as you do, surely you must realize how attached I've become to Jennifer." She decided to risk some of the truth. "Scott wasn't home very much. His job was demanding, as well. I spent every evening with her and all of the weekends when he was off doing training. I could never replace her real mother. But we've become very close. Can you understand that?"

His jaw hardened, and the green eyes came back to penetrate hers. Lost in his own thoughts, he didn't really answer her question. "Jennifer is the only family I have now. I'm the only one who can make sure she has everything she needs."

"That's not true."

Appealing to reason hadn't worked, and Tracy spit out her defense now, ready to fight. "I may not be as wealthy as you are, but I can give her love. I was a little girl myself once, and I can be a positive role model for her. If you were a reasonable man, Mr. Leigh, you'd see it's possible to share her. Why can't we both be family to her? She needs as much love as possible."

His own face reddened with anger now, and Tracy realized she'd lost all chance of negotiating.

"If I leave her here," he boomed, "I can't oversee her medical care. I can't watch her grow up. If I take her, I can send her to the best schools, give her music lessons or whatever she wants. Everything I have will be at her fingertips.''

Feeling tears beneath her eyelids, Tracy could no longer remain sitting in the chair. She stood up, hands on hips, backing up to the counter.

''My little house is not a palace. But it's clean and comfortable. I'm planning to turn the upstairs den into an office to work at home.'' As soon as she could afford a computer, she almost added. But she didn't want to admit to her dismal financial situation in front of him.

No matter what she wanted to admit, he seemed to realize the truth of the matter. He brushed her efforts away with a flick of his manicured hand.

''Starting a home business will hardly support a child with Jennifer's needs. You'll burn out in no time. No, Jennifer will get what she needs with me.''

''How do you know what she needs?''

They glared at each other, and Tracy gritted her teeth. She tried to think frantically of what to do. Surely Andrew couldn't just whisk Jennifer away? Or could he? She would need to obtain a lawyer right away. And that meant legal fees. She tried to stifle her inward groan. She tried not to believe the man in front of her could be a kidnapper.

Andrew scraped his chair back and stood up, as well. ''Maybe we should ask Jennifer.''

Tracy squared off with him. The logic of what he said warred with her protective instincts. In her mind, this man had become a monster out to tear her fragile family fabric apart. But some small trace of emotion parted the curtain of his obstinacy. She suddenly realized that he was desperate himself. Andrew Leigh was lonely. Her puffed-up anger deflated. Jennifer was family and he wanted her. It was as simple as that.

Her words were choked off as she realized the selfishness of her own arguments. Some of what he'd said was true. And at the moment, Jennifer was being kept in a fortress because *she was in danger*. Andrew Leigh had the money and power to keep her safe.

Tracy reached behind her for the counter beside the sink for support. It would make sense to hand Jennifer over to her grandfather until she resolved the threats that were putting both their lives in danger. If it made so much sense, why couldn't she do it? Why couldn't she say the words?

Instead, all she could do was numbly nod and follow him as he turned and headed toward the hallway. When he reached the staircase, he peered upward. Tracy summoned what strength she had left and spoke with dignity.

"If you'll wait in the living room, I'll bring Jennifer down."

She found Jennifer with Rene, occupied over a scrapbook of photographs. As she went in to join them, Rene exchanged looks with her.

"Jennifer," said Tracy, sitting down next to her on the floral-print bedspread on Rene's queen-size bed. "How would you like to spend the day with Grandfather Leigh?" She tried to ignore the lead weight dragging at her heart.

Jennifer shrugged, then turned her round eyes and chubby cheeks up to her. "What will we do?"

"Um, I'm not sure. What would you like to do?"

Jennifer swung her legs, bouncing her tennis-shoed feet off the edge of the bed. "We could go to the zoo. Will you come?"

Tracy pressed her lips together. Of all the awkward moments, why did Andrew Leigh have to show up today? Matt needed her to help him. There wasn't a minute to waste in getting to the bottom of the deadly threats that surrounded them. In all fairness, she would have to warn Andrew Leigh in case someone saw an opportunity to abduct Jennifer out from under his hands. The bizarre possibility even crossed her mind that the threats had come from Andrew himself in some crazy attempt to intimidate her. But she pushed that thought aside. He didn't strike her as an unbalanced or violent man. On the other hand, admitting that she was frightened for their lives only strengthened his position as the best guardian for Jennifer.

Rene watched her over Jennifer's head and seemed to sense some of the battle going on inside Tracy's mind. She gave them both a friendly smile.

"Tell you what. Maybe your grandfather would let me go along to the zoo," said Rene. "I'm off work for the holiday weekend. We could pack a lunch."

Thank you, Tracy wanted to cry out. Instead, she smiled down at Jennifer. "Do you like that idea? I know Rene makes very healthy lunches."

Jennifer nodded excitedly. "Yes. If you can't go with us, that is," she said loyally to Tracy.

"Well, Matt needed me to help him with something today."

"Oh." Jennifer's gray-eyed gaze took on some endearing coyness. "If he needs you, then you'd better help him. We'll be fine by ourselves. We can meet you back here this evening." Her last words sounded so grown-up that it made both Rene and Tracy laugh.

Satisfied with this plan, she got up. When they all trooped into the living room, Tracy announced the suggestion. Andrew nodded politely, though she could see in his eyes that he preferred to be alone to get to know Jennifer better. But there was also a flash of relief, and Tracy saw the awkwardness that he must have felt at having to communicate with a young girl all by himself.

Her mixed emotions became suffused with compassion. He was nothing but a lonely man. His wealth and power had failed to bring him family. She had no idea what his wife had been like. Remembering that he had said Jennifer was all he had left confused her. She remembered that Scott had told her that Jennifer's mother had had a sister. And Andrew had just said that he hadn't had time for his daughters. But now wasn't the moment to ask.

While Rene went to make the lunch and Jennifer went upstairs to put on play clothes, Tracy instructed Andrew on what to do should Jennifer have an asthma attack. They would carry an inhaler to use in the event of emergency. Then Tracy interrogated him on how close he would watch her.

"I'd like to reassure myself that you won't let her out of your sight," she began. "You know the dangers of having children in public places. I don't want to sound paranoid, but there have been occasional kidnappings in this city. Will you make sure nothing happens to her?"

He met her gaze soberly. "You needn't worry on that account. My driver and bodyguard will be with us. I completely trust Domenico."

"Oh, I didn't know." She knew Andrew Leigh considered himself important. She didn't know he traveled with a bodyguard.

While the idea should have been reassuring, it gave her a shiver. What kind of dangers did a man like Andrew Leigh fear? She tried to reassure herself that his stature in the business community must warrant a bodyguard. Many prominent citizens had to guard against threats. It was the same reason that key executives in large corporations were heavily insured for their lives.

"What time will you bring Jennifer back?"

Andrew glowered at her, but she no longer felt him such a formidable enemy. Perhaps that moment when she'd seen through his gruff exterior to his own inner losses and needs had softened her. But she still couldn't let down her guard until matters were resolved.

"I thought I might take Jennifer and your friend to the Brown Palace for tea at four." Then, grudgingly, he added, "Would you care to join us?"

"Thank you, no. But Jennifer will need a nap if she's tired."

"I'll see to it she gets one either in my suite or back here, whichever she prefers."

"Thank you."

Tracy told herself she shouldn't worry. Jennifer's own flesh and blood would never harm her. And Rene knew the score. She would keep her eyes peeled for trouble. Then there was this bodyguard Domenico. Where was he? Deciding to risk Andrew's wrath by trying his patience, she stuck her nose further into his business by asking to meet Domenico. After all, if a man she'd never heard of was to be entrusted with Jennifer's security, she would be less than responsible not to meet him.

"Domenico is outside. I'll introduce you."

They found the bodyguard in the backyard tossing a ball to Paolo. Seeing his employer, the dark-haired, bronze-complected bodyguard called to the dog, who brought the ball and meekly dropped it at Domenico's feet.

Bright white teeth flashed in a smile when he was introduced to Tracy.

She reacted warily to him, but he looked her in the eye and bowed slightly while shaking her hand. Then he stood respectfully, waiting for orders. She noticed out of the corner of her eye that the lean, black-and-fawn-colored dog thumped his tail once and sat down beside the man he had obviously befriended.

"Well," she said to all of them, "if Paolo is willing to trust you gentlemen, I'm pretty sure I can."

Andrew pulled his mouth sideways in an ironic smirk. "If you would feel safer, the dog may accompany us."

She actually considered it for a moment. But in the end, she decided an army with canine-attack support might be overkill for a visit to the zoo and a picnic. She faced Andrew, strangely feeling less afraid of him and more on an equal footing now. She realized with a sudden swell of pride that in spite of his money, she had her own resources.

"That won't be necessary," she told him. "But I'll send the Doberman after both of you if you don't have Jennifer back in time for dinner."

As they drove away in the rented black limo, she prayed she had done the right thing.

Chapter Ten

Friday morning, Matt's squad met their physical-fitness training requirements. On the obstacle course, he clambered over the six-foot chain-link fence, jumped the ditch, crawled through sand, hoisted himself over a seven-foot wall, used a battering ram to knock down fifty-gallon drums, dragged a two-hundred-pound dummy carrying forty pounds of gear twenty-five feet and then ran a quarter mile in under three minutes.

When he crossed the finish line, Commander Udal was leaning in the shade beside the concrete-block building that contained showers, locker room and small office. Matt huffed and puffed as he jogged over, catching his breath from the workout. The sergeant clocking him marked his time on a clipboard. Then he handed Matt a towel to wipe down with.

The commander pushed himself away from the wall and strolled over to meet him.

"Good job, Matt," said Udal.

He waited for the sergeant to disappear around the corner before placing a hand on Matt's sweaty shoulder. He steered him away from the building to where they could talk near some trees that shaded cars in a gravel driveway.

As Matt's heart rate returned to normal, he tried to assess the familiar lines in his commander's placid face. But Udal spoke before Matt had time to prepare for what he had to say.

"How's your personal life going, Matt?" asked Udal in his easy, nonthreatening way.

"Fine, sir." He still drew deep breaths as he toweled some of the sweat off from the extreme workout.

"You know I don't interfere in my men's personal lives unless I think it has an effect on the job."

"Yes, sir. That's been my experience."

Udal's penetrating blue eyes bored into Matt as he spoke. "You're seeing Tracy Meyer—that right?"

Resentment flared in Matt, then he swallowed, trying not to appear defensive. He was beginning to see where this was headed.

"Yes, sir, I am. Is that a problem?"

"Not to me, personally. It's you I'm worried about."

Matt looked away at the junipers and pines climbing up a low rise toward the hogback ridge west of Denver. He inhaled a deep breath and returned his gaze to Udal, waiting for what he had to say.

Udal glanced away, too. "You're a little on the edge, Matt. Ever since Scott Meyer's death. I worried that I should have taken you off the team for a while then. But you're one of my best men. There's no question about your abilities. You know the rules. If you're emotionally involved in something too close to home, you're likely to get jumpy on the job."

He looked back into Matt's eyes. "I should have offered you time off then. I'm doing so now."

Suspicion slithered up Matt's spine, but he kept his face from betraying any thoughts. "Will this go on my record?"

A hint of a smile curved Udal's lips. "You're due for

vacation, in case you haven't noticed. No need for anything on the record. You've just been working too hard and need some time off.''

Udal puffed up his chest and then let out the air. Hands on hips, he gave his orders. "Starting now, you're on vacation for two weeks. Does that work for you?"

Matt began to relax. "Why yes, it does, sir. I don't mind taking some time off, to be honest with you."

"Good." Udal seemed as though he wanted to say more, but they started walking back toward the showers. Before they reached the corner of the concrete-block building, Udal halted.

"And, Matt."

"Yes, sir?"

The commander didn't quite meet Matt's eyes as he gave his final warning. Instead, he shoved himself off by pushing a hand against the concrete wall. "Don't do anything illegal."

He didn't look back as he left Matt staring after him. Matt watched him go, then tossed the sweaty towel over his shoulder. He grunted. The man was smart. He knew Matt needed some time to look into things. If he was doing it on his own time, then the SWAT team wouldn't be held responsible for any rules Matt might break. Matt nodded to himself. Good man, Commander Udal. He could read his men like a book.

After his shower, he called the Baker residence, but no one answered. When he tried Tracy at home, she picked up. She explained that Jennifer's grandfather had shown up and taken the little group out for the day.

"I'm in the den," she told him over the phone. He realized she didn't want to say too much over the open airwaves of his cell phone.

"I'll be right over." He shut the cell phone and sped back to town.

Pulling up at her curb forty-five minutes later, he scanned the neighborhood for potential danger. What he found instead was a quiet, sunny afternoon with very few people and cars in sight. A woman across the street in shorts and a wide-brimmed hat pulled weeds in her flower beds. The few cars parked curbside had no occupants. Birds twittered in the trees, and the hot afternoon sun baked the grass. In Tracy's yard, shade from an old, overhanging silver maple offered relief from the blinding sun.

When Tracy let him in, it took a moment for his eyes to adjust to the cool interior of the brick house. He let his vision focus on her luscious figure clad in a lime-green, cropped T-shirt and denim cutoffs. His pulse lurched at the sight of her bare midriff and her tanned legs, and he had to fill his lungs with air in order not to give away the lust he felt.

Her brown eyes wore a slightly worried expression, and he wanted to take her in his arms and soothe her worries away. Her full lips half parted as she drew in a breath, and he felt the spark leap between them.

In the shadowy house, cooled by a fan in the window, he almost thought she might walk into his arms. He was ready to plant a kiss on her mouth, taste and feel of her as much as he pleased.

They were alone, and he sensed that she wanted him as much as he wanted her. With more self-control than he would have credited himself as having, he didn't move a muscle, but let Tracy brush past him and lead him through the house.

He stared at the gentle sway of her hips, the inviting crop-top T-shirt and the cascade of curling auburn hair. In the kitchen, she held out the desk blotter from upstairs, and he forced his mind to business. He was more determined than ever to resolve matters surrounding them. For when he did, he wanted to have a serious talk with Tracy about how he felt about her. Would she be ready for another man in her life? He realized now that he wanted to be in her life for a very long time.

She carried the desk blotter out to the screened porch where the sun poured in. He took it out of her hands and held it at an angle so he could see the indentations made from writing on sheets of paper on top of the blotter. From the look on Tracy's face, he could tell she'd found something she wanted him to see. He frowned at the squiggles and marks indented in the soft fibers of the surface.

"Help me out," he said. "What've you found?"

She pointed a long, graceful finger at several tilted lines in the middle of the blotter. "Look at this."

He shifted the blotter to get a better look, then opened his eyes wider. "Bingo. It looks like a list of names. Get a piece of paper."

"I've already written them down, at least what I could make out. Maybe you know some of the names better than I do."

Realizing they might be onto something, he shoved his physical desires to the back of his mind and squinted at the impressions that came into focus as names. He whistled softly through his teeth.

"What've you got?" he asked Tracy as she brought the white pad of paper from the kitchen.

As she read her interpretation of the list, he nodded. Though he didn't know them all personally, he recognized the last names of officers of the Denver Police Department. He corrected some of her spelling and filled in where she hadn't been able to read them. When they were finished, he looked over the names and then met Tracy's anxious look.

"Good work," he told her. "Now all we have to do is find the connection between these men and why Scott wrote their names down." Another chilling thought occurred to him. "Any idea what happened to the original list?"

She shook her head. "I just started looking through the desk again. But so far, I haven't found it."

But someone did. He didn't want to say it out loud. Someone must have laid hands on the list and knew what it meant. Matt shook his head, feeling a deep sense of regret creep into his gut. Once Scott had made his list, for whatever reason, he should have destroyed it. He sighed, not wanting to depress Tracy any further.

"Come on. Let's go look."

They tore the desk apart and then looked through the closet in the den. "Did you keep any of his clothes?"

She shook her head. "No. I gave those away as soon as I could. If the list was in one of his pockets, it's gone."

Matt felt grim. "I doubt it. Whoever got the list had it before they killed him."

He got up off his knees and then offered her a hand to pull her up from where they'd been crawling around on the carpet looking under the desk. He didn't want to let go of her hand. She stood still for a minute, very close to him, and he felt the warmth of her body. If there'd been time…

He swallowed and satisfied himself with laying a hand on the silky skin of her arm. "There's something I need to do downtown. I'd better keep you with me. I don't like the idea of you being alone in this house."

She lifted her face to his, but her eyelids remained half-lowered. "It's the middle of the afternoon," she said.

Did he imagine it? Or was she slightly breathless?

"Nothing's going to happen."

He gritted his teeth, cursing his luck. If they didn't have such urgent business, he'd like very much to make something happen while they were alone this afternoon. The rush of desire was almost too much.

"Tracy," he said in a husky voice. He slid his hands around to her back.

"Mmm?"

"I—" He didn't know how to phrase it. "Damn," he finally muttered.

A wicked grin formed on her lips, and she raised her eyelids, meeting his gaze with a teasing one of her own. Then with pretended innocence, she repeated, "Damn?"

A surge of emotion bowled him over. Her humor was a delight and a relief. He pulled her into the circle of his arms, not caring if his lust made itself felt against her thighs.

"We have things to talk about, Tracy," he said, pressing his chin against her temple. His hands coursed over her back. "I'm attracted to you. You must know that by now."

"I know." Her own voice was choked, too.

"Do you?" He brushed a kiss along her ear and felt tongue-tied. Damn it, he'd never bothered to ask a woman before. He was used to having sex with girlfriends when things took their natural course. Why was it that Tracy had him wanting to jump through hoops to make everything just right for her? It wasn't a casual affair he wanted here. He wanted her respect. He wanted to be her white knight.

"I want you," he finally admitted.

Her breasts hardened against the material of his T-shirt, and he gently pressed her against his burgeoning loins. "I want you, Tracy," he repeated.

"Hmm," she murmured against his neck.

Hope surged in him.

For answer, she lifted her head and half parted her beautiful lips for a kiss. He gladly responded. They embraced each other madly, heatedly. His need hardened, and he moved his hips against her. His hands found their way under her T-shirt to press against the athletic bra she wore.

"Matt," she said breathlessly.

She pressed her hands against his chest. "I...can't."

He stopped his caresses instantly, removing his hands from her breasts and gripping her arms instead. His chin pressed down heavily on her lowered head.

"Why not?" He struggled with the urgency he felt. "I care about you, Tracy. We could..."

He swallowed, confused. He hadn't had time to plan what he wanted to say. "We'd be good together."

"I know."

He heard the choke in her voice, saw regret written on her face as she turned away and sniffed as if she were about to cry.

"What is it?"

He reached for her again, but this time he gently held her back to him, wrapping his arms around her waist in a comforting, protective manner and swaying with her, back and forth. They weren't going to make love today. Not until she was ready. But he realized in the depths of his soul that he cared about her. That she was becoming part of him.

"Is it Scott?" he said in a rumbling voice. "Does he still stand between us?"

"I...yes...no..." She was obviously struggling to sort out her own emotions. "It's very hard to explain."

She turned around again and faced him, looking earnestly into his face. She lifted a hand and brushed some of his hair off his forehead.

"You were his partner," she said with emotion in her voice. "And I was his wife. That's a little uncomfortable, as it is. And..." She hesitated, dropped her eyelids to cover her eyes. "You have the same profession."

He could tell she had things she wanted to tell him but was too afraid. "Go on."

"I just don't know if I can do it," she said.

"Do what?"

"Be with...another cop." She dropped her head, as well, and let her hand slide down to his chest.

It was what he'd expected. His hopes plunged, but he continued to hold on to her for a moment before he let go. "I see."

She hadn't been entirely happy with Scott and didn't want to repeat that life-style. How could he blame her? He walked toward the middle of the room, blowing air out through puffed cheeks and rubbing the back of his neck. She wasn't ready for an intimate relationship with him because he was a cop.

"I'm sorry, Tracy," he said without turning around.

This time she came to him. She moved up behind him and pressed her body against his back. Her arms encircled his waist. She laid her head against the base of his neck. "Me, too."

He didn't want to move. He wanted her to stay there forever, close to him, her body warm against his. Finally, he turned, reached around and squeezed her shoulders with one arm. His other hand caressed her cheek.

"You don't want to get involved with a cop because you're afraid that every morning when I go to work, I won't come back that night."

She sighed and nodded. "I just don't want to get something started that we wouldn't be able to stop. There's too much at stake."

She took a step away from him, reached the desk and pressed it with her fingers.

"You mean the custody suit with Andrew Leigh."

"That, and being threatened." She turned her deep brown eyes on him again. "I can't live like this."

"I know." He felt a tightness in his throat and restrained himself from reaching for her again. "Okay. Then we have to do something about it. When matters are settled, we'll talk about this again."

He thought he saw a blush rise in her cheeks as she pressed her lips together and nodded.

"Let's go, then," he said. "There's something we need to check out."

Before he let Tracy come out onto the porch, he did a sweep of the neighborhood with his eyes again. Nothing moved. The woman pulling weeds had worked her way down to the flower beds at the curb. She looked up and waved at Tracy as they walked to the car.

As TRACY FASTENED her seat belt, she still throbbed from Matt's sexy presence in the car. Now that she'd sampled the feel of his hands on her and the hard muscles of his thighs and arms, her body ached for more. Next time she might not have the strength to say no. Letting the hot wind blow in through the window, she didn't mind how it tangled her hair. She needed the warm summer wind to distract her roaring blood.

Matt Forrest is just another SWAT team cop. Never mind that he was going after whatever and whoever threatened them. Never mind that she felt safe when she was with him, would trust her life to his skills and experience. Never mind that he seemed to like children and that he had a reputation for being steady and reliable. He wanted to take her to bed and she wanted him. She knew they would have intense pleasure there.

As she viewed his healthy, fit body out of the corner of her eye, she knew beyond a shadow of a doubt that making love with Matt would exceed her wildest dreams. But she could not reconcile that act with what would follow. The logical part of her did not want to burden him with her financial dilemma or with Jennifer's health problems. After the first sexual rush, then what? Life would become a grind for him just as it had been for Scott. Scott had turned away from family life because he couldn't deal with having a sick little girl. He'd wanted a boy he could play football with and take to hockey games. He hadn't been able to cope, and so had buried himself in work.

Would Matt do the same? Given the fact that a sexy, attractive man like him was still single, she had the feeling that he, too, had shied away from further relationships after his last girlfriend had dumped him. Had the woman wanted more of his time than he could give? Was that why she found someone else? As they rode through traffic, Tracy didn't give any indication of what she was thinking.

They parked in the underground garage at the police administration building. Walking into the precinct, Tracy didn't feel as self-conscious about being with Matt as she had before. New personnel didn't recognize her anyway, but as they passed through the corridors, some of the old-timers spotted her and smiled or nodded. She returned their greetings, having gotten over the sensation that she was a secluded widow.

The next minute, Matt took hold of her hand and didn't let go. She looked up at him in surprise. Although the sizzling feeling that raced from her heart to her toes was dizzying, she wondered why he chose this moment for such a public display. The handhold could mean only one thing, that they were together.

Her heart looped around like the roller coaster at the amusement park. It was pleasurable to hold Matt's hand, and she matched his grip with her own. But she had to caution herself against wanting more from him. A relationship wasn't possible, she had to keep telling herself.

On the fourth floor, Matt swung left into the office of staff assistance. A chest-high counter separated them from an open room with windows opposite. Three women worked at computer stations stacked high with papers.

"Hi, Mindy," Matt called to one of them.

"Hello, Matt."

A middle-aged woman with short gray hair swiveled in her chair. When she saw Tracy, she wrinkled her brow as if trying to place her, but gave her a pleasant smile.

"Do you know Tracy Meyer?" Matt asked. "She was Scott Meyer's wife."

With thirteen hundred cops on the force, personnel staff could hardly be expected to remember all of them. But when one of their own was killed in the line of duty, all attention was directed toward the officer's family.

Recognition dawned in the other woman, who nodded. "Oh, yes, of course. What can I do for you?"

Matt grinned at her sheepishly, as if half-embarrassed by the obvious fact that he was now seeing Tracy. As she watched him put on his act, she was amazed. It made her wonder if he would really behave this way if they were lovers. The tingle that rippled through her at the thought seemed beyond her control.

Then he frowned seriously and cleared his throat. "I'm helping Tracy finish up her husband's affairs." He glanced at her with a look of caring and concern. "Minor details that she didn't get around to just after Scott's death."

Tracy nodded, confirming his story, unsure where he was going with this.

He wrinkled his brow at Mindy. "We can't seem to find his bowling ball. He was on one of the teams in the league last year, wasn't he." It was more a statement than a question.

Mindy stared at him blankly for a split second, then creased her brow. "I don't remember, Matthew. Let me check the lists."

Tracy's pulse jumped, and she and Matt exchanged glances. This was what they wanted. She kept a neutral expression as Mindy slid open her bottom drawer and fingered the files. When she pulled one out and flipped it open, Tracy could feel Matt straining over the counter. Then he did better than that. He pushed open the swinging gate that marked off the public area and walked in as if he belonged there. He stood behind Mindy's chair looking over her shoulder so that she couldn't turn around.

"He played on Tuesday nights," he said as if reminiscing to himself. "Did many of the teams in the league play then?"

Tracy didn't feel comfortable following him, but waited. From her position with her elbows on the counter, she could just barely see the papers Mindy was shuffling. Finally, the woman and Matt both stared at a piece of paper with names in several groupings. Matt was taking his time, obviously looking for the one he wanted.

Mindy shook her head. "His name isn't here. Are you sure he played?"

Matt grunted, picking up one of the lists and studying it. "I was sure he did."

Then he shook his head doubtfully. "Maybe it was a different year I had in mind." He chuckled again. "We were going bowling tonight and could only find one ball in the house. I thought maybe he left it with his gear at the SWAT unit, but I didn't find it there. That made me wonder if I was wrong about him playing last year. So, while I was here to check on something, I just thought I'd stop by."

Mindy seemed to fall for the story. At that fortuitous moment, her phone rang. While she answered it, Matt spent a few more minutes looking at the names on the page. There were obviously too many to memorize. He spied a photocopy machine, and Tracy felt her adrenaline pump. Surely he wouldn't try to copy it in front of the staff.

Evidently deciding not to, he replaced the paper on Mindy's desk. Not waiting for the woman to get off the phone, he shrugged congenially, waved at her and strode back through the swinging gate. Then with his hand on Tracy's elbow, he steered her out.

They didn't stop anywhere else, but hurried down to the car where he pulled a pen and pad of paper from a pocket in his visor. He quickly wrote down the names he could remember, pausing once or twice. When he had exhausted his memory, he handed it to her.

"These are the men he must have been watching last year at the bowling alley. Some of them were on the list he made on the blotter."

She shook her head over the list. "What could they have been doing that got him into trouble?" She lifted her eyes to Matt. "If he suspected some kind of corruption, wouldn't he have reported it to internal investigations?"

Matt rested his elbow on his rolled-down window and rubbed his chin with his fingers. His face took on a grim look, and he finally met her gaze. She could tell by his look that he hesitated to say what he was thinking.

"What?"

His hand reached over to take hers and squeeze it. "He would report it unless he had a reason not to."

His meaning pierced her heart like a .38-caliber bullet. "You mean, unless he had something to hide himself."

Matt nodded slowly. "I'm not accusing him of anything. It's just a possibility."

The air seemed to rush out of her chest, and she slammed back against the seat. "Scott, a dirty cop? I can't believe it."

But she had to confront the hard truth of her relationship with her deceased husband. It hadn't been as close as it should have been. She hadn't known him as well as she should have when she married him. She'd bonded with Jennifer because Scott had begun to withdraw into his own world. She realized now that, had he lived, the marriage probably wouldn't have lasted. She swallowed a lump in her throat.

Matt kept a respectful distance. "I'm sorry." His own voice was hoarse. "I know how you must have felt about Scott. He was my partner, too. I didn't think he was dishonest."

"Maybe he wasn't," she croaked out.

Matt squeezed her hand again. "I hope not. I'm sorry I brought it up. But if we're going to get to the bottom of this, we have to consider everything."

She tried to arrange her tumbling thoughts into a semblance of order and looked wide-eyed at him. "What next?"

He drew in a breath and exhaled it on a long sigh. His hazel eyes held a longing look as if he wished they weren't caught up in something so deadly that they had no time to explore the feelings passing between them. His look made her lower her eyelids. She felt suddenly naked under his gaze, more vulnerable than before. She hadn't asked for this, and she'd sworn she'd never fall in love with another cop. Confused emotions tugged at her, and she tried to inhale deep breaths to control herself.

Matt straightened up and faced the front, and the moment passed. He rested his powerful arms on the steering wheel and glared at the row of cars facing them.

"I need to pick up some gear. You'd better wait here." He glanced over at her. "In full view of people coming and going from the entrance to those elevators, I don't think anything will happen to you. But don't move, okay?"

She nodded, but didn't ask where he was going. He hopped out and pulled a black leather bag from the back.

"Be back in a minute," he said, slapping the open window on the driver's side with his hand.

Then she watched him walk nonchalantly to the glass doors, push them open and disappear into the bowels of the building when the elevator came. Feeling slightly nervous in spite of Matt's reassurances, she glanced around. A few police personnel came and went. Car doors slammed. Nothing seemed out of order.

Running out of things on the outside to keep her occupied, she began to study Matt's car. It was a reflection of himself, she thought. The same masculine, outdoorsy scent permeated the vinyl seats and upholstered interior. She closed her eyes and imagined his arms around her again.

She was sharply awakened from her reverie by the sound of the door opening, which caused her to jump. Matt tossed the black bag in back, shut the door and scooted into the front seat. He didn't waste any time getting away.

They didn't speak as they drove east on Fourteenth Avenue. Only when they'd left the dense Capitol Hill area behind them and crossed Colorado Boulevard did Matt say anything.

"You doing okay?" he asked her.

"Yeah, just mulling things over."

He nodded in understanding.

The single-family dwellings that lined this street sat on small lawns shaded by tall, old leafy maples and oaks. They passed a small residential shopping area, then took the jog across the wide Monaco Parkway.

Once in Rene's neighborhood, Tracy glanced at Matt. "What's in the black bag?"

"Something I needed for some work I have to do tonight."

"Do I get to know what that is?" She could tell from the tense muscles in his cheek that he was going to do something off limits.

"No need," he said. He gave her a swift glance. "There's one name on that list that gives me a bad feeling."

She didn't need to ask. "McAllister."

He nodded, but didn't say any more. Finally, they came to the Bakers' driveway. Paolo barked as if he were ready to chew their legs off, until they got out and went to the fence. Recognizing them, he simmered down to an exposure of sharp teeth and a growl, his tall, pointed ears forward and alert.

The house was empty, and Tracy experienced a sudden attack of worry. It wasn't time for anyone else to be back home yet, but she realized she wouldn't rest easy until Jennifer walked through the front door.

Matt reached into the refrigerator for a bottle of seltzer water and poured out two glasses. The bubbly liquid helped cool them off, then he pulled out a chair and indicated that Tracy should sit down. He did the same. His gaze on her face was riveting. But in spite of the invitation in his eyes, she saw something else there. A predatory look like a hawk about to attack.

But before he could voice what was on his mind, the doorbell rang. Matt got up. "Stay here," he told her.

She didn't miss the way he glanced out the kitchen windows at the backyard before he walked down the hall to see who was there. She herself moved away from the windows. Then she swore to herself. She hated this. She hated hiding out, and she hated the entanglements that had drawn them into danger. She waited as Matt disarmed the security alarms and opened the door. Then she peered around the corner to see him talking to a man in a gray sport coat and open-necked shirt.

She stepped out when Matt said her name. "Special Agent John Metcalf. He's investigating the bank robbery and has some questions."

She sighed, but walked into the living room, offering the agent a seat. Matt looked on warily.

John Metcalf was an average-looking man with light brown hair. He was the kind of man who easily blended with any background. He showed her his badge and then flipped his wallet shut and took out a pad of paper.

"Sorry to bother you, Mrs. Meyer. We're still looking for Carrie Lamb, and we thought you might be able to help us."

"I don't know where she is."

"How well did you know her, Mrs. Meyer?"

Tracy exhaled a breath. "She tutored my stepdaughter, Jennifer. We were friends. I can't believe she's done anything wrong."

The agent nodded sympathetically, but persisted in his questioning like a hound hunting for a fox. "Did she ever say anything about her past to you?"

Tracy shrugged. "She was from Chicago. She told me she'd been a teacher there."

The agent frowned. "And yet she didn't take up that profession here. Did she ever say why?"

Tracy shook her head. "Amanda Fielding gave her the job at the bank. Maybe there weren't any openings in elementary schools. I really don't know."

"Did you ever check her references?"

Tracy's heart thudded, but she tried not to show her irritation. "I felt a personal recommendation from my bank's president was enough. And I am a good judge of character."

"I'm not saying you're not, Mrs. Meyer. It's just that we need to follow up on any leads to find her. I understand she telephoned you when you weren't at home."

Tracy swallowed. A sudden suspicion burned in her mind, and she didn't answer the agent's question. Rather, she asked one of her own. "How did you know where to find me?"

He smiled, but she didn't like the thinness of the smile. It said they knew everything. That there was no such thing as privacy.

"Your neighbor told us you'd left with Lieutenant Forrest and I tracked you from there." Though he didn't make it sound snide, Tracy felt her privacy intruded upon.

"What neighbor?"

"Mrs. Gaffney."

She blinked, then remembered that Dolores Gaffney had been working in her flower beds when they'd left the house this afternoon. The tightness in her stomach frightened her, but she was determined to remain calm.

"I see."

The FBI agent tried to soothe her ruffled feathers. "You might let us know if you plan to go anywhere else."

"Why? I'm not under investigation for anything, am I?"

"No, of course not. You're free to move about. But we would like to know if Carrie Lamb attempts to contact you again."

Tracy thrust her jaw forward. "I don't see why she should."

"She's under investigation for being an accomplice in the bank robbery."

"That's ridiculous."

"I understand your feelings, Mrs. Meyer. She was your friend. But the very fact that she didn't speak to you of her background makes it appear she had something to hide."

The niggling truth that Carrie might have had something to hide bothered Tracy. Ever since the hostage crisis, she'd begun to wonder about that. But they'd had too much else to deal with to worry about Carrie. What happened to Scott a year ago, Matt's suspicions about police corruption and Carrie's part in Wednesday's bank robbery had nothing to do with each other.

Or had they?

Chapter Eleven

As she promised Special Agent Metcalf that she would stay in touch, she felt Matt's gaze burn into her. He seemed just as glad as she was to see the agent's back when he walked away from the house.

And she held her breath as the black limo turned the corner and pulled into the driveway just as Metcalf drove away. Then she stepped out onto the porch to watch Jennifer tumble from the car, followed by Rene and Andrew Leigh.

"Tracy, Uncle Matt!" squealed Jennifer while she raced across the lawn. "We had tea at the Brown Palace. I had scones and strawberries and clotty cream. The waiter had on a white suit, and I sat on a queen chair. We had chocolate and short cookies, but Rene said they were made out of bread."

Rene smiled. "Shortbread," she explained to Tracy.

Jennifer continued to bubble on about her day. "Grandy Leigh has three big rooms at the hotel, all to himself. I took a nap on a big bed."

She bumped against Tracy's legs, and Tracy gave her a squeeze. "I'm glad you had a good time."

Andrew Leigh crossed the grass while his bodyguard closed all the limo doors and stood behind the car, arms crossed, scanning the neighborhood. She met Andrew's eyes across Jennifer's head, realizing how relieved she was to see all of them return safely.

"Come into the house," she offered after having introduced Matt to Andrew. "You all must be tired."

Rene assumed the duties of hostess. "If you don't mind a home-cooked dinner, I'll put on the pot for spaghetti. Roland will be home soon, and there'll be plenty for everyone." She tipped her head in the direction of the bodyguard. "Him, too."

"Thank you," said Andrew. "I won't inconvenience you. I'll just step in for a word with Mrs. Meyer, and then I'll be on my way."

"Whatever you say." Rene lifted eyebrows at Tracy and then went into the house. Matt didn't seem inclined to leave Tracy with Andrew Leigh, and so followed them in.

"Thank you for entertaining Jennifer," said Tracy when the three of them were in the living room.

Andrew mopped his brow with a monogrammed handkerchief and then sat down on the couch. Tracy followed suit, but sat erect, on the edge of the sofa facing him. Matt stood, arms crossed, in front of the bay window behind her.

"We had a pleasant time," said Andrew. "Jennifer is a very intelligent child."

Tracy confronted him directly. "Indeed, she is. I'm glad you noticed."

The lines in his face cramped as if he knew she would always misunderstand him. "I'm sorry we are at odds, Mrs. Meyer. Do you mind if I call you Tracy? After all, you were married to my son-in-law."

"A son-in-law, I gather, of whom you didn't approve."

He moved his head from side to side. "I didn't want Jennifer's mother to marry a policeman, it's true."

He leaned back against the sofa, and she read the regret in his light green eyes. "I failed with my children. I don't mind saying it. Now I've lost them."

Tracy blinked. Had seeing Jennifer aroused his innermost guilt and nostalgia? Was he going to try to use sentimentality to win his arguments about having Jennifer? In trying to secure her own defenses, she wasn't listening carefully to what he was saying.

"We all make mistakes," she said by way of sympathy.

"I know you think I'm a selfish man. Used to getting my way."

"Well, aren't you?"

He looked at her with obvious sadness in his eyes. "If I had my way, I wouldn't have lost two daughters."

Tracy felt confused. "Two daughters? I didn't realize...."

"Neither did I, until day before yesterday."

"I'm sorry, I don't follow you."

He leaned forward, elbows on thighs, hands dangling between his knees. But his sharp gaze held her eyes. "Perhaps you didn't know that Carrie Lamb is Jennifer's aunt."

Astonishment nearly slammed Tracy off the edge of her seat. All she could do was stare at him openmouthed. She glanced toward the stairs, not wanting Jennifer to come into the room right now while her mind struggled with this new fact. Was he serious?

She swallowed and found her voice. "Carrie Lamb is your daughter? Jennifer's mother's sister?" Her voice rose in disbelief.

He nodded slowly, frowning seriously. "I assure you, what I say is true."

Tracy jumped up from the couch and paced toward the fireplace. "Why didn't anyone tell me this before? I can't believe it."

"Nor could I, until I saw her picture on television night before last. Odd coincidence that she was in a hostage situation with her niece's stepmother."

Tracy's hand pressed against her heart. "*Odd* isn't the word for it. Why didn't she tell me?"

"Because she wasn't telling anyone. She disappeared two years ago. Lamb is a false name. I assure you I did everything I could to locate her then. But it became evident to me that she didn't want to be found."

He shook his head. "When I understood that she wanted to be left alone, I let it go, hoping she'd contact me when she was ready. I prayed that she wasn't in any trouble."

Tracy was still in shock, but she breathed out a realization of her own. "Then she came here to be close to Jennifer. I didn't know. Oh, my heavens, Carrie…"

"I'm sorry to startle you, but it's true. I'm acquainted with Amanda Fielding's parents through the country club. Miss Fielding must have known her identity and provided her with a job. Unfortunately, Miss Fielding's doctors will release no information unless I have a court order, and she has not been staying at her home since she was released from the hospital."

Tracy focused on him again. "Then you came to Denver to find Carrie."

"I did. And, of course, to see Jennifer, as well."

She slumped back to lean on the hard edge of the mantel. "When you said you didn't have any family left, I didn't know…."

"Nor did I know that Jennifer's aunt was her tutor until today."

"I'm sorry. I would have told you if I'd known."

"I'm not blaming you. I just want to find my daughter."

Now images of Carrie being yanked across the grass by the bank robber began to replay in Tracy's mind. Her last sight of Carrie was on the motorcycle as the robber drove away.

"They haven't found her, then," she murmured to herself.

Matt finally broke into the conversation, stepping farther into the room. "Mr. Leigh, you realize that your daughter is suspected of being an accomplice in the attempted bank robbery."

Tracy looked at Andrew in time to see the pain that statement caused him.

"I'd not like to think she's part of any such crime," said Andrew gruffly.

"I hope she's innocent," added Matt. "But until she's found, we can't prove that."

"I'm going to try to assist in that endeavor," said Andrew. "Believe me, I'm putting all my resources toward finding her."

Tracy moved back to the sofa and took a seat. She leaned forward. "Mr. Leigh, do you have any idea why she ran away? Why she didn't want to be found?"

The sorrow welled out from behind Andrew Leigh's carefully constructed armor. Even so, he did a fair job of hiding it.

"If I knew that, I'd be able to sleep nights."

Tracy's compassion flowed toward him. How awful to suffer the death of one daughter only to lose the second one for some unexplainable reason. She choked on her pity. But she didn't know what else to say. Should they tell Andrew about the obsessed caller looking for Carrie? Something made her hold back until she could discuss this with Matt. This information was too new. And she didn't know Andrew Leigh very well. Better to proceed cautiously. It also explained why he so desperately wanted Jennifer with him.

"I'm going to be occupied until I find my daughter," said Andrew. He cleared his throat. "I'm glad I had today with my granddaughter."

"Of course," said Tracy absently.

"Business demands that I return to Chicago Monday. But I swear to you, I will not leave until I know something about my daughter's whereabouts."

She nodded. "I hope you can find her."

Present realities began to spring back into her mind now that some of the facts were coming to light. "Special Agent John Metcalf was just here asking questions about the hostage situation we were in."

"I've already talked to the FBI." His look seemed to say he preferred to do things his own way.

He got up and exchanged a swift glance with Matt, who continued to ponder the situation seriously. Then, refusing further offers of refreshment, Andrew went to the front door. Outside, his bodyguard still leaned on the limo.

"I'll certainly call you if I hear anything," Tracy said weakly.

Andrew gave both Matt and Tracy a brief, sharp glance, nodded his head and walked outside. Paolo barked and leaped up to the fence as Andrew crossed the lawn, until Domenico went to the fence and calmed the dog, speaking in a Latin language Tracy didn't recognize.

As soon as Andrew was gone, Tracy turned to Matt. "Do you think we should have told him about the man who's looking for Carrie?"

"Not yet. Not until we know why Carrie doesn't want to be found."

Tracy shivered and hugged herself. "If she's hiding from a pursuer, maybe her father could help her."

"If she thought that, she would have gone to him two years ago."

"I suppose."

Rene came to announce dinner and, to Tracy's surprise, Matt said he wasn't staying. He squeezed her shoulder and kissed her on the forehead as if the gesture were one he performed every day.

"Stay here and don't go outside. I have something to take care of."

Suddenly, Tracy didn't want to see him leave her sight. "Where are you going?"

"I'll tell you about it when I get back."

"Then you will be back?"

He met her gaze seriously, and Rene slipped back into the kitchen, leaving them alone. Tracy felt a huge need well up in her. She didn't want him to go yet. They had so much to talk about with this new twist in their lives. Or her life, she corrected herself.

"Don't worry," he said in a sensual hush, pulling her into his arms. "I promise you I'll be back tonight. This should take no more than a couple of hours. Three at most."

She closed her eyes and let him pull her into his embrace. If he didn't want to tell her where he was going, she wasn't going to force him. Swallowing her arguments, she knew she had to trust him. Matt knew his business. Let him go, she willed herself. But the old unpredictability of seeing a peace officer she cared about walk out the door sank to wrestle with her heart.

MATT KNEW he'd never get an official wiretap on Captain Brad McAllister's phone line. The red tape alone would put the police captain on the scent, and he'd then simply prevent any calls that might reveal what Matt was after. If he were caught performing an illegal wiretap, he could go to jail. His job was on the line. He questioned himself as to why he was determined to risk so much.

The answer was that he was angry. Even though he had questioned his late partner's ethics earlier, in his gut he couldn't believe that Scott had been dirty. As a trained cop, Matt had to consider all the possibilities. But deep down, he couldn't accept that one. His buddy had accidentally found out something dirty on one or a bunch of cops and gotten shot for his trouble. Scott had most likely tried to play by the rules and lost. Now the rules were for breaking.

Matt waited until the evening shift was on duty at the central office where McAllister's phone line was routed. It was an easy matter to pass all the security requirements using the forms he'd filled out so he could bluff his way through. The technician was a man he'd met, and he thanked his good fortune that Charley was the sort that wouldn't talk.

There was nothing unusual about leasing a line to carry the signals from McAllister's phone to the location of Matt's choice for monitoring. The fact that the police department would be billed for the leased lines wouldn't become evident for weeks.

After leaving the central office premises, Matt stopped by an electronics store to pick up the rest of the equipment he needed.

As he drove through the darkened residential streets returning to the Bakers' house, he slowed warily. He could see the house in the next block. Lights in most of the windows gave the impression that everyone was home. Paolo barked in answer to the yips and yaps of the neighborhood dogs. Matt double-checked his auto pistol, then left the Blazer and crept along the shadowed sidewalk, keeping next to the line of trees by the curb. Crickets chirped loudly in the summer night.

A dark Ford sedan was parked facing the house half a block away. Two figures sat in the darkened vehicle, and one of them looked to be a woman. Since the two weren't entwined in each other's arms, Matt's internal warning system told him they were trouble. They were watching the Bakers' house. He waited until he was sure they didn't have any other friends in the vicinity.

They didn't even hear him until he'd slid into the back seat. The 9 mm handgun rested on the skull of the woman in the front seat.

"Freeze," he said quietly. "And lift your hands up slow where I can see them."

He felt their surprise. The woman lifted her hands steadily and didn't move, but the round-shouldered man on the driver's side started to growl and turn around. Matt saw the silencer end of the gun in his lap, and shifted his gun to the man's sleazy face.

"If you want to keep your eyes in the front of your face, don't move. I don't have a problem with mixing your eyeballs with your brains and leaving the whole mess here in the car."

"Do what he says." The woman's voice was brash and hostile. But at least she had some sense.

Her partner grimaced, showing missing teeth, but he stuck his hands up beside his ears.

From his position in the back seat, Matt couldn't reach for the gun in the man's lap without risking the couple grabbing him. He had to remain in the back seat with his gun out of their reach.

"Who sent you?"

The tough guy grunted. "We don't know things like that."

"I see," said Matt. "So your boss doesn't have a name."

"Not one you'd know," snarled the man.

"Try me."

The woman half turned around, her hands still raised. "He ain't lyin'," she said. "He calls himself the Duke. But we don't know what he looks like."

"Keep talking."

"Look." The man now tried to smile, but it was more a broken-toothed leer. "We're freelance. We ain't here to hurt anybody."

"That's good," said Matt, keeping the threat in his voice. "Then if I find out what I want, we can all go home happy. What did the Duke want you to watch for?"

The thug's gaze shifted out the window toward the house, but Matt didn't fall for that trap. "Said there's a nosy cop stayin' here we should keep an eye on. See where he goes."

The surge of anger almost made Matt want to grab the man by his throat and shake the information out of him. But he didn't know what the woman would do. The sleazehead turned back and grinned at him. "That wouldn't be you, would it?"

The woman suddenly dived for the gun in the front seat, leaving Matt no choice. He shot the gun out of her hand and peeled out of the car, ducking behind it for cover. Cursing his bad luck, he darted behind the solid tree trunk five yards away as they fired at him, the thump from their silencer hardly waking the sleepy neighborhood. He quickly shot out their tires so they couldn't get away. Then, in answer to his prayers, he saw Roland run out his front door. His lightning dash to the cars in the driveway drew their fire to the big side yard, away from the houses.

The big thug opened his door and attempted to take up

a position behind his car, firing at Roland now, while the woman in the front seat screamed. She catapulted out of her side of the car and sprinted down the street. Matt was on her in no time and rolled her down on the pavement. When he came up, his gun was in her back.

She didn't fight anymore as he got her up and pushed her to the curb and concealment behind some trees. Her boyfriend had left the cover of their car and had made it farther along the row of cars, working his way up the block. Roland joined Matt behind the big tree trunk.

"Let him go," said Matt as he secured handcuffs on the woman. "We're going to have enough trouble explaining this."

Then he pushed the woman up against the car and made sure she wasn't concealing any other weapons.

"Get out of here," said Roland. "There'll be a police convention on this street in seconds. Tracy's getting Jennifer into the Blazer."

Matt felt a surge of gratitude. Complications with police were the last thing he needed. Roland would be able to hold them off.

"I'll tell them I caught her prowling about my property."

"That ain't your property," she spit out, jerking her head toward the house where the shot-out car was parked.

"I'm afraid it is," said Roland. "It's a rental property, and I happen to own it."

"Thanks, pal," said Matt.

"Not a problem."

Sirens churned the night air a few blocks away. They were cutting it close. When he saw Tracy come out of the house holding Jennifer's hand, he dashed across the street. They got into the Blazer, and he started the engine.

"Fasten your seat belt, Jenn," said Tracy.

Matt pressed the mechanism that locked all the doors, then backed out of the driveway. Out of the corner of his eye, he saw Roland steer the woman out into the middle of the street. The patrol cars would have to stop in front of them, giving Matt the chance to drive the other way.

"Are we going to be in a chase?" asked Jennifer from the back seat as her seat belt snapped shut.

"I hope not," answered Matt.

"Hang on, anyway," said Tracy as she twisted around to make sure Jennifer was belted in.

Matt resisted the impulse to screech away. The last thing he wanted was attention. Pulse throbbing in his ears, he forced himself to pause at the stop sign when he saw another patrol car flashing its lights two blocks away. When its siren rent the night air, he paused, following the rules of the road and let the patrol car approach and turn the corner. If only Roland could keep the woman quiet long enough and confuse the hell out of everyone, they might be able to avoid pursuit.

He turned the corner as soon as he could, then turned onto the next side street. After several more turns, and a circuitous route, he approached busy Colorado Boulevard. There were no more sirens and no one was following. He let his breath out in a rush.

"I think we're okay," he said. He exchanged a quick glance with Tracy and took Colorado Boulevard to the highway, then headed west.

Tracy grasped the back of her seat and leaned around to check on Jennifer. "Are you all right, honey?"

"Of course. We can't get hurt in Uncle Matt's car, can we?"

"No," answered Tracy, sounding somewhat doubtful. "No, of course we can't."

Then she turned around again and pressed her back against the seat. "Where are we going?"

"I'll tell you when we get there. Sorry to drag you out so suddenly."

In spite of his concentration on getting away, his gut twisted. He knew Tracy hated being on the run, and he wished with all his might there was something he could do about it. It reinforced his determination to catch the rats at their own game and bring everything out into the open.

"Nothing will happen to you," he said with a fierce determination to protect his own that reverberated through him, heart and soul. "I promise you that."

"I know."

But her voice was weak with worry. He tried to tell himself this wasn't his fault. That he was only trying to fix what was already started. That she and Jennifer could still have a normal life, if he had anything to say about it. But he wouldn't know until this was over whether that would prove true.

Chapter Twelve

The car lights behind them pressed forward in a swarm. Once on the highway, it was harder to tell if they were being followed. Tracy felt trapped, torn between the need to get away from whomever Matt had snuck up on and the need to protect Jennifer.

Oddly enough, Jennifer seemed fine. As soon as Matt felt it safe, he pulled off the highway so Tracy could tuck a blanket around Jennifer and give her a pillow.

"Matt's getting us away from the bad men, isn't he?" Jennifer said, her eyelids drooping now that the excitement of getting away was behind them. They had stopped in a shopping-center parking lot, but Matt kept the engine running.

"Yes, he is," said Tracy, making sure she was warm enough, but not too warm, and that she had the seat belt strapped around her even if she lay down.

Matt stood beside her, scanning the parking lot, and she was aware of the protective shield he formed. He'd told her they were going to a cabin where they'd be safe for a day or two, just until he found out what he needed to know about Brad McAllister.

She bit back the accusation that they were supposed to have been safe at Rene and Roland's house, and now here they were, running again. But voicing her fear and resentment wouldn't help any of them. She got Jennifer settled and then shut the door. Matt helped her into the front seat, and in spite of her worries, she felt his strength as he leaned across her to check that her seat belt was tight.

He paused before withdrawing, and she felt an impulse to reach for his torso. But she clamped her hands in her lap, fighting the tingling sensation that danced along her skin as the night air bathed them from the open door.

"All right?" he asked in a deep, husky voice.

"Yeah."

His face came closer, and her lips remained half-open of their own accord. She thought he was going to kiss her, and she was surprised at her response to his evident caring about both her and Jennifer. After all, he was putting his life on the line for them. His job was probably already on the line. She swallowed a dryness, realizing her response to this bold, impulsive man was deeper than she could do anything about.

But he must have known there wasn't time, and he pulled himself out of the car to shut her door. Once he was back on the driver's side, he used the mechanism to lock them all in tight.

She would have liked to have enjoyed the romantic ride from north Boulder up to the little town of Lyons, nestled in the foothills. From there, they turned deeper into the mountains, following a winding mountain road that carried them beside rocky slopes clothed in juniper and pine. Tiny lights from residences were tucked into the folds of the hills scattered along small settlements. Then they passed through a wide valley with only the moon for company.

They eventually swung down into the town of Estes Park, a resort town not far from the continental divide. Matt bypassed the brightly lit village and took a road leading north. Finally, he left the pavement, and the Blazer scrambled up a long dirt driveway. She could just make out the shape of a cabin at the end.

"Whose is it?" she asked when he pulled the Blazer behind the cabin and turned the engine off.

"It belongs to my uncle. I know where he leaves the key." He paused to lift a hand and brush her cheek. "Just to be on the safe side, let's not turn on any lights when we go in. I have some things to unload after I get you two settled."

She waited while he disappeared around the corner of the cabin to make sure the area was clear, then returned and helped them out of the car. Going in without any light bothered her. How did they know what manner of natural enemies might be in an empty cabin? It wasn't unheard of for bears to visit cabins on the edge of a town in the mountains. And there was the possibility that bugs or snakes might have decided to make the place their home. Still, she had no choice but to follow his advice.

Matt carried Jennifer in, and to Tracy's great relief, there was enough moonlight to see fairly well. The cabin was clean and fresh smelling. While Matt held Jennifer in his arms, Tracy pulled back a handmade quilt from the bed. Crisp white sheets gleamed at them.

As if sensing her concern, Matt said, "My uncle has a caretaker come every week. No need to worry."

Jennifer fell into the welcome bed almost without waking up, and it only took seconds for Tracy to assure herself that everything was all right. She put the bag with her inhalers on a pine dresser and then unzipped the duffel bag she'd thrown everything into in the two minutes she'd had before Rene had hustled them out the door.

Then she felt her way around and located the bathroom.

Her eyes were adjusted to the darkness now, and she quickly familiarized herself with where everything was.

But when she slipped out of the bedroom into the living room, she was surprised to see Matt on his knees under a table full of equipment, hooking up wires against the wall. The window shades were drawn, and he allowed himself only a penlight, which he pointed at a phone jack.

She felt her way across the room as he crawled out from under the table and stood up.

"It's a listening post," he said, running his hands up her arms.

"A listening post?" she repeated. Her tired mind was more aware of his strong hands caressing her chilly shoulders than she was of what he was saying.

"I tapped McAllister's phone line before we left."

She wanted to give a hysterical laugh. "Just like that."

She felt him tense and instantly wanted to apologize. "I'm sorry, Matt. I know you're risking your life for us."

She felt his mood soften as his fingers worked their way to her face. "I would risk everything for you."

She held her breath. The mountain air must be making her light-headed. Suddenly, she wanted nothing more than for him to take her in his arms and tell her everything would be all right.

As if in answer, his head lowered and his mouth hovered near hers until she let her arms slide around his waist.

"Matt," she whispered, no longer able to fight her need for him.

"Tracy," he replied in a whisper of relief. He held her tight and they swayed together in the moonlight. The isolated cabin invited cozy intimacy that Tracy realized she wanted very badly. Thankfully, Jennifer was sleeping soundly, and she desperately wanted to believe they were away from their pursuers. Matt's solid support and electric kisses on her neck made her want to drink in what he offered.

"Is there anything you can't take care of?" she asked in what she meant to be a teasing voice. But it came out shaky.

"Nothing," he growled into her ear. "You tempt me, Tracy. Right now, all I want is to take care of you."

She wanted that, too, her fuzzy mind realized. She wanted to forget about everything, to lose herself in him. He was winning her over, as her weak knees attested. He was everything Scott hadn't been, or so he was proving himself to be. Did he really want to stay by her side this way forever? Now wasn't the time to ask. Or was it?

"Tracy," he whispered huskily. "I care about you. And Jennifer. I'm not doing this for Scott anymore."

"No?"

"No."

"Then who are you doing it for?"

"For me. For us."

Suddenly, he let go and turned to a sofa she'd barely noticed against the wall. He tossed the cushions onto the floor and then unfolded it into a bed. She knew he wasn't just showing her where she was to sleep. Her heart pounded fast, and the shivers of sensation in her limbs told her what was going to happen. Matt folded back the white sheets and then came to stand close to her, his hands on her hips, his lips against her forehead. She knew it was the ultimate invitation.

She had to do it. She had to go to bed with him and end this cat-and-mouse game. She wanted him with all her heart, even though it was crazy. Even though they hadn't resolved anything. Maybe the added desperation was what sizzled her blood.

Before he could kiss her again, she said. "I need a minute."

"I brought protection if you didn't," he said. His voice was still husky with desire.

"It's okay. I remembered, too."

Then she fled into the bedroom to retrieve her diaphragm. She'd refilled the prescription several months ago, in a moment of whimsy when she thought she might date again. She also took a moment to observe Jennifer, who was sleeping soundly.

When she reappeared in the shadowy living room, wearing only bra and panties, Matt was already between the sheets. She drew in her breath at the sight of his muscular silhouette stretched out in the moonlight. He was propped on one elbow, the sheet just covering his waist. He stretched out a hand as she moved toward the bed.

The coolness of the sheet greeted her naked legs as she sat down on it.

"Wait," he said.

He scrambled out from under the covers, and she glanced at the rest of him revealed against the tight whiteness of the fitted sheet. It stole her breath away as she laid a hand on his muscled thigh, his desire so evident and bold.

Every fiber in her trembled as he reached his arms around her and gently and sensuously caressed her skin, warming every inch of her. He took his time unfastening her bra, then gasped in his own shallow breaths as he gazed at her.

"You're beautiful," he said as he worshipped her body with tender touches and delirious kisses.

She closed her eyes and let him kindle the fires between them that she'd been holding in check for too long. She wanted him with all her heart. Even if there were no tomorrows, she wanted this one ecstatic night, to be joined with this man who was so insistent on taking care of everything in her life.

"Matthew," she whispered, liking the sound of his name rolling off her tongue. He laid her on her back for more intimate, tempting pleasures. When he tasted her breasts with his teasing tongue, explosions rocked through her. His firm, muscular torso stretched out next to hers, his solid erection dancing in her shaking hands. "Make love to me, Matt. Make love to me now."

He did.

MATT RELUCTANTLY LEFT the warm bed with Tracy snuggled against his back. He hated having to disentangle himself in the middle of the night, and allowed himself a moment to gaze at her lovely face on the pillow. Her rich hair sprawled around her head. Her face in sleep was more peaceful than he'd seen it in the past days. He couldn't resist the urge to touch her face. When she moaned and moved against his hand, he had to pull her warm body against him for one more moment of the closeness that was now filling his life with new meaning.

But when she settled into slumber once more, he unwrapped the sheets from his legs and pulled on his jeans. Still not lighting the room, he crept across it. He knew Tracy would want him to check on Jennifer, so he pushed the door wider to see her sleeping peacefully. The night protected them for the moment.

Back in the living room, he slid into his listening post. The cabin was eerily quiet, and he tried to operate his equipment carefully so as not to wake Tracy. The red light on the tape recorder told him that the equipment had recorded one or more calls from McAllister's house. *We'll just find out who he's talking to,* Matt thought grimly as he positioned the earphones.

Two of the calls were meaningless. But the third one piqued his interest. He replayed it, listening intently.

"That nosy cop has been asking questions," said a grating, coarse voice. Matt wasn't even sure he caught all the words.

"What do you want me to do about it?" asked the voice Matt recognized as McAllister's.

"That's up to you. But I don't want him interfering with my plans. You understand our arrangement."

"Yeah, I know," said McAllister. "In another three days, I'll be out of here and no one will know where to find me."

"I'll know where to find you."

Matt could hear McAllister's shallow breathing, as if he were nervous. Then the coarse, distorted voice continued.

"Just make sure the nosy cop doesn't connect you to me. He won't find me, but as far as anyone else is concerned, I never heard of you."

"I understand."

"Good."

"I'll take care of the nosy cop."

"Do it soon."

The line went dead. Matt replayed the tape, making sure he heard everything. He had no idea whom the coarse voice belonged to, and he wondered if the speaker had had throat surgery. He knew, without a doubt, they were talking about him, and his survival instincts flooded every fiber in his body. He wished he could think of a safer place to leave Tracy and Jennifer and go after these bastards alone. He knew this must have been the caller harassing Tracy about Carrie Lamb's whereabouts. If this man thought

Tracy knew anything, it sounded like he'd stop at nothing to get what he wanted.

It filled Matt with cold, deadly rage. But it was an emotion he could control, because he needed every shred of his training and quick thinking to handle this. It was time to go above McAllister's head if he could do it without stepping on the toes of McAllister's friends. So he had to know who those friends were.

Other thoughts occurred to him, triggered by the conversation he had just heard. A year ago, McAllister could have found out ahead of time when a high-risk warrant was going to be served, keeping SWAT busy. He could have let his boss, Scratchy Voice, know. The boss man could have set the wheels in motion for the Crestmoor State Bank robbery. Scott had responded because he was in the area, but had no backup. McAllister must have used the opportunity to get Scott out of the way for knowing too much.

Matt checked the cabin again to make sure it was secure, and when the thin grayness of dawn began to creep over the mountains, he opened the cases that held his SWAT equipment. His mind was clear now, and he made coffee so Tracy could have some when she woke up. His chest tightened with the desire to hold her, but he knew with certainty that if he ever wanted to hold her safely again, he had to win this day.

When she began to move, he went to her, stretched across the bed so that she'd see him when she opened her eyes. She smiled at him, and when he saw her come awake, he touched her face. Her eyes widened, and then she turned her face into his hand and kissed it. He felt a tremor rock him and had to hold himself steady. Then she started to sit up and glanced toward the bedroom.

He took her in his arms and whispered in her ear. "Jennifer's still asleep. I checked on her a few minutes ago."

Tracy sank into him then, and he heard her deep sigh. They held each other for a few seconds.

"Hmm," he murmured, his head beside hers. "Much as I'd like to crawl back in between the sheets, we've got work to do."

She responded to his serious tone and sat up, holding the sheet in front of her, making his hands want to pull it down. But the questioning look in her eyes made him concentrate on business.

"I monitored a call to McAllister," he said. "I want you to listen to the tape. Then I need to take it to the lab to get a voice print made."

He hated the lines of anxiety that crossed Tracy's face. But when she turned aside to find her underwear, he moved to the listening post while he still had presence of mind.

After she'd slid into shorts and a T-shirt, she took a seat in the chair and placed the earphones over her head. "Ready," she said.

As soon as he began replaying the phone call, Tracy widened her eyes and nodded. "That's him," she whispered.

He let her listen to the end before rewinding. Then he popped the cassette tape out and stuck it in the pocket of his T-shirt.

"I'll take you and Jennifer into town. You'll be safe enough in the crowds there. Just stay in public view while I get this to the lab. I have a friend who owes me a favor."

"I'll get us ready."

Tracy poured herself a cup of bracing coffee and then disappeared into the bedroom to get Jennifer up. Matt's pager beeped and he checked the display. Roland. He knew his friend wouldn't bother him unless it was important. He couldn't risk using his cell phone now, so he'd have to wait until he dropped Tracy and Jennifer off in town.

A half hour later, Matt, Tracy and Jennifer pulled into the public parking area in the village of Estes Park. Next to them was the river, which coursed through town behind the shops. The water from mountain runoff was high enough that the big water wheel was cranking full speed. Tracy had explained to Jennifer that while Matt took care of business, they would get to eat breakfast and shop in the gift shops that lined Elkhorn Avenue.

As soon as Tracy and Jennifer had placed their breakfast order at the Grubsteak Restaurant, Matt used the public telephone.

"Roland," he said when his friend answered. "Matt. What's up?"

"Bad luck," Roland drawled. "Division chief wants to see you. Udal told him you were on vacation, but it doesn't matter. Chief Bartola says he wants you now. He's at his weekend place in Allenspark."

Matt shifted the phone and snagged a pencil from the bar next to the phone. "Shoot."

He wrote down the address, then cursed his luck. Before he hung up he asked Roland to track down Percy Ferrens, and tell him he needed a special favor today at the lab. Matt would contact him after he stopped to see Bartola in Allenspark. He also let Roland know where he was keeping Tracy and Jennifer. Some instinct told him that before this day was through, he might need backup.

That machinery turning, Matt hustled out of town on Highway 7, headed for Allenspark. He considered dropping the tape off at the lab first, but Allenspark was on the way to Denver. He hoped he could enlist the chief's help in what he was doing, but Chief Bartola wasn't exactly an ally. Matt had always had the feeling that Commander Udal had to walk a tightrope to get what he wanted for SWAT.

The stunning mountain scenery along Highway 7 made him wish Tracy were with him. But he didn't know what he was getting into. She was better off in public view in town. Craggy Longs Peak towered above him with snow in its crevices. He slowed and turned into a restaurant parking lot in Allenspark to ask directions. Bartola's house was up a mountain road another mile.

Caution made Matt pass Bartola's mailbox and climb on up the road to a turnaround. He left the car in the shade of some aspens and walked back down. The house sat below the road. When he heard a car on the driveway, he stepped into the trees to see whose wheels were spinning up Bartola's gravel driveway.

A Subaru station wagon crested the driveway and paused before turning into the road. Matt's blood pulsed when he saw the stocky driver turn his head to check for cars on the road. Out of uniform, Captain Brad McAllister glanced both ways, then stepped on his gas pedal to cruise into the curving road.

McAllister socializing with the division chief? Or was it something else? The timing made Matt glad he was being cautious. And glad he'd locked the cassette tape safely in the glove compartment of the Blazer.

By the time he rang Bartola's doorbell, he had himself composed. The chief himself opened the door, glanced outside and let him in.

"I don't see a car," commented Bartola. His thin smile didn't fool Matt, who decided his boss's boss didn't deserve any more information than he needed to give.

"Hiked up the hill," said Matt. "Needed the exercise."

He stepped down into a Southwestern-style living room decorated in natural wood. As he'd suspected, wide glass windows from the dining room opened onto a view of a small lake below.

"Nice place here," commented Matt.

"Thank you."

Chief Bartola was a big man with slightly thinning hair. Matt imagined he'd been quite a tough character in his earlier days. He was a career man with an unbroken record of service. Now Matt wondered about that service.

"What did you want to see me about, sir?"

Instead of answering the question, Bartola offered refreshments. "Coffee? Soda? Something stronger?"

Evidently someone had stocked the wet bar, and the smell of fresh coffee blended with the piney scent of the room. Matt declined the offer.

Bartola settled himself on the Navajo-patterned sofa and waited until Matt sat down in the matching easy chair opposite. A multicolored braid rug separated them.

"I was wondering if there was something you wanted to tell me," said Bartola.

"How's that?" asked Matt, keeping a look of innocence on his face.

"Come, come, Forrest. I know your commander just gave you some time off."

"Anything wrong with that?"

"No. I just hope you use it well."

Matt studied the sharp features of the man opposite him. The man wasn't stupid.

"I didn't know you'd be so interested in what I do on my vacation," said Matt, lifting an eyebrow just slightly.

"It's more what you were doing before the vacation that has me concerned."

"Oh, really? Commander Udal didn't mention it."

"Maybe that's because I didn't mention it to him."

"Why not, sir? I thought you had to go through channels."

"The same could be said of you, Lieutenant. Why were you asking about Scott Meyer at a liquor store on Colfax Avenue the other night and at a bowling alley on Leetsdale?"

Who told him? Matt wondered, clenching his teeth. He sighed, gathering his thoughts.

"It's Mrs. Meyer, sir," he said. "It's no secret I've been seeing her. I was a friend of the family before her husband's unfortunate demise a year ago. She had some questions, and I was just trying to put her mind at ease."

"What questions? Has she come up with new evidence in her husband's case?"

The question sounded so sincere, and the way Bartola frowned made Matt almost blurt out the truth. Only years of caution and training made him hold back. He had to know what Bartola had been doing with McAllister first.

"It's just that she's never been satisfied that the whole SWAT squad was engaged elsewhere when that bank robbery that killed Scott took place."

Was it Matt's imagination or was there a flicker of resentment in Bartola's watchful blue eyes? But then the ripple of whatever it was he'd seen on the chief's face settled into wary compassion.

"I can understand Mrs. Meyer's concern, even after the elapsed time."

"I'm not accusing anyone," Matt said. "I think Mrs. Meyer just questions why so many of the SWAT team were training that day, while the rest were delivering a high-risk warrant."

Bartola smiled as if he were reassuring a child. "That was unfortunate. I believe the deployment of the SWAT team has changed since then. Your commander keeps a number of men on call in town now, doesn't he?"

"He does." Matt's mood darkened. He was tired of this game. Time to spring the trap.

"I didn't know Captain McAllister had a cabin up here," he said without warning.

Bartola's face froze in surprise. But he quickly recovered. He gestured broadly toward the stands of aspens out his front window.

"I thought you might pass him on the road. You say you left your car at the restaurant?"

"I didn't say." So who had called the chief from the restaurant to warn him that a visitor was on his way?

Bartola watched Matt watching him. The slack jaw loosened to form a pleasant mask. "As a matter of fact, Captain McAllister had some reports to turn over to me, and I asked him to bring them here since my wife and I won't be returning to Denver until after next week."

"I see." He let it go at that.

Bartola swooped in for the kill. His mask sharpened into a predatory look. His eyes narrowed, and a muscle twitched on the top of his left cheekbone.

"Don't get carried away, Forrest. If you have anything to report, use proper channels. And whatever you're doing, forget about dragging Roland Baker into it. He tells a good story about intruders trying to break into his rental property. But witnesses saw you drive away with Mrs. Meyer in tow. Consider this a warning. If you have any grievances, go through channels. Or else you may find yourself transferred off SWAT. You know we only allow the most stable men on SWAT. It's too risky otherwise."

Too risky for whom? Matt felt the throb of anger in the set of his jaw and the clench of his hands on the nubby upholstery of his chair. But he was wasting his time. If

Bartola were playing good ole boy to McAllister, then let him. He had things to do.

He sprang to his feet, his back ramrod stiff, and looked out the window over Bartola's head.

"Yes, sir," he said, jaw thrust forward. "I'll keep it in mind."

Chapter Thirteen

It was easy to entertain Jennifer all morning, wandering in and out of the artisans' shops along Elkhorn Avenue. An old church had been converted into a gallery of gift shops, restaurants and a place to get old-time photos taken. When Jennifer got tired, they stopped to watch the glassblower. Jennifer was enthralled with the colorful shapes spun on the end of the long metal tube.

It was while they were sitting on the raised benches in front of the glassblower's screened-in studio that Tracy became aware of a man who had taken a seat outside the shop. There was something familiar about his curly-brimmed cowboy hat and the silver snaps on his black shirt. She tried to control her jitters as she glanced at him out the shop's side windows. When some leggy teenage girls walked by in a huddle, he grinned at them, revealing a gold tooth.

Her body tensed as she faced the hot ovens into which the glassblower thrust his work. But when she looked out the window again, the man was still there. She'd seen him in the Old Church shops, too. Was this coincidence? Or was he following them? Her mind flashed back to Elitch Gardens and the man who'd broken off from those coming off the roller coaster just before she'd been assaulted. Was that where she'd seen him?

She realized her mistake now. She'd wanted Jennifer to sit and rest where she could be entertained by the glass-blower. But this shop was at the end of the shopping district. Across the street, a rock wall ran the length of road out of town. To get back to the main shopping area, they would have to recross a parking lot and then the bridge beside the water wheel.

Stay calm, she told herself. There were only a few customers in the store. A clerk worked on displays behind the counter. Nothing was going to happen in broad daylight.

But she couldn't help the suffocating feeling that closed in on her. Slipping off the bench, she stepped over the other way, pretending to examine the delicate glass bowls and vases balanced on shelves brightly lit by windows on three sides.

She spotted a second stranger on the sidewalk in front of the shop. He was dressed in golf shirt and khakis with sunglasses covering his face. His purple-and-silver baseball jacket seemed out of season for such a hot day. Why was he standing there as if he was waiting for someone? He ran a hand through slicked-back black hair and walked over to lean against a post.

Tracy moved back to where Jennifer was sitting and scooted up beside her on the bench.

"We need to go, Jenn. I don't want to frighten you, honey, but I don't like the looks of a couple of men outside. I want us to walk very quickly along the sidewalk back to the shops. You sit here while I make a purchase."

"Okay." Jennifer straightened as if realizing the importance of what Tracy had said.

The glassblower finished his vase and tapped it off the long pole. He spoke to them through the screen.

"Are you in some kind of trouble, ma'am?" he asked, having overheard their conversation.

She looked up at him through the screen. "I'm not sure. There are some men loitering outside. I just wanted to take my stepdaughter back to town to avoid any trouble."

"You wait right there," said the glassblower. "I'm stopping now for lunch. I'll walk with you."

"Thank you. That's very nice of you."

Tracy quickly purchased a glass dish, then slung her purse strap over her shoulder, holding the package by the plastic handles. If she needed a weapon suddenly, she would break the glass.

Then she helped Jennifer down, took her by the hand and waited for the glassblower. When he emerged, they walked out into the sunlight, passed the men outside and walked briskly across the parking lot. She didn't look back until they'd crossed the bridge. Once past the water wheel, the glassblower left them.

"Thank you," she called after him as he darted up some wooden steps. He gave them a wave.

"No problem."

She risked a glance backward and shivered when she saw the first man walking over the bridge. He seemed in no hurry and paused to lean out over the tumbling water to watch the water wheel. *Just the way someone would who was following and didn't want to draw attention.* They needed to get away quickly.

"This way, Jennifer," Tracy said. She conveyed some urgency, but not enough to frighten her.

Once inside the Old Church shops, it shouldn't be hard to evade pursuers. The galleries twisted above each other, and they hurried up a set of stairs. Tracy had to slow her pace to accommodate Jennifer's, and at the top, they darted into an antiques shop. The owner greeted them and then engaged Jennifer in conversation.

"I have a wooden horse like that," said Jennifer, pointing to a large painted carving.

"Do you?" The older woman came over to visit with Jennifer.

While they chattered, Tracy glanced out the front window down to the street. Both suspicious men were making their way through the crowds on opposite sides of the street. Though they didn't look at each other, a sixth sense told her they were working as a team. Had they seen where she and Jennifer had gone?

She interrupted the woman's conversation. "Is there a back way out of here?" she asked.

The saleswoman didn't seem all that surprised. "Why yes. If you go out that way, you'll come to an exit. It takes you down outside."

"Thank you. If some men come looking for us, I'd appreciate it if you didn't say we were here."

The woman gave her a look of total support. "Don't you worry. I'll send them the other way."

"Thanks."

They sped along to the next set of stairs and down, then out through a restaurant. Turning quickly into an alley, Tracy had no chance to check if either man had seen them. A narrow passage ran behind the next building, and she led Jennifer in the next door she found. They were in a long covered corridor with stuccoed wall on one side. Turning into the next entrance she came to, they found themselves in the sandwich shop.

At least she could breathe easier, for tourists thronged this place.

"Want something to eat?" she asked Jennifer.

"Sure. Can I have a fish sandwich?"

"You can if they make them here. We'll ask."

She ordered lunch for the two of them at the counter and then slid into a booth while they waited for their food. Tracy's heart still raced, and her adrenaline pumped. But if the men barged in here and tried to grab Jennifer, she'd be able to make such a racket she doubted the bystanders would let them get away with anything.

She thought about calling the local police, but she knew darn well that police could do nothing unless a crime had been committed. They would not ask suspicious-looking men to move along. Anyone had a right to loiter on the sidewalk. It was what tourists did.

As they munched on their sandwiches, she tried to plan her next move. An idea struck her. She didn't want to hire a taxi to take them back to the cabin. All that would accomplish would be to lead their pursuers to their hideout. But she could take a taxi to some other public place. A place that was well staffed and could offer assistance if she needed it. A place where Jennifer could rest if she needed to, and where Matt could find her if she got word to Rene to let him know her whereabouts. She couldn't call him directly on the cell phone. The frequency would be too easily monitored. After they finished their fish sandwiches, she found the phone and ordered a taxi.

When the local taxi pulled up in front of the sandwich shop, she tried to use the crowds to conceal them getting in. She saw the man, now carrying his purple-and-silver jacket, turn from the storefront he'd been gazing at, just as she shut her door.

"The Stanley Hotel," she told the driver. "Take Spruce to Bighorn Drive and then Wonderview Avenue." That way, they'd avoid turning around and going through downtown again.

"Yes, ma'am."

She tried to conceal herself in the shadows of the cab, but as the driver pulled away from the curb, she saw the gold-toothed cowboy standing at the top of the steps by the water wheel. She couldn't know if he'd seen the cab. Only when the cab left the main street and climbed up the side streets did Tracy look back. They left the shopping district behind and wound past cottages and summer homes above the village. A grand view of the stunning valley unfolded before them.

The historic Stanley perched on a scenic rise. But as the cab pulled into the circle in front of the hotel's wide verandah, Tracy looked at Jennifer. Her face looked almost as white as the glistening hotel.

"Are you all right, Jenn?" she asked.

"I feel tired," said Jennifer.

Tracy handed the driver the money and then helped Jennifer out. As soon as they had climbed the steps to the porch, Jennifer crawled up onto a wicker settee. Tracy's heart raced, and she dug into her bag for the bronchodilator. She recognized the early-warning symptoms and needed to take action before they became worse.

Jennifer coughed and Tracy's heart clenched. But she retrieved the inhaler as fast as her hands would work, shaking it to mix the medication.

"Ready?" she asked Jennifer.

Jennifer nodded, wiping her nose with the tissue Tracy handed her. Then Jennifer tilted her head back and opened her mouth, holding the inhaler the way she'd been taught. Tracy steadied the apparatus as Jennifer breathed out and then began her slow, deep breath as Tracy pressed the inhaler to deliver the mist.

"One, two, three, four, five," Tracy counted off the seconds. "Hold in now."

Jennifer held her breath for another ten seconds, allowing the medication to settle in the airways.

"Okay," said Tracy when it was all right for Jennifer to resume normal breathing. She waited to see if another puff might be required, but Jennifer's color returned, and her breathing seemed normal.

Tracy patted Jennifer's knees. "Just rest awhile, honey."

She packed away the inhaler and then took a seat beside Jennifer on the settee. Her pulse still pounded, and with Jennifer out of danger, she concentrated on the people in the surroundings. Tourists with cameras emerged from the hotel and walked to cars in the parking lot. Bellboys hoisted luggage up the steps. If the two suspicious men knew where she'd gone, they weren't visible.

"I'm sleepy," said Jennifer. She leaned against Tracy, who wrapped an arm around her.

"You need a nap," she said, frantically wondering how to accomplish that.

They sat for a few more moments on the settee, and then Tracy roused Jennifer. It should be time for Matt to be returning. If he didn't find them in town, he'd go to the cabin. If they weren't being followed any longer, it might be best to try to get back to the cabin, where Jennifer could lie down and Matt would find them.

"Let's go inside," she said. "I'll find a place you can rest."

Early in the century, the Stanley had rivaled European mountain resorts. Recent renovations had included original 1909 furnishings. Tracy and Jennifer walked down a long hallway off the lobby and turned into an alcove, where Jennifer climbed up on a comfortable love seat to stretch out.

While Jennifer shut her eyes, Tracy gazed out the mullioned window. Driveways left the hotel from behind adjacent buildings. She studied the town map she had with her and ascertained the way they'd have to go. It was too far to ask Jennifer to walk. Sitting still in the quiet, old hotel, she waited a quarter of an hour to make sure no one lurked around a corner or watched them from a staircase.

Then she roused Jennifer and they took a back staircase, walking along the path to an outbuilding that had been made into the concert hall. Slipping into a side door, she sighed with relief when she spotted a telephone. While Jennifer went to look at the old photographs on the wall, Tracy called Rene.

"Rene, it's Tracy. Have you heard from Matt?"

"He just called. Are you all right?" Rene's voice conveyed her concern.

"We're fine. But I think we were followed in the village."

"Matt's on his way back to the cabin. Sounds like things didn't go too well at the chief's house."

Tracy felt a clench of anxiety at her words. Was it all going to end here in Estes Park? She fought the swell of panic as she envisioned their enemies closing in on them. If only Matt had had time to drop that tape off to someone who could help them. But she didn't dare ask too many questions over the phone.

"All right," said Tracy. "I've got to get Jennifer into bed for a nap. I'll see Matt when he gets to the cabin then."

"He should be there soon. He left town an hour ago."

"Thanks."

Her decision made, she peered out the door at a parking lot behind the hotel. A woman emerged from what appeared to be the kitchens and waved as a man drove up in

a beat-up Buick and stopped. It gave Tracy an idea. She
darted down the steps to the parking lot.

"Excuse me," she called out, sprinting across to them.
"My little girl is ill. Could you give us a ride to our
cabin?"

The couple responded in Spanish, and Tracy was afraid
she wouldn't be able to communicate her need. But apparently the couple was just discussing her plight between
themselves, for the man turned to her and said.

"Of course. Where is your daughter?"

"Wait here. I'll bring her."

She darted back to where Jennifer waited and told her
they were getting a ride home. Then she slowed her pace
so Jennifer wouldn't have to race across the parking lot.
With every agonizing step, Tracy wondered about the wisdom of leaving the well-populated Stanley for the isolated
cabin. But the urgency of talking to Matt drove her forward.

Jennifer smiled and charmed the couple, and the woman
entertained her in the back seat while Tracy gave directions
from the front seat. When they reached the cabin, Tracy
offered to pay, but the man refused.

"I hope your little girl is better," he said.

The black-haired woman smiled and waved as they
drove off.

SEEING MCALLISTER at Bartola's had left a bad taste in
Matt's mouth. He had waited a long time to make sure
there was no one about to follow him and then took the
opposite direction. He wound over the mountain before
descending into Boulder and through heavy traffic to Denver. Before he reached the city, he phoned Percy Ferrens,
who agreed to meet him at a fast-food restaurant to pick
up the tape. That way Matt could hightail it back to Estes

Park faster, and no one would see him near the lab—something he needed to avoid, since he'd been officially warned away.

He pressed along the highway, keeping his eye on the rearview mirror. Once he thought he spotted a white Mercedes that stayed behind him too long, but when he passed through Boulder again, he lost it. Then he sped along the road, making it back to Estes Park in record time. It was late afternoon. A call to Rene informed him that Tracy was back at the cabin.

He didn't realize he'd been holding his breath as the Blazer scrabbled up the rocky driveway. But when he saw her crack open the door at the sound of his approach, the air rushed out of his lungs and he stepped inside, clasping her to his chest. He felt her trembling and buried his face in her hair.

"Everything all right?" he asked.

"Actually, I don't think so." He didn't like the worried sound of her voice.

She set out some dinner she'd prepared. "I found spaghetti and sauce in the cupboard," she said. "Jennifer and I already ate. I hope you're hungry."

"Famished," he replied, sliding a chair out and taking a seat at the painted table near the small kitchen area. "Tell me what happened."

As Tracy served the food, she related her story.

"You weren't followed back here?"

She shook her head, her tousled hair rippling around her worried face. He wanted to kiss the worries away, but he knew they had to be more practical than that. He didn't recognize the men she'd described, but their pursuers could hire thugs to do their dirty work.

"It's McAllister, all right," he said after swallowing

enough food to sustain him. "He was just leaving Bartola's when I approached."

Her eyes widened. "Did he see you?"

Matt shook his head. "No. But it's possible that Bartola will tell him I was there."

"But just seeing McAllister at the chief's house doesn't prove anything," she said.

"No, but the voice giving him orders to take care of us proves he was into something nasty. I have a hunch that Scott must have witnessed McAllister taking payoffs at the bowling alley or at the liquor store. That's why he made those notations in his appointment diary."

He got up from the table and pulled a folded section of newspaper from the jacket he'd tossed on the sofa. Tracy spread it out and looked at it, then lifted curious brown eyes to his.

"It's from Wednesday. The day of the bank robbery," she said.

He sat down again. "Look on page two. What do you see?"

She furrowed her brows and turned to the page. When she looked up again, understanding filled her eyes. "The same day Jax Schaffer escaped from the police van. Do you think there's a connection?"

He nodded slowly. "The attempted bank robbery went bad. McAllister delayed the hostage takers long enough for SWAT to get there. Most of our squad was engaged in that call-out. Only a couple of our guys were off that day. Schaffer's accomplices spring him, SWAT is busy, so only local cops give chase. Schaffer gets away."

Matt glared at Tracy. "Sound familiar?"

He saw her sway and grip the table for support. But her gaze was steady. "That voice. You think it's Schaffer?"

"The voice print will tell us. The tape is safe in Percy's

hands. They have tapes of Schaffer being interrogated, so we'll know soon enough if it's a match.''

She nodded slowly. ''So you think McAllister is taking orders from Schaffer?''

''Makes sense, doesn't it?'' He told Tracy what he had thought about after listening to the taped conversation. That McAllister could easily have found out ahead of time when the high-risk warrant was going to be served, keeping SWAT busy. He could have let his boss, Schaffer, know.

''Schaffer could have set the wheels in motion for the Crestmoor State Bank robbery,'' Matt said grimly. ''Scott responded without backup. McAllister couldn't have planned that Scott would be there, but he used the opportunity to get him out of the way. If he knew Scott was snooping, McAllister had to get rid of him somehow. This way, he could make it look like an accident. It all fits together nicely. McAllister was a dirty cop receiving payoffs for Jax Schaffer's crimes. When Scott got too close, he was eliminated.''

''And now they want to eliminate us.''

''Not if I can help it.''

''How? You can't even be sure of the division chief.''

''Then we'll go above his head. Udal's on my side. He'll support me.''

She shook her head, reached across and squeezed his arm. ''How can he when you've broken every rule in the book?''

Gazing at her and feeling the pull toward her with every fiber in his body, he knew why. Because it was worth everything to nail her husband's killer any way he could. For his buddy, gone beyond this life now, for his sense of right and wrong and for the beautiful woman sitting across from him who needed him so desperately. At least he hoped she needed him. Last night's act of passion had sealed the unspoken bond between them. But he wasn't so foolish as not to know that a lot was yet undecided.

"One step at a time," he murmured, taking her hands and lifting them to his lips to kiss them.

Instead of tossing Tracy across the bed the way his body was urging him to do, he checked the listening post while Tracy cleaned the dishes. He replayed the tape that had been activated every time McAllister had had a call, but there were no more incriminating calls. An hour later, he risked a phone call to Percy Ferrens, using the code they had set up so that neither of them had to risk using his name.

"Maroon Bells here," said Matt. "What did you find out?"

"Bingo, Maroon Bells. We have a match."

Matt's skin prickled. Percy had been able to get access to Schaffer's interrogation tape. He knew better than to mention his name, but gave Matt the information he needed.

"Good. Keep those tapes under lock and key. I'm coming down tonight. By tomorrow morning, internal investigations will have to reopen the case."

"No problem. I've made copies for safekeeping."

As evening shadows claimed this side of the mountain, they left the lights out at the cabin. Tracy rested with Jennifer in the bedroom, making up a fairy tale. Matt listened wistfully to their voices. He knew now, without a shadow of a doubt, that he wanted to make them his family. But it wasn't the right time to ask.

The sound of an approaching helicopter was still distant when Matt first became aware of it. But it only took a few seconds to send his heart spiraling in his chest. He snatched his load-bearing vest, which carried his handgun and extra ammunition. He put it on and slung his M-16 across his back as he appeared in the bedroom door.

"We've got to get out of here now," he said. "We need to get clear away from the cabin toward the trees."

His eyes lifted to the ceiling as he tried to assess the exact direction the helicopter was coming from.

Tracy sprang up, and Matt lifted Jennifer off the bed. "Run."

"Hang on to Matt, honey," Tracy instructed Jennifer, then she sprinted toward the door. She grabbed the bag with Jennifer's medical supplies, and only glanced at Matt once before flinging open the front door and dashing across the porch.

The pounding of helicopter blades burst over the top of the ridge as the three of them reached the trees fifty yards away.

Chapter Fourteen

As soon as they were under cover, Matt set Jennifer down, and Tracy grasped her hand. Matt pointed to some boulders farther up the slope, still covered by trees. She could barely see them in the near darkness.

"Up there," he shouted. "Get up there behind cover. If they open fire, get as far away as you can."

Tracy's instinct took over, and she tugged Jennifer up the hill, her eyes surprisingly accustomed to the summer night from being in the shadowy cabin.

"Hurry, Jenn," she cried as they negotiated the pine needles and rocks under the roof of boughs overhead.

She was out of breath when they reached the rocks and terrified of what else might lurk in the woods. She pulled Jennifer into her arms behind the rocks, but peered over, searching for Matt, who had taken cover a little below them behind the trees. She covered Jennifer's ears with her hands as the helicopter circled the slope. She couldn't believe their pursuers had chosen such an overt method to track them down.

Matt held his assault rifle at eye level, covering the helicopter's descent. Tracy held her breath, clinging to a shred of hope that this was all some mistake. She could just barely see the silhouette of a man leaning out the open side of the chopper against a sky that still held summer light. But when a projectile shattered the cabin windows, the explosion sent her heart bursting through her ears.

Matt crouched, moving up the hill toward them. "Run," he ordered. "Keep to the trees."

She didn't need to be told twice. Her heart pounded in terror, the more so for Jennifer. "Can you run?" she screamed over the noise.

Jennifer nodded, but already Tracy could see her fright in the girl's eyes. If Jennifer should have a serious attack now, they were without help. Frightened for their lives, she gripped Jennifer's hand and helped her climb higher, deeper into the trees, clutching the bag full of medications.

Behind them another explosion made her turn. The gunman from the helicopter was firing into the shattered side window. How long before they realized no one was firing back?

Below her, Matt moved from tree to tree, covering their position. She prayed no one would discover them and they could get away. The road twisted around this ridge. If they could make it to the top and down the other side, they might have a chance.

"Can you make it?" Tracy asked Jennifer anxiously.

Round eyed and pale, Jennifer nodded. She didn't waste any breath on words, but scrambled up the hill beside Tracy.

The ground rose steeply, with loose rocks sliding underfoot. A grassy patch ahead was less covered by trees, and Tracy worried that they might be sighted against the pale prairie grass. She steered Jennifer around the clearing, and they sprinted beside a stand of aspens, stopping to rest against the smooth white bark to catch their breath. She could no longer see the helicopter, but the engine roared louder, as if the blades were slicing the branches as it descended.

Matt ran up the hill to them. "They won't be able to land on the hill," he shouted. "But they're dropping some men to the ground."

Tracy's chest ached, but she drew enough breath to speak. "They'll see we aren't there."

He slid the M-16 to his back and reached down for Jennifer to carry her. "Our only chance is to get to the road."

She nodded. If they made the road, they might be able to make it to help.

A burst of fireworks suddenly illuminated the sky, and Tracy realized their pursuers' ploy. The gunfire would be indistinguishable from the fireworks.

Now flashlights behind them in the woods told her their pursuers had searched the cabin and had seen they weren't there. She tried to hurry her pace, but already Jennifer's coughing was causing her grave concern.

"She can't go any farther," Tracy said when she caught up to them. She slid her shoulder bag down and dug for the inhaler with shaking hands.

"It's going to be all right," she told the frightened little girl. "Don't worry. Matt will take care of us."

And she believed it. Even though the whirring helicopter that now danced upward over the trees could fly directly overhead at any moment, deep in her soul she believed that Matt could handle it. Matt could handle anything.

The one slipup must have come after he'd left Chief Bartola's house. Just as he'd predicted, Bartola must have let McAllister know that they were in the area. Somehow McAllister's men must have followed Matt back to the cabin unseen. Once they knew which road Matt had taken to get here, they'd known where the cabin was tucked away.

Jennifer leaned against a boulder and tried to exhale slowly. She clutched Tracy's arm desperately as Tracy brought the inhaler up to her open mouth. In her fright, she gasped in too quickly, and Tracy mistimed releasing the medication. It took every ounce of courage for Tracy to speak slowly and calmly.

"Breathe out, honey. Slow now."

Jennifer had more control this time and exhaled slowly. She nodded quickly, and then Tracy waited for her slow, deep inhalation. This time, she pressed the inhaler at the right moment, releasing the mist. Jennifer held her breath as Tracy counted with the fingers on her left hand.

"We gotta move," said Matt, coming next to them. "They're getting too close."

"Right."

Jennifer breathed again, and Tracy stuck the inhaler back in the bag. She whispered. "We're ready."

"This way," said Matt. "I'll stay behind you."

He had to cover them in case anyone fired at them, which left Tracy to blaze the trail. She bent low to avoid branches and to better see the rough ground, holding Jennifer's hand tightly behind her.

The next blaze of fireworks showed her they were on top of the rise. Directly ahead was a wire fence, marking someone's property.

"I can run," said Jennifer bravely when they came to the grassy open space.

A spray of rifle fire from behind them tore the ground to their left. *They were going to die.* Right here on this mountain, Jennifer would see them shot to death before taking a bullet in her young heart.

The sharp return fire from Matt's semiautomatic rifle

was so loud, Tracy's head nearly burst. But some survival instinct made her pick Jennifer up in her arms and hurry to the fence. She thought Matt had stayed back to cover them, but when she dropped to her knees, gasping for breath, he was miraculously beside them. Wire cutters appeared from one of his pockets, and with a couple of strong cuts, the wires broke free. He reached for Jennifer and set her on the other side. Then he helped Tracy through.

As the first of the flashlights crested the hill, Matt leaped over the fence. But rather than shooting to give away their position, he grabbed Jennifer again and veered off at an angle down the hill. Tracy followed on the steep angle as thorny weeds and shrubs cut her ankles. She stumbled, grabbed a bush to hold her as her feet slid, then regained her balance and half slid, half ran down.

Pink star bursts blossomed overhead, and Tracy no longer knew whether rifle fire or fireworks followed their progress. They slid into a gully and she felt Matt's arm reach out to pull her to him. She pressed against his chest, feeling Jennifer whimper against her.

"You okay, Jenn?" she asked. Her own voice shook, and tears of anguish mixed with dirt and sweat on her face.

Her heart was thundering so loud, she at first didn't realize they weren't being shot at anymore. Instead, flashlights swept the hill, but farther to the west. Could it be possible that they'd gained precious seconds by sliding down in this direction?

"This way," whispered Matt, taking Jennifer again.

Her feet found the edge of the road. At least they could make faster progress now. Town was the other way, but so were the pursuers. Their only chance might lie in circling back.

She fled along the road with Matt carrying Jennifer, certain that at any moment a bullet would whiz toward them.

They rounded a curve, and Tracy recognized the long dirt road that led to the cabin. Matt crossed it, heading for some trees.

She looked over her shoulder only to see headlights turn off the main highway, onto this road. "Lights," she gasped, out of breath from the dash.

Matt glanced back. "Head for those trees, but watch your step." He led the way off the road through weedy, rutted ground.

They crouched beside some pines just as the car topped the rise and descended toward the road to the cabin. Her heart jumped into her throat when it turned up the dirt road, but in the ambient light, she thought it looked familiar.

"Roland," said Matt, setting Jennifer down.

"He's headed for the cabin," she warned anxiously, taking Jennifer's hand. "They'll kill him."

"No, they won't," said Matt. "Stay here."

His rifle in his hands, Matt stayed low and crept up the side of the road toward the cabin. Tracy shivered as she held Jennifer in her arms.

"Will Matt get hurt?" asked Jennifer.

She stroked the little girl's head. "I hope not, honey."

"Will the bad men get us if Matt doesn't win?"

Tracy tried to draw a deep breath. "Not if I can help it."

She was faced with the greatest decision of her life. Matt would want them to get away. But to where? The pursuers were covering the road from here to the highway. That way lay danger. Her instinct to protect Jennifer was as strong as her instinct to stay close to Matt. She felt ripped apart on the inside.

"Do we have to stay here?" asked Jennifer. "Maybe we can help him."

Tracy swallowed to try to ease her dry throat. "I wish we could. If he gets to Roland in time, at least there will be two of them."

But they had to move. Summer nights in the mountains were chilly, and they'd left too quickly to take jackets. Tracy made her decision. "Let's move up closer, but stay deep in the trees. Go slowly and don't make any noise. Okay?"

She felt Jennifer's silent nod. Carefully and slowly, they crept along the line of trees, pausing to try to listen to the night sounds. A final burst of multicolored fireworks signaled the end of the display. The helicopter had timed its departure well. Its deafening engine could no longer be heard.

A blast of gunfire made her grab Jennifer and duck. She heard voices shouting and then more gunfire. Running footsteps approached, and she pulled Jennifer in behind the trees. A man sprinted along the road, coming even with them. He turned and fired. Then, to her horror, he veered off the road, plunging into the trees, headed right toward them, not twenty yards away. She had to stop him.

"Get down flat," she whispered to Jennifer, and then seized a dead branch, rising to her knees, prepared to defend her stepdaughter.

"You can't get away with this," shouted Matt, close in pursuit.

McAllister dropped into the foliage, and she saw Matt make a dash for trees on the other side of the road. A bullet zinged toward McAllister's position covering Matt's approach.

Terror choked her. They didn't know where McAllister had gone, and if they fired in this direction, they might hit Jennifer or her. If she shouted to Matt, McAllister could get to her first. Her only chance was to create a diversion.

But evidently McAllister had decided to play bully. He yelled at Matt, uncomfortably close to Tracy's position.

"You won't win, Forrest. For all your fancy training, you're outnumbered."

A gun exploded, and a bullet whacked into a tree, splintering bark. "Turn yourself in," Matt shouted. "It'll go worse for you if you don't."

"You're out of your league, Forrest. This thing is bigger than you think."

"I know who you're taking orders from," Matt shouted back. "If you kill me, it'll be one more murder charge. Give up now."

For answer, McAllister scrabbled farther into the woods, and Tracy held her breath. He was coming this way. Suddenly, a cough erupted from Jennifer's throat, and McAllister's movements stopped. Jennifer coughed again, and Tracy dropped the branch to try to help her.

"Who's there?" called out McAllister.

In a minute, he'd find them. They'd both be dead.

But a crash of undergrowth distracted him, and then Matt was on top of McAllister, ten yards away. She was dimly aware of sirens growing louder. Fear paralyzed her as Matt rolled with McAllister. Metal glinted in the moonlight that filtered through the trees.

"Drop your weapon, McAllister," Roland shouted as he entered the woods.

Then in the next instant, McAllister was on his feet, his gun aimed at Matt's head. But Matt drove an arm forward, gripping McAllister's gun arm and forcing it across his body. With a knee to his groin, he stepped past his right leg, twisted McAllister's body and brought him down with a knee holding his head. While Roland covered him, he got the gun away.

With lightning speed, Matt had McAllister on his stomach, his hands cuffed behind him and a gag tied around his mouth. Headlights blinded them, and two county sheriff's vehicles ground to a stop as officers emerged, ordering, "Hands up."

Rene Baker appeared out of nowhere, evidently having followed the sounds of gunfire until she deemed it safe. She crashed through the undergrowth to reach Tracy, the whites of her eyes visible in the darkness as she knelt down to put a reassuring arm around Jennifer.

"It's all right, honey," said Rene. "You've got your friends here."

A burly officer fanned out his men as he strode forward. Tracy stood up as the sheriff approached. "Are you all right, ma'am?"

"Yes, but this little girl needs to get to a hospital. She has asthma. The man taken hostage tried to kill us." She pointed at McAllister. "His accomplices are still at large."

"You can let him go," she continued, nodding toward Matt. "He's with me. And his friend and his sister helped us."

"We'll sort it all out, ma'am. We have to follow procedures to make sure no one gets hurt."

The sheriff's officers disarmed Matt and Roland and led them to the cars.

"I'll go with Jennifer," Rene said in her ear. "You stay here with Matt."

An ambulance arrived and took Rene and Jennifer, and McAllister was led away. She heard more shots exchanged in the woods, some shouts, and then the shooting stopped.

Still unable to believe it was over, Tracy climbed into the back seat of the car with Matt. His hazel eyes swam with emotion as he looked at her, unable to hold her with the handcuffs keeping his hands behind his back. She touched his perspiring face.

"It'll be all right," she whispered, her own emotions at the end of their tether.

He turned his face to kiss her fingers. She knew what he was thinking. He'd broken the rules. The evidence they had wouldn't stand up, gathered illegally as it had been.

"It doesn't matter," she said, her body pressed against his side. "McAllister tried to kill us. He's a maniac. That much we can prove."

"I'd do it again," Matt said with that stubborn edge to his voice. "I'd do anything for you."

She closed her eyes and reached around him to hold him close. The wounded prisoners were brought up and taken away in a van. The sheriff interrupted them.

"Time to go, ma'am. The deputy will drive you downtown."

She stifled her irritation at being separated from Matt, but this wasn't his jurisdiction, and she'd better cooperate and give her statement to the authorities. The sooner they told their story, the sooner the truth would be brought to light. Then tomorrow, they would untangle their personal lives.

With one last glance at Matt that said everything, she backed out of the car.

Chapter Fifteen

Late Monday morning, Tracy began packing up Scott's den. With plans to remodel the room, she made a new resolution that allowed her to put away the past. The future held some hope.

After a tiring day at the sheriff's department in Estes Park on Sunday, matters were straightened out and Matt and Roland were let go. When Jennifer was released from the hospital, they drove back to Denver and spent a long evening at Commander Udal's home. The chief of police listened to their story and immediately opened a full investigation.

McAllister was now in jail awaiting a hearing. Faced with the voice print that matched escaped criminal Jax Schaffer, McAllister confessed to carrying out Schaffer's orders. The murder weapon that had been in Tracy's safe-deposit box was found hidden in McAllister's basement. The evidence was strong that he'd killed Scott the day of the Crestmoor State Bank robbery.

Tracy had been so tired last night when Matt tucked her into her bed that she fell asleep instantly. By the time she'd awakened this morning, he'd been gone. But it was best that way. In spite of the bond between them, she knew in her heart that she just couldn't have another relationship with a cop. She just couldn't do that all over again.

An hour later, she heard a car stop in front of the house and looked out the dormer window to see Matt striding across the lawn. She decided to wait upstairs and let him find her here. Her heart felt like lead as she thought about telling him she just couldn't be with him. As much as he meant to her, she couldn't do it again.

In moments, his footsteps climbed the stairs. Then he stood in the doorway, gazing at her, one hand on the door frame.

Her heart cracked, and she dropped the curtains she'd just removed from the window. His gaze swept her figure, and his eyes looked into her soul.

"Everything all right downtown?" she asked breathlessly.

His sober lips twitched upward as he stepped toward her. They met in the center of the room, and he let his hands rest on her back as she clamped her hands on his strong shoulders and leaned back so she could see his face.

Then he smiled and pulled her to him. "Tracy, I love you."

Her voice trembled as she murmured into his shoulder, "Oh, Matt."

He began to caress her, kindling their deep passion. She didn't resist. She longed to make love to him one last time. It would be a beautiful goodbye. He kissed her lips and slipped his thumbs around her rib cage and under her short knit top to graze her skin.

"Mmm," was all he said. "We're alone."

Within minutes, they lay on the daybed. His look grazed her face, and he took his time disrobing them both. Then their demanding passion overwhelmed him, and they spent the next half hour giving and taking, pleasuring each other as if there were no tomorrow.

When at last he lay next to her, he propped himself up on one elbow and brushed her hair from her face.

"I'm not a cop anymore," he said.

She sat upright. "You're what?"

He grinned in amusement at her disbelief. "I decided I needed a new profession, one more suitable for a family."

Her wide brown eyes blinked. "But what will you do? The SWAT team was your life."

He pulled his mouth to the side in a wry expression. "I broke the rules, and I've been suspended. But I'd do it all over again." He looked at her more seriously, his eyes hiding a smile. "And I had an offer I couldn't refuse."

"Doing what?"

"Running a camp for teenagers outside Estes Park. An old friend offered me the job a while ago. I didn't have a reason to take it then. I do now. It would be a great place for Jennifer."

He rolled over her, off the bed and got on his knees. "Tracy, I'm proposing. Will you marry me?"

The look of love he gave her told her it had all been worth it. She reached for him again, running her hand through his tousled hair.

"I love you, Matt. I thought we couldn't be together. I knew in my heart I couldn't go through all that again."

She shook her head, tears coming to her eyes. "I never expected this. I mean, I knew you'd broken too many rules to be on the force without suspension. I knew they would set you back. But I never expected you to give up police business entirely."

She cried as he held her, but he knew they were tears of relief, of unspent grief and of joy. He was happy at last. Justice would take its course, and he no longer felt burdened by the guilt that had consumed him until he'd learned who his buddy's killer had been. In some mysterious way, fate had led them through this and blessed him with true love. They had won.

AFTER A LONG AFTERNOON of intimacy and renewing joy, Tracy finally left Matt soaking in the bathtub. She showed him a letter Amanda Fielding had faxed to her this morning. The bank president had decided on her own to arrange a loan for Tracy so she could buy computer equipment to be able to work at home.

On the heels of that, Andrew Leigh called and offered to pay for Jennifer's medical expenses. "I've decided to drop the custody suit," he said.

Tracy felt stunned by this news. "What made you decide that?"

There was a pause on the other end of the line, and then Andrew's voice sounded full of emotion. "Jennifer herself. She didn't like the idea of being without you."

Tracy felt renewed tears in her throat. "I see," she finally said when she got control of herself.

"I understand the wish to be with someone you care about," he said. Then he cleared his throat. "I'll expect to see her for holidays."

"Yes, of course. She'd like that."

She slowly lowered the phone. So much was happening so fast.

She reread Amanda's letter as she went out to the back porch and down to the yard, breathing in the scent of the Russian olive trees along the back fence. Evidently, Amanda had resolved some situations of her own for the tone of the letter was much softer than when they had last spoken.

The letter took Tracy back to the morning of the attempted bank holdup the previous Wednesday. That seemed a lifetime ago. And Andrew Leigh was still looking for his daughter, Jennifer's Aunt Carrie.

"Where are you, Carrie?" Tracy whispered to the wind.

Deep down, Tracy believed that Carrie would turn up soon and be all right. Deep down, she had faith in her friend.

She turned around when she heard the screen door open. Matt stood on the redwood deck, barefoot, in jeans. The sun glinted off highlights in his dark blond hair. He gave her a very satisfied grin and lifted one eyebrow as he came down the steps to the backyard.

"Come here, woman," he said as the grass tickled his feet. "We've got wedding plans to make."

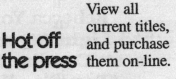

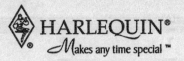 **HARLEQUIN®**
Makes any time special ™

WIN A DREAM

In celebration of Harlequin®'s golden anniversary

Enter to win a *dream!* You could win:

- A luxurious trip for two to *The Renaissance Cottonwoods Resort* in Scottsdale, Arizona, or

- A bouquet of flowers once a week for a year from **FTD**, or

- A $500 shopping spree, or

- A fabulous bath & body gift basket, including **K-tel**'s *Candlelight and Romance* 5-CD set.

Look for **WIN A DREAM** flash on specially marked Harlequin® titles by Penny Jordan, Dallas Schulze, Anne Stuart and Kristine Rolofson in October 1999*.

FTD

RENAISSANCE. COTTONWOODS RESORT
SCOTTSDALE, ARIZONA

K·TEL

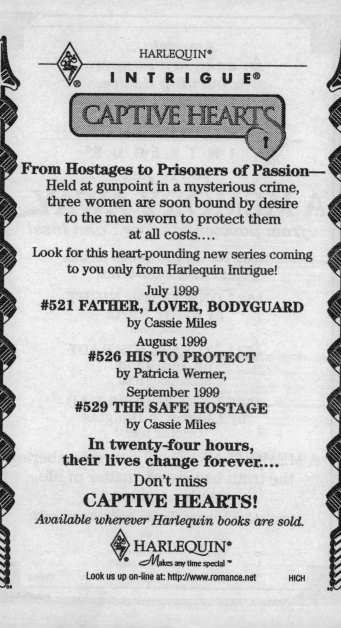

COMING NEXT MONTH

#525 AFTER DARK by Rebecca York and Caroline Burnes
43 Light Street and Fear Familiar—a special 2-in-1 Intrigue!
Two couples must hide from the day...and anything can happen after
dark....
Counterfeit Wife by Rebecca York—When a madman comes after
her, Marianne pretends to be Tony's wife—and can no longer deny
the desire burning between them....
Familiar Stranger by Caroline Burnes—When Molly's son is
kidnapped, she has no choice but to find her mystery lover—and tell
him of their son's existence....

#526 HIS TO PROTECT by Patricia Werner
Captive Hearts
In twenty-four hours, three women's lives were forever changed in a
hostage crisis. Now Tracy Meyer must put back the pieces and fight
to keep her stepdaughter, while sexy cop Matt Forrest moves in to
protect them from the hostage taker's revenge....

#527 ONE TEXAS NIGHT by Sylvie Kurtz
A Memory Away...
In the heat of a Texas night Melinda Amery found herself staring into
the double-barreled blue eyes of Lieutenant Grady Sloan. And he
wanted answers about the murder of her neighbor. Only, she didn't
have them—didn't have any. She had amnesia. But Grady was the
type of man who wouldn't let go until he got what he wanted. And
that included Melinda....

#528 MY LOVER'S SECRET by Jean Barrett
Only one man could protect Gillian Randolph from the madman who
stalked her: private investigator Cleveland McBride. Their sultry past
aside, Gillian trusted Cleve with her heart, but could she trust him with
her secret child...?

Look us up on-line at: http://www.romance.net